Isle of Ancthia

Rachel Adkins

CONTENT WARNING

This book contains depictions of death, murder, violence, and suicide attempts.

1

"Mama, I'm home! Only for a second, though!" I shouted, the front door bouncing off the wall as I raced into the house.

"Why are you late, Sadie?"

Mama stood in the kitchen, hands on her hips. Dinner had clearly been sitting out for quite some time on the table. Food that I knew was hard to come by. I abruptly paused the trek toward my room, guiltily chewing on my lip in response, fiercely avoiding eye contact.

"What did you do this time?" Mama huffed, slapping the towel she'd been holding onto the counter.

Oh, she was *mad* mad. I immediately rushed to my defense. "It wasn't even my fault!" I whined, "Lander was shooting spitballs at my face, and—"

"And you got put in detention for the third time this month?" she interrupted, raising an eyebrow and crossing her arms in that way moms do when they're about to give you a lecture.

"No, I didn't get put in detention! We only had to scrub the bathroom floor."

"It doesn't take that long to scrub a bathroom floor," Mama replied skeptically, "especially if Lander was scrubbing with you."

I admitted sheepishly, bracing for the blow of disappointment to finally land, "We had to use a toothbrush."

Mama sighed heavily, pinching her nose with a shake of her head. Her lengthy brown hair rippled with the movement, matching the flow of her thick, long linen skirts. "If you get in trouble again, I'll be the one making you scrub the bathroom floor with a toothbrush. Except this time, you'll be using *your* toothbrush." She narrowed her eyes at me.

Gross. Not my own toothbrush. She meant it too. "Yes, ma'am."

Her glare softened, and she reached out to gather me into a tight hug. "I love you."

"I love you, too, Mama." She'd let me off easy, even though I'd wasted her efforts on dinner. An expensive one, from the looks of it.

"Now off you go. You're late." She pulled out of the embrace, reaching to pat my back to usher me along. My attempt to dodge her failed, and I burst into giggles as I rushed to my room.

Small as our house was, I reached my room in seconds, yanking the beaten violin case out from under my bed. Right before I opened the front door to leave, Mama stopped me, holding out a small wooden box neatly wrapped in cloth.

"Here's some food for the road. It's still warm."

I grinned widely, planting a kiss on her cheek, vowing internally that I wouldn't let her meal go to waste. "Thanks!"

She anxiously waved me off as she always did, waiting in the doorway until I was out of sight. I waved exuberantly back, hoping to soothe the nerves she always had about letting me go off on my own.

Tyben's Square was a good fifteen-minute walk from our home, but I was determined to make it in ten. I was grateful for the cool spring air rushing past my hair as I ran, hair that everyone said matched my mother's light brown hue. Save for the colors of our eyes, our neighbors here in Ancthia always gushed that I was my mother's twin. They meant well, and I couldn't exactly blame them since they'd never had the chance to meet my father, but their statements never failed to ruffle my feathers. I was the spitting image of Papa, not Mama, and it didn't matter how many times someone said otherwise, it would never become the truth.

The cobblestones clattered under the soles of my worn shoes as I ran. So narrow was my focus on trying not to fall flat on my face in front of the entire city that I failed to notice the commotion until I was right up on it. Icy dread filled my veins.

I jogged to a stop, approaching a rather dense crowd that had gathered to watch the source of the shouts ringing out across the streets. I knew what it was—as did the onlookers—having seen this sight numerous times before. But it didn't matter how many times I saw it. The thirtieth time was as jarring as the first, watching a family torn apart in only a matter of minutes. Similar to the way mine had been only five years prior.

"It's not the fever, I swear to it! He's teething!" a woman wailed, her voice carrying over the shocked din of the crowd. I pushed past the onlookers, trying to get a peek at the unfolding situation. I knew I should turn around to cross the last few streets to the square. However, curiosity always tended to get the better of me, so naturally, I had to watch.

"Watch it, kid!" An older man shoved me.

In the chaos of the crowd, I hadn't noticed that I had stepped on his shoe. His push sent me tumbling into another woman's skirts as the wall of people broke apart enough to give me a decent view.

A group of gate guards stood in a circle around the woman. She had fallen to her knees on the street, a young child clutched to her chest, wailing as loud as her, if not louder. The guardsmen's black leather uniforms were a stark contrast to the white garb of the medics, four of whom stood between the woman and the guards. Covered head to toe in protective waterproof material, hoods, and masks meant to protect them from exposure, they didn't fear the virus that threatened our city. Our world. The outside of which we had long since abandoned.

The woman's pleas fell on deaf ears.

"I'll not repeat myself again. You've been ordered to hand him over," said the medic closest to where she kneeled.

He reached forward, heavy, thick gloves clinging tightly to his fingers, meaning to rip the child right out of the woman's arms. Unsurprisingly, she did not comply, throwing herself backward instead to cower against the stone walls behind her. Her tear-laden eyes darted left to right, searching for an out—a way to escape—despite knowing that it would be fruitless. That it might cost her and her child their lives. I saw him then—her son—whose cheeks were glossy and red, telltale irritation brought on by a constant onslaught of drool and rubbing. Something I'd seen many times on our neighbor's three young children when their teeth painfully burst through sensitive gums.

"No!" she shouted, shrill and desperate. "He isn't ill—he's teething! You can see right there he's got a brand-new molar coming in!"

She held him up for the medics to see, and as if on cue, the child coughed. Not a singular one, either, but a full-on fit of deep, congested coughing. It might've been brought on by the excess of drool dribbling from his lips, or it could've been a run-of-the-mill cold. I'd spent many a day holed up in my room with one, as Mama kept me hidden until the symptoms passed. Because no chances could be taken here. Not with the consequences that may arise should the virus infect the city.

The crowd emitted a collective gasp—myself included—taking a number of chaotic steps back and away from the child now officially deemed contagious. I was bumped about, this way and that, my small size adrift among the surrounding adults, a leaf caught in a turbulent current.

"Come on now, stay back!" a guardsman sighed, shoving against the line of curious onlookers. Meeting resistance, the guard clocked a younger man on the side of the head with his metal stick, the crowd stumbling back in response. I fell on my bottom against the hard stones below, the heavy violin case throwing my balance off. I didn't mind the spot I'd landed on much, as I had a better view down here around their legs. Though the side of my hip now boasted a generous throb. Hoisting myself onto my knees, I crouched below the city folk, intently watching as this poor woman was swarmed by the medics. I was committed now. I had to find out how this ended. The chilly temperature of the ground pierced through my layers of thick skirts, numbing my knees and adding to the shiver that gripped my spine.

"You damn barbarians, why won't you listen to me? It's not the fever!" she screamed as he was ripped from her hands. A medic shoved a gag in the child's mouth, while two other medics held his mother down and did the same to her. They wouldn't be speaking directly to her again, nor to her child, that much I knew, not after hearing him cough that way. Rumors floated along the breeze that even exchanging a conversation with the infected was a means of spreading the fever. The truth of that was up for debate, but I couldn't blame them for being extra cautious. Grateful for it, even.

For the third time, the crowd was disturbed, and I was shoved about beneath the feet of the group. I held my violin case protectively to my chest, dodging the shoes that threatened to trample my most prized possession as a man tore through the people and into the guards.

"That's my son, not some rabid animal! You can't do this!" he hollered, frantically attacking the guardsmen with a handful of frenzied punches.

They tolerated his assault with the same tired disappointment a parent might show to a child throwing a tantrum. At least until he pulled the knife. The woman's shrieks were muffled by the gag, her eyes flitting rapidly back and forth between her son and her husband as the guards rushed him. I wondered if she was screaming for him to stop, to think of their future. Or perhaps she was egging him on, thrashing to be free of her own bonds in a final act of revenge. But there wouldn't be any revenge today.

His shrieks didn't last as long as hers.

Obviously, I should've left long before the gate guards grabbed the man firmly by his head. But morbid curiosity and horror had me glued to the ground as firmly as the people around me. Squeezing my eyes shut, I slapped my hands over my ears to block the resounding crack of his neck. But I was half a second too late. I heard it from beginning to end. Saw the defeat in the woman's eyes as she watched her husband slump to the ground, lifeless, her fight coming to a stop as abruptly as his life had. I couldn't bear to witness her silent, broken sobs for a moment longer. I scrambled away on my hands and knees, tripping over my skirts once, twice, as I got to my feet. Brisk, early spring air blasted across my skin as I cleared the oppressive heat of the mob.

I was no longer motivated by the fear of being late; rather, the need to get as far away as possible from the man's lifeless body as it was dragged out of the streets. The despair on the woman's face as she fought a useless battle. And from possible exposure to the life-shattering sickness that plagued the world. I sprinted away, lungs burning as I cut corner after corner, rapidly closing in on the peace that was Tyben's Square. I reached my destination in record time despite my unexpected detour, pausing by the fountain to catch my breath.

The square was bustling in the early evening, with market stands set up in all directions along the cobblestone buildings. Warm light filtered from under the awnings. The scent of baking bread and the din of gentle conversation intertwined to create an atmosphere of comfort and normalcy—a far cry from how things were beyond the peaks. And as of only a few minutes ago, how they were down the street. I found relief here in the square from the brutality of Ancthia everyone collectively tried to ignore. This was the city I pretended was reality, where we were safe from any resemblance of the chaotic anarchy on the outside.

I squinted up into the late evening sky. Despite there being two hours of daylight left, the shadows of the sharp, jagged mountains circling the valley of Ancthia created the appearance that sunset was already underway. The mountains weren't always there—nor was the valley—despite appearing as if they'd stood tall for millennia. Only fifty years had passed since their creation, back when the virus made its first appearance across the world. Whenever the ground lifted away from the Earth, infected by a means that wasn't yet understood, it left behind valleys and peaks, carving out the landscape into something new and unexpected. I found it hard to believe that miles upon miles of land could become infected with a sickness, causing it to separate from the solid, immortal ground on which it lay. Anything stricken with the fever—people, plants, and even land—would float off into the sky never to be seen again. But I'd witnessed it before, back when I lived outside the safety of Ancthia. Back on the day my entire life flipped upside down. Or rather, floated away in the form of an old oak tree.

Despite the comforting calmness of the square, a sense of heaviness had settled over me after witnessing the gate guards tear another family apart. The mother's pleas echoed in my ears, and I jumped each time I heard a sudden noise around me, fearing it were that man's neck snapping all over again. With a firm shake of my head, I turned to the only thing I knew that could erase the pit of dread in my stomach.

Plopping down onto the fountain's smoothly carved marble border, I flipped open the latches to my violin case. I was grateful for tonight's sizable crowds, for we were short a good handful of gold for this month's groceries. I hoped to make up for what Mama's salary couldn't cover. The fountain bubbled and gurgled, splashing cool mist into the air. The fresh scent of water and the peacefulness of the market easily set the mood for my music tonight. It gave me something to channel other than the darkness I'd carried in on my shoulders. Flickering candlelight from nearby lampposts cast dancing shadows over my violin, making the instrument appear alive.

After checking that everything was still in tune, I lifted the bow expertly in my hand, gently pulling it across the strings with controlled chaos. I let my heart flow into each finger without restraint.

Lander once mentioned I had a knack for giving even the most upbeat of songs a melancholy tang. The sadness had to come out somewhere. Tonight's performance lasted hours. I played until my neck ached from squeezing the wood between my chin and collarbones. Until my arm was hard to hold up. I played until the turmoil from the past five years of my life had poured out completely. Releasing this tension left me both empty and satisfied, though I knew it wouldn't last forever. It always found a way to come flooding back in, but letting it go every few days made it bearable.

I didn't pay much mind to the people who lingered and listened. I only hoped that these songs somehow assuaged any pain that they held onto as I played my heart out directly into theirs. Yes, I did it to make ends meet. But I also did it to bring some light into the dark streets of Ancthia, to honor my promise to my father, and to speak my mind without words.

Toward the end of my performance, stars twinkled in the void of deep, blue darkness above. The square was still heavily populated with shoppers, but their numbers had dwindled, leaving more space between visitors. Children no longer played in the street, and the air had grown colder, a nighttime chill rolling in the way mist did off the lake in the city's center.

I completed my last song, letting my arms drop to my sides as the final note reverberated on the stone walls. Out of habit, I glanced over at the small alleyway facing west. It was cloaked in darkness, at first glance empty, but I knew he'd been there for the last three hours at least. Sensing the end of the performance, Lander pushed off the wall, sauntering out into the dim, golden light of the square. He slowly clapped, the sound muted by the leather gloves he always insisted on wearing.

"Your squeaking has improved greatly, but you still have a lot of work left to do," he remarked, casually rifling through the pocket of his thick brown canvas jacket. He pulled out a small golden coin and flipped it into the open case, the metal clinking against the large pile I'd accumulated over the evening.

I rolled my eyes. "Lander, take that back. You need it as much as I do."

I picked out his coin and threw it at him. He was too slow to catch it as usual, and it dropped to the ground, bouncing and rolling away.

"Come on!" he sighed, and chased after the coin, dodging quite a few people on the way. Once he finally seized it, Lander slipped it back into his pocket, hovering over me as I shoveled the remaining bounty into a small bag.

"Sorry! Almost forgot you're half turtle!" I jeered. He narrowed his eyes at me. The mist from the fountain hung in my hair, creating a halo of lengthy frizz—much to my irritation. I sat back down on its marble border, listening to the water's quiet trickle while raking my fingers through my unruly hair in an attempt to tame it. Seeing as I wasn't yet ready to leave, Lander joined me on the fountain's edge, plopping down heavily. A few moments of comfortable silence passed, and I watched in fascination as a rare workhorse clopped across the square, a gate guard sat atop. It had been months since I'd seen a horse. They tended to remain outside of the city limits, plowing fields and guarding livestock, a rather important task. Often, the desperately hungry snuck out of the confines of the tall buildings, attempting to snag a rare meal of meat to make it to the next day. An attempt to extend their lives that typically resulted in a premature end.

Lander's soft voice drew me out of my thoughts. "I knew you wrote it down. It sounded pretty," he commented.

My brows knitted together. "What?"

"The song you were tapping out earlier, in class. You played it."

His deep brown eyes glittered in the dim torchlight, matching the shimmery water behind us.

"How'd you know I played it?"

He shrugged. "I remembered the beat. And there was only one song that you played the same verse five times in a row, wrong," he said matter-of-factly.

Of course he'd noticed. Lander never missed a beat. "Rude," I muttered. "I haven't finished it, clearly. How would you even know it was wrong if you haven't heard it before?"

"Some of the notes didn't exactly match. And the squeaking. That one had extra."

"Shut up," I said, shaking my head. Mama's disappointment replayed behind my eyes, bitter shame coursing through my veins. I'd almost forgotten. "Thanks for getting me in trouble, by the way. Seriously, Lander? Spitballs? I can't believe you got us kicked out of class!"

"You mean your temper got us kicked out of class. You could've accepted my spitballs as a welcome distraction, but you *had* to explode instead." Lander said playfully.

"Spitballs are disgusting. I can't believe you'd even pretend that was 'welcome!'" I fumed, angrily whirling away from him. He peered around my shoulder, and I pursed my lips together, trying hard not to laugh when he crossed his eyes. Lander always knew how to egg out a giggle, but I vehemently resisted. I was supposed to be angry, after all, and twisted further toward the fountain.

"If it makes you feel any better, I didn't use actual spit. And I know the look you had on your face. You couldn't stand sitting there another minute listening to Mrs. Fenter drone on and on." He made his voice high and shrill to create a mocking rendition of our teacher. "Thirty years ago, two random people picked their noses..."

I snorted involuntarily, falling victim to a fit of giggles at his sheer goofiness, and much to my dismay, the irritation dissolved as quickly as it formed. Lander joined in until the laughter stole our breath away. I wiped the tears from the corners of my eyes when I was finally able to inhale properly.

Lander said, "You should've seen your face when that first spitball hit you."

I shoved his arm playfully, his dark, wavy hair rippling in the candlelight. "You're an annoying slug."

"Thanks for the compliment."

Lander stretched out his legs, his leather boots thudding heavily atop the cobblestones as he glanced over in my direction. He had that trademark half-smile plastered onto his face, his white teeth bright in contrast to the olive tone of his skin and the dim lighting of the square. His long, dark eyelashes flickered as he met my gaze, my heart frantically skipping a few beats in response. I fought the urge to shy away, my palms suddenly sweaty. *It's only Lander. You've known him forever. He always looks at you this way. There's no reason to feel ... whatever this is.*

He spoke, oblivious to the unexpected fluttering of my heart and the heat that was slowly creeping its way into my cheeks. "You gonna treat me to a pretzel tonight? That smell has been torturing me for at least three hours." Lander inhaled deeply, staring longingly over at the bakery stand adjacent to his hiding spot.

"I guess I can spare some of my hard-earned money for you," I told him, handing over three copper pieces. He'd treated me plenty when I was hungry and weak from playing all night. Back when the threat of losing our home and place in the city was a regular occurrence. It had taken time before Mama found steady work, being outsiders on the brink of a reemerging pandemic. The mistrust and mistreatment were frequent then. Nearly three years passed before we created a comfortable living here, after coming to the city with almost nothing. Even now, food could be hard to come by.

All we arrived with were the clothes she'd haphazardly shoved into a satchel, a few odd coins and food, and this violin handcrafted by my father. He had been both a musician and a woodworker, specializing in small, intricate pieces such as musical instruments. He taught me my way around the violin at an early age, almost as soon as I could walk, and after many years of practice, I became quite proficient. *You have an ear for it,* he'd tell me after hearing me sing along to his music. *You only have to put in the work. An artist can't craft a masterpiece simply by looking at the canvas.*

I took this to heart, making it my personal mantra after we'd left him.

At the age of eight, roughly one year after we'd come to the city, I took to the streets, hoping to make enough for food. I wasn't sure if it was the quality of my music or the pitiful presence of a starving young girl playing music for scraps, but it turned out to be a lucrative endeavor of which I continued multiple nights a week.

"Thanks, Sadie!" Lander pushed himself off the edge of the fountain, trudging across the square to his favorite bakery.

A pretzel was how Lander and I met. Well, not precisely, as we'd been in the same class since arriving, but it was how we noticed one another. Two young kids searching the streets for scraps, he had waited in an alleyway nearby, watching me closely. After realizing I'd made enough money for something to eat, I purchased a warm, soft pretzel, the first real food I'd had in almost two days. But that night, right before taking a bite, we locked eyes. Those eyes told me everything I needed to know, reflecting what I saw in the mirror every day. The loss, the loneliness, the desperation. I broke my treat in half despite my aching hunger, and that's where it all began. We took care of each other. We were a team. When one of us was in need, the other was always there, an unspoken oath bound that day with a single pretzel.

Lander didn't have to come see me play every night, as now he and his mom were established enough to have a decent supply of food, but he never missed a performance. A fact that I'd never admit meant the world to me. Not with words, anyway.

As he purchased his favorite treat, I unwrapped my dinner and dug in. Mama had given me a modest baked potato with a small pat of butter, and a rare piece of chicken on the side. After all the hours I spent playing, it was cold now, but as Lander always said, hunger was the best seasoning. Dry as the potato was, each bite was a chore, the butter having solidified ages ago. I forced it down as though my life depended on it—because in all honesty, it did, with as little food as we had available. I should've gotten a pretzel instead. They weren't my absolute favorite—that honor belonged to apple streusel—but Lander's passion for them gave the doughy treats a special place in my heart.

He returned to his spot, and we ate in peaceful silence for a while, watching people go about their business. At some point, a woman walked by holding a small, sleeping child in her arms. A boy, roughly the same age as the one I'd seen on my journey here.

I suddenly found the potato stuck fast in my throat. Lander paused in tearing into his pretzel, eyeing me as I guzzled the rest of my water in a matter of seconds.

"Are you still dead set on becoming a gate guard?" I asked him once I'd gotten the tuber down, gripping the half-empty lunchbox tightly in my hands.

"About as dead set as you are on being a musician," was his reply.

I raised an eyebrow at him. "I don't exactly have any plans to go back on my promise."

"And neither do I," said Lander.

Lander and I had spent many nights exploring the city, having snuck out after our moms had gone to sleep. Under the cover of darkness and adrenaline we'd made many confessions to one another. One of mine being that I promised my dad when I was little that I'd one day become a famous musician. His that he'd protect his mom, no matter what.

"You'll have to get less squeaky on that violin though if you want to keep that promise," he joked. I went to jab him in the ribs in retaliation. He jumped back, almost falling into the fountain, and I missed.

I stared down at the half-eaten food, my appetite having completely left me despite the ever-present hungry ache in my middle. Lander tilted his head, squinting at me as he regained his balance.

"Does it taste that bad? You can have some of my pretzel if you want," he offered, ripping off a rather large piece and holding it out for me.

I shook my head. "It's not that. I . . . I saw some gate guards kill someone on the way here," I said quietly. I hated the thought of him becoming one of them, even if they were meant to protect us. He was too kind. Too gentle. I could never imagine him breaking someone's neck in such a barbaric manner.

"Damn, what for?"

He shoved the piece of pretzel he'd offered me into his mouth, chewing rather loudly. I frowned. It didn't matter how many times his mom smacked him on the head with her wooden spoon. His manners were as abhorrent as ever. What was it about him that had made my heart race again?

"What do you think? The medics thought his son was infected," I explained, handing over a napkin to wipe the crumbs off his chin. Thankfully, he took it, knowing he'd be in for a lecture if not. "His cheeks were bright red, but I'm pretty sure he was only teething. You know how babies are—the drool gets all over them and chaps their skin all up. He did have a terrible cough, though. Maybe they were right."

Lander chuckled, shaking his head as he said with absolute certainty, "He didn't have it."

"How could you know? You didn't see it! That was a sick cough if I ever heard one!" I retorted.

"You don't get a cough with the virus, or a sore throat, stomachache, nothing. Only fever. That's why they call it 'the fever,' Sadie, duh," Lander told me, dusting the crumbs off his leather gloves onto the street. "And then, once it breaks, you float off into the sky, never to be seen again." He waggled his fingers playfully at the starlit sky, the peaks only visible in the darkness where the stars ended and a jagged void of black began. His tone grew unusually serious as he added,

"Remember, I've seen it up close and personal. Seven times. I know it when I see it."

A pang shot through my chest. Lander was the sole survivor of a family of seven children, his father and six sisters all victims of the virus. I wasn't sure how many succumbed to the fever and how many were released, as any time Lander spoke about it he'd get too choked up. What I did know was that only he and his mother were spared, fleeing when their home was attacked by regulators. They arrived here around the same time my mom and I did, right before the gates were closed off again. He always believed that it was his fault, after his father was infected, that he couldn't protect his sisters as the next man of the house. That's why he wanted to become a gate guard, to protect the last member of his family. He had no one else left but her. At least until I'd come along, he once told me.

He'd been incredibly lucky. How he and his mom made it out unaffected when his entire family went down, I'd never understand. But I was grateful they had.

"I'm sorry, Lander," I whispered, rubbing at my chest as though I could soothe his aching heart for him. An ever-present pain of his that I felt as if it were my own.

"No need to be sorry. It means I have the insight that others lack," Lander winked at me cheerfully. "There won't be any of that ridiculousness going on when I'm a gate guard! We'll be nearlies next year, so it won't be much longer!"

He'd lost more than most in his life, yet he could always find a reason to smile. Next year we'd attend the big school as nearlies, for our ninth through eleventh years of education. We were almost finished with our last year of middles, and, despite him being eleven months older, Lander and I had been lucky enough to share the same classes since we were in littles. He'd be fourteen this September — my favorite month. My favorite because it was the only month of the year we got to be the same age. After my thirteenth birthday this August, we'd finally be the same, and then he'd leave me in the dust again to age another year. Lander and I were inseparable other than that one simple fact. And being separated from him in any manner pained me to no end.

"I can't wait," I said sarcastically. "A few more years and then we get on with the rest of our lives. Going to work instead of school, stuck in an endless loop of wake up, go to work, go to bed. All the while held behind the same old peaks that confine us in this disgusting, boring city, waiting to be taken down by guards the instant we cough on a bite of dry potato."

It was true, honestly. There was nowhere else to go, or to do. Nowhere else to dream. Sure, my mother and I were alive, and Lander was safe and sound thanks to this city and its rigorous protocols. I had no right to be bitter about it. Yet I wondered what I was missing out on. Was this all life was going to be?

Lander fought back a smirk. "Shit, tell me how you really feel. I thought you loved your job as a musician."

"I do! But you know the city will expect me to get a 'real job.' That way I can contribute to society or whatever. They'll kick me out otherwise," I said.

"You can't leave the city, remember?" Lander pointed out. "No one in, no one out since the gates were closed. That's practically Ancthia's motto."

"Okay, correction. They'll *kill* me. There aren't enough resources in the valley to support someone who only takes and doesn't contribute."

Lander smiled sweetly, sending my heart back into that irritating fluttering frenzy.

"I disagree. I think your music is an excellent contribution. It gives this 'disgusting, boring city' a little bit of joy."

His sweet smile became a wide grin when my cheeks flushed a bright scarlet red. I wished I could rip my skin off for being such a traitor to my thoughts—to the smooth warmth that filled my heart when he complimented me. I muttered a rather embarrassed thanks, grateful that a stray, skinny dog chose that moment to appear at our feet. He hungrily licked up the crumbs Lander had scattered on the street, and we each donated a morsel out of my forgotten meal. Its pitiful face tugged a chord of sympathy in our hearts.

"Doesn't look much different than we used to," Lander remarked as the dog slinked off to beg from others.

"At least we wore clothes," I snorted, in an attempt to make a ridiculous joke to lighten his dreadful observation.

"Look at that creature again and tell me he doesn't have clothes on."

I raised an eyebrow. "You mean his fur?"

Lander stood, nodding, and held out his hand to help me up, an unnecessary but kind gesture characteristic of him. One I simply adored.

"I have to admit, the clothes we used to wear were far scrappier than his fur," I observed, taking his hand.

"The way you sew, I'd have to agree."

I glared as he laughed himself silly at his ridiculous joke. Though I'd never admit it, it was a good one.

He led me down the street, heading in the direction of my house, dodging a rat here and there. We chatted aimlessly about anything and everything as the darkness closed in around us. For some reason, speaking our minds was easier under the cloak of night—a bandage concealing the rawest parts of our hearts. Our conversation shifted from lighthearted jabs to a heavier pace until our journey came to an end. Even though we'd said our goodbyes at the doorway of my small cabin, I sensed he still had something on his mind.

I put my hand on the doorknob and paused. He wasn't going to come out and say it. Not without some prying first. "What is it?"

He lingered behind me, likely searching for words as he often did. His face was barely visible in the scant candlelight that filtered through the window. He stepped forward, meeting my eyes, my heart thundering as he grew closer. His whisper softly caressed my face. "Promise me I can trust you."

"Promise," I said, my cheeks heating up, acutely aware of how little space separated us.

He grew quieter this time, peeking around us before speaking; an unnecessary measure given how dark it was. "I found an exit."

The warmth in my cheeks and the electricity of the moment rapidly subsided as the implication of his reveal hit my chest with the force of a ton of bricks. "What do you mean, an exit?"

"You know exactly what I mean. There's a way out of this city, and it's not even hard to get to."

I was silent, chewing on my lip as I processed this information. We were safe here. The sickness—the other kingdoms that had fallen into anarchy couldn't get to us. Right? "You're telling me the city is compromised?"

"Yes. I mean, no. I don't believe it's compromised. And honestly, I don't think it ever was."

"I don't understand." He wasn't making any sense, as usual. "What are you trying to say?"

He sighed heavily, scuffing his feet in the dirt at the bottom of the step as he searched again for the right words.

I impatiently raised an eyebrow. His vagueness annoyed me to no end. Could he never get to the point? "Lander?"

The worn leather of his gloves scratched against my skin as he grasped my upper arms firmly. His tone was as hushed as it was intense.

"Meet me tomorrow night by the south-side apothecary when the sun falls below the peaks. The one with the sea-nymph carved over the doorway. I'll explain it all then."

His eyes darted around, as if something or someone was watching, waiting, listening in somewhere nearby. I'd never seen him this nervous before. But if he truly knew of a way in and out of this fortress, that kind of information could be both dangerous and damning.

"Okay. I'll be there," I replied, even more confused than before.

He released his grip, pivoting away, making to go back home. And as he retreated into the darkness, his voice carried on the wind, floating out from nothingness as the night swallowed him up. "See you then."

"See you."

I wasn't sure if my reply even reached him through the stifling darkness, and I stood there for a moment, blinking into the night, thoroughly bewildered. Lander had only ever wanted to protect the last member of his family. Why then was he suddenly interested in an exit out of the walls of safety? Unless he meant to report it for a reward. But if he did, the investigation might find him in a difficult place. How did he even discover it? Would they suspect he'd been exposed?

I shuddered at the thought, remembering again what I'd seen on the streets. What I'd seen many times before. Sometimes, the exposed were treated exactly like the infected and killed on the spot. As ruthless as this city was about protecting its residents, he might be at risk, but no one knew for sure what the consequences would be on any given day. It depended on the mood of the gate guards, whether there was any fighting back, or the level of symptoms. There were reports of people attempting to scale the fences being killed, their bodies burned to prevent possible spread, but I had no proof of that. Shaking my head, I turned to enter the small cabin, gathering these concerns to warn him tomorrow about his possible recklessness.

On a typical night, when I arrived home, Mama was already in bed. But tonight, she sat at our modest dinner table, two candles lit in the middle. This wasn't entirely unusual, as she did occasionally wait for my safe return. However, I found myself startled by a stark difference, stopped in my tracks when I laid eyes on the guest she had sitting at the table next to her.

He was broad and muscular, linen sleeves tight on his forearms, with long dark hair tied back with a piece of leather. Streaks of gray peppered his hair, and the early hints of wrinkles were evident on his face. I guessed he was a few years older than Mama, who was in her early thirties, and couldn't shake the observation that the pair had been rather relaxed until my entrance. Much too relaxed. Close to a point that was unusual for a simple guest.

"Who are you?" I blurted out the instant I saw him.

"Oh! Is it that time already?" Mama exclaimed, abruptly hopping to her feet in surprise. She wrung her hands nervously on her skirts as if my presence was particularly unexpected, despite the fact that I lived here. She gave me a smile that didn't quite reach her eyes, brows furrowed in trepidation as she reluctantly gestured to her guest.

"Sadie dear, I . . . um, this is one of my friends," she explained, her guest as uneasy as her. He followed Mama's example and stood, giving me a curt nod, hands clasped so tightly on the back of the wooden chair I thought he might break it. "His name is Thamus Hodges. He's a farmer who supplies the shopkeeper down on the west side, near Tyben's Square. You know the store I'm talking about—the one with the pair of fish on the sign."

I frowned at the pair, eyes darting suspiciously between them, the way they'd been sitting close together setting off alarms in my gut. Was he a friend? Or something more? "No, I don't suppose I do."

Mama shuffled her feet at my curt response and paled as if she might faint.

"That's quite all right. Um, we planned to tell you soon about everything, but I guess since we're here I suppose I can explain it all now. You see, over time we've gotten awfully close, and . . ." she rambled, and reached out to take Thamus's hand. He obliged, the lines in his face softening at the touch.

Over time? What time? My heart sank as a shy smile played at her lips and a glint flashed in her eyes. To say I was disappointed was an understatement. She'd told me for years she had been waiting for Papa's return, that she believed him to be alive. Yes, that likelihood was extremely low, as was the possibility he could enter the city. The gates had only ever been opened once since the virus's appearance in the world, fifty years later when it was thought to have finally disappeared. Unfortunately, unbeknownst to Ancthia, the resurgence had already begun, a mysterious event where the virus suddenly came back to the world after disappearing for nearly two decades. And that's when we arrived. We'd been among the last to cross the gates before the city caught wind of this devastating event. *But is it really that unlikely? After all, what Lander had revealed only moments ago . . .*

I shook my head, trying to throw the thought out. No. Every resident had to be documented in the city. Ancthia had order and protection. And most of all, Papa would've found us by now had he snuck inside. He'd have sorted through the seventy thousand people scraping by in this isolated valley. Or, he would've been used as a public example of the consequences of illegal entry. He likely wasn't coming back. I'd known that deep down for years.

I would never let go of Papa for as long as I lived. No one would ever be worthy of replacing him. Mama might be able to move on, but I never would. I understood her need to seek the warmth of love in this lonely, isolated place but I couldn't squash the grief that erupted within me at the sight. I never thought I'd see that glint in her eyes again—one that had always been reserved for Papa. Confusion swirled around inside of me, quickly filling the emptiness I'd created playing my heart out. I pushed it all down, biting back the prickling in my eyes, and mustered the nicest smile I could manage for Mama.

"You don't need to explain. It's nice to meet you, Mr. Hodges," I choked out over the lump in my throat. I fleetingly wondered if I'd managed to get that entire bite of dry potato from earlier down.

"It's nice to meet you, too, Sadie," he replied, kindly but warily. He put his right fist to his left shoulder and tapped it twice, an alternative to the old-fashioned handshake that had become extinct at the emergence of the virus. I did not engage in a return shake, still reeling from what I had walked in on.

"I do wish I could stay and further meet your acquaintance, but I'm rather exhausted from my performance. Excuse me." I pushed past the pair to my bedroom, wishing I could've managed to be a hair less rude. But the shock was a tad overwhelming, and I didn't think I could participate in any type of conversation without bursting into a fit of tears.

The voices outside of my thin wooden door were hushed but soft, and thankfully unintelligible. I heard the front door open and close, and then a slight pause before Mama's footsteps pattered toward my room. The doorknob rattled a second before I heard the hinges to my room squeal.

"Sadie," she said quietly, peering around the wooden slab. I was sitting on the edge of my bed, having taken off my shoes, attempting to smooth out the frizz that had taken over my head. If I didn't get to it before bed, my hair would be an absolute mess by morning. That wasn't a chore I had the energy to tackle. She cautiously crept into the bedroom and slowly sat down next to me. The straw-filled mattress sunk in slightly with her presence. "I'm sorry this is how you had to find out. I hadn't yet found the right time to tell you."

I set the brush in my lap, running my fingers across the bristles again and again. *Sure,* I thought. *Sure you would've told me.* "Would there ever have been a right time?"

She sighed and shook her head. "No, I don't suppose. Please, are you angry with me? It's been forever since I've had this. With Thamus, I finally have that spark that I've been wishing for, that life might be worth pursuing."

I bristled. "Yes, I'm angry!" I glared at her glittering blue eyes, the spark she'd mentioned visible within them at the mention of his name. A spark that should only be reserved for Papa. "How long has this been going on behind my back?"

"Only a few months," admitted Mama quietly.

I nearly came unglued. She'd been actively hiding this for that long? "Months?" I shrieked. "You've been hanging around him for months and only now told me?" I threw my hands up in exasperation. "What about Papa? You've said you were waiting for him! What happens if he shows up the way I did? He's not going to take too kindly coming home to find a stranger in his house!"

Mama's jaw twitched. She took my hands, rubbing her rough fingers over my smooth skin. "Listen. There's not a day I don't think of your Papa. And not a day that I don't feel guilty for leaving him that way. I always believed he would catch up with us, as fit and fast as he was. He knew the way to the city and our escape plan by heart. How long it would take to travel that distance. But when he didn't show within the first few nights, I realized there was no way he made it out alive. The fever was spreading fast in our town, and he was directly involved with the infected tree, and I . . . I should have told you."

I frowned deeply at this admission. Mama had never spoken of this. She'd always held out some hope that he might be out there. At least, that's what she'd always told me. "Mama, what . . . ? All this time, you've known? You've known that he was dead?" I yanked my hands away as she nodded slowly, unable to meet my eyes. I gripped the side of the bed to ground myself, my world suddenly spinning out of control.

"I'm sorry. I truly am. I couldn't bear to see you lose any more hope than you'd already lost. I wanted to wait for the right time, but it hadn't come yet, and—"

"Stop it." I squeezed my eyes shut, grimacing against the sting in my heart. I grabbed at my chest, at the pain. "I get that you didn't want to hurt me. I get waiting for the right time. But what is wrong with you? Obviously now isn't that time, yet here we are! Don't you think it hurts worse to find out in the middle of all this that you knew all along? That you've been leading me on with a bunch of false hope?" My voice grew incredibly shrill, the shock of both admissions in one night far too much.

"I wasn't leading you on, I was planning to tell you—"

"No, you weren't!" I hollered. "You're a liar! You only told me because you got caught!" I hopped to my feet, needing to pace, to find some sort of distraction to the chaos in my mind.

She was silent, picking at the pills of fabric on the worn quilt.

"What, do you have nothing else to say for yourself?" I demanded, my eyes prickling.

"I'm sorry." Mama tried to pull me into a hug, but I pushed her away. I didn't want her apology. I wanted my dad.

"Sorry isn't enough! You just told me my dad is *dead*! And that you've known this for years! Ever since you dragged me out of our old house without him! Why did you do that, anyway? He would've been home in only a few hours!" My voice broke into a sob. I stood as far away from Mama as possible, who had sat back down on the side of the bed.

"Please understand, Sadie, there simply wasn't enough time. We couldn't afford to wait for hours. You saw that tree, rising up to the sky faster than we could run! Is that what you wanted? To die floating off into nothingness? No! Especially not with your fear of heights," Mama shouted with a sarcastic laugh, her jaw tense as she pointed fiercely at her chest. "I did what I had to for your protection! You should be thanking me!"

"Thanking you? What about Papa's protection? Did you not care about his wellbeing? Do you even now? I mean, you didn't even care to tell me he's dead until you found a way to replace him!"

"Thamus is not his replacement," Mama hissed through gritted teeth, fingers blanched from gripping the bedclothes tightly.

"You're right," I spat. "You can't replace someone you never loved. I can't ever remember a time I saw you sitting that close to Papa. Looking at him with such fondness in your eyes."

Mama hopped to her feet, aghast. I'd struck a nerve, and I wanted to punch myself for being pleased about it. "You'd better watch your mouth, Sadie Elizabeth!" she warned me.

I glowered harshly up at her. "Well? Did you love him?" I shot back.

She paused, matching the intensity of my stare. Horror surged in my stomach. Was this really such a difficult question?

"Give me an answer!" I demanded. She was going to give me one if it was the last thing she did. Even if it was one I didn't want to know.

"Yes! My answer is yes!"

The knot of burning dread in my stomach tightened. "That's not enough! I want to hear you say it! Say you loved him!" I exploded, fresh, hot tears pouring down my face.

"Stop being ridiculous!" Mama said.

"I'll never stop! Not until you tell me the truth! If you can even do that, with as many lies as you've caught yourself in lately!"

She inhaled sharply. "Yes, I loved him!" she finally shouted, giving in to her own angry tears. "I loved him, do you hear me? And I now love Thamus! There! Is that enough for you? Are you happy now?"

My shoulders heaved as I stared at her, wide-eyed. She'd finally said it. And yet, I couldn't find it in myself to believe her.

"Get out of my room."

"Don't you dare speak to me that way," she growled, her damp cheeks glistening in the candlelight. "This is my house, and I'll not be disrespected by my own daughter in it."

"It's my house too! I spent the last three hours of my evening working to pay for it. I've been helping you pay for it since I was eight!" I fumed. I stomped my foot, planting it to the floor. To *my* floor.

She pursed her lips, unable to argue against this point. But she didn't leave.

"I said, get out!" I sobbed, hands curling into fists at my side. "Get out! Go away! I don't want to see you right now!"

She wordlessly got to her feet, each step heavier than Lander's boots as she complied with my demand. And when she slammed the door behind her, my window rattling from the force, I collapsed onto my bed, burying my face in my pillow until I cried myself to sleep.

2

"Sadie! Stop walking so fast, wait up!"

Lander's footsteps thundered from behind me with such a racket I nearly mistook him for a horse. I ignored him, still reeling from the conversation Mama and I had the night prior, wanting to have some time alone to process. But Lander was never one to leave me alone no matter how much I might protest. With a resigned sigh, I accepted his presence, slowing my pace to match his.

The fog this morning was dense, having rolled in during the night off the city's lake, obscuring our pathway. It swirled around our feet wispy and skittish, as though it were a kitten winding between our ankles.

"How did you even find me?"

Lander panted hard at my side, obviously having ran the entire way here. "We take the same path to school. It wasn't exactly a challenge."

"Run any further and you're likely to breathe out a lung," I quipped, side-eyeing my friend. "When was the last time you exercised?"

"Mind your business," he grumbled, hands on his knees. I paused to let him catch his breath.

Finally getting ahold of himself, Lander rose, and we continued, shadowy forms visible around us between the tendrils of fog as other students rushed to class. The sound of their chatter was far away despite our proximity, the mist swallowing up their voices. We walked along in silence, words rolling around on my tongue but not quite forming. I was still stuck deep in my mind, the image of Mama and Thamus as fresh as rotten porridge behind my eyelids.

Lander intently watched the path ahead of us, hoping to scope out any obstacles in our way. He wasn't what I'd call successful, though, judging by the way he tripped over the edge of someone's garden and almost slammed into a wall. He was successful, however, in distracting me to the point that I'd failed to notice he'd been watching me as closely as the road this entire time.

"Hey. Look at me."

The sudden break in silence nearly made me jump right out of my tightly laced shoes. I did as instructed—albeit hesitantly—gaze settling on the gentle furrow of his dark brows, rested atop long eyelashes that would make any girl jealous. He studied me for a moment, eyes darting across my features before coming to a conclusion. I willed my heart to slow down, something in his face causing it to sputter unceremoniously, and turned away the instant my cheeks heated up.

"You've been crying."

"No I haven't," I quickly denied, knowing full well that the lie was as feeble as my elderly neighbor Mr. Kneiss, who stood bent at a ninety-degree angle. The old man always hobbled along with a stick as a cane, the wood as twisted as his back.

He detected the lie before I even said it, launching his accusation right as I launched my denial.

"Liar."

I was thankful that he didn't press for an explanation, knowing that if I wanted to talk about it, I would. The knowledge that he'd noticed, that he was right there if I needed him was enough to soothe the painful knots in my stomach. He instead went back to his feeble attempts at seeing through the fog, and I went back to wallowing inside the confusion and sadness inside my head.

He thought it was me at first when laughter rang over our shoulders the instant he tripped over an upturned stone. But the pitter patter of multiple pairs of feet drew his attention to another direction.

Lander and I peered backward in unison, searching for the source. Two girls, one with waist length, shiny blonde hair and the other with a long dark braid dashed up to us. The blonde, named Cyntha, had the most beautiful green eyes I'd ever seen on a person, with white lashes accentuating their ethereal beauty. The brunette, Inala, was seldom without her best friend, and she wore a splash of adorable freckles on her round cheeks. She was shy, unlike her outgoing other half, making the pair a good combination.

I'd asked her once why it always appeared as though she wanted to hide from the world. After lots of probing, she'd finally admitted embarrassment over her accent. As many years as Ancthia had been locked down, most everyone here spoke the same exact way. During the short period of opening, people poured in from many parts of the world. Because of the city's seclusion, the sound of a novel accent was both intriguing and a blaring mark of difference, one that often made her a target for various unkindness and suspicions.

Difference or not, they were both wonderful girls, and I'd noticed on more than one occasion that Cyntha was sweet on Lander. A fact that had me wanting to yank her perfectly blond hair right out of her head. I immediately regretted this call to violence, as Cyntha had always been nothing but kind.

The two approached us, Cyntha giving a cheerful greeting. "Good morning, Lander! Sadie!" Inala simply smiled, giving a small wave as they both came in between Lander and I, slowing down to match our pace. Cyntha took the spot next to Lander, no surprise there, and quickly engaged him in conversation. I was glad to have gotten Inala, due to my lack of desire for social interaction this morning. Though my fingers twitched themselves slowly into fists as I repeatedly peeked over at my best friend who was apparently having a great time with Cyntha.

She tightly clutched her notebook, working her thumbs together, awkwardly chewing on her lip as she typically did. Inala and I met about a year prior during a group project at school. She was a good friend, and we often sat together at lunch hour. Whenever we were lucky enough to get our hands on a book, we'd share it between us, our conversations typically revolving around the latest story we'd read.

Books were a rare commodity in Ancthia due to the scarcity of materials causing terribly high prices. Isolated as we were, any and all materials had to be grown in the tree farms and fields surrounding the city. We'd learned in school how Ancthia once had places called libraries, where anyone could walk in and choose a book to take home for a short while. After the virus, libraries were no longer allowed in the city, locked down and boarded up to prevent exposure from one to another by the sharing of books. While it was known for sure that physical contact could spread the virus, there was suspicion that secondary contact could also facilitate contagion. Currently, none of the research done into the virus had borne an accurate representation of how it could jump from one person to another. Even more so, how it could infect the ground beneath our feet. All that was known was once infected, always infected, and even after the fever passed, the survived could still pass it on. Its origins remained a mystery, as did a cure, and once common social commodities of everyday life—such as libraries—were a thing of the past. Not that any were left to mourn over. When the original city lifted off into nothingness after its infection fifty years ago, these mythical buildings went along with it.

Our secret sharing of books was a welcome distraction to the blandness of school. Inala had a large collection, as her family was wealthier than mine and Lander's. On the rare occasion I could save up enough extra money from performing, I'd sneak to the bookstore on the far end of the city and indulge in extravagant purchases such as literature. Inala was always thrilled to see a new title, her shyness dissolving at the sight of an aged leather-bound book. She aspired to be a writer, and from what I'd seen of her writing, she was a fine one.

"My mum found me a new notebook," Inala told me, sensing that I wasn't up for initiating any sort of conversation.

"That's wonderful, have you written anything yet?" I smiled, happy for her good fortune. Inala was a lucky one, and I was lucky having the opportunity to bear witness to the joys most weren't privileged to.

She shook her head. "Not yet. I want to make sure that when I do, it's with words I truly want to memorialize, like how artists carve a stone. You can't un-carve it, the same way you can't pull ink out of paper." She paused for a moment, contemplating what she'd said while chewing harder on her lip. "Does that sound silly? I fear it does. Truly, tell me." Inala lifted her gaze, eyes wide with the desperate fear that her words had sounded ridiculous.

"It doesn't sound silly. Not even close. I wouldn't want to write willy-nilly either on something so special."

Her shoulders relaxed, and she gave me a nose-crinkling grin.

Cyntha laughed then, the sound equivalent to the pealing of a dainty bell, and Inala and I peeked over. Lander was holding back a chortle, I supposed to appear manly, but the way his cheeks were puffed up around pursed lips made him resemble a frog. I only hoped Cyntha found it as goofy as I did. I averted my eyes, trying not to laugh, and focused instead on the emerging school ahead of us, a large sea of white parting around a dark fortress.

Right before entering, Lander grabbed my shoulder, pulling me aside for a moment, checking around us to make sure no one was listening. He whispered, "Don't forget to meet me tonight," and then rushed off into the doorway before I could even respond. I was grateful for the reminder. I'd almost forgotten. The chaos and turmoil from last night had taken over the forefront of my mind.

We took our usual places, and I watched as the sun broke through the fog, the warmth lifting away the cloak to reveal its hidden secrets. I stared out into the cloudless sky, feeling strangely alone in what was otherwise a crowded classroom.

***

The day ticked by, slow as usual. I swore Mrs. Fenter refused to put in even a molecule of effort to make her lessons entertaining. Lunch hour couldn't come fast enough, and I sat outside in a sunny corner, the wooden fence keeping us unruly children from escaping. I always loved this corner. The small cedar tree nearby reminded me of my father, who always came home carrying the sharp scent of timber.

Mama had packed me another potato, and much like the one I'd had last night, it was far past the point of being warm. I couldn't complain. Potatoes were the easiest crop to grow in our small garden. At least I had something to eat. I tried to wolf it down quickly, not yet hungry enough for the flavor to be anything but gross, and guzzled water in an attempt to get it down.

Lander sat with some of the boys, something he tended to do after any interaction with Cyntha. Their chatter was ridiculously loud, louder than a pack of dogs chasing a squirrel. I watched as Lander repeatedly glanced over at the pretty girl, who was sitting daintily at the picnic table next to Inala. Usually, he'd be glancing at me instead. Shaking my head, I swallowed back the bitter flavor of disappointment, focusing instead on the increasing ridiculousness of the boy's hoots and hollers. Cyntha was unaware of what was going on around her, although I truly didn't understand how she could be oblivious to such obnoxious noise. Lander was clearly talking about her, the tips of his ears tinged red as the boys playfully roughhoused him. It appeared they were trying to egg him on to speak with her again. He finally relented, and with the redness spreading, approached Cyntha. I couldn't make out what he said, but she blushed a fine cherry in response, and took his outstretched hand.

He led her over to the fence where they sat together on the sun-kissed grass, the distance between them about as large as a hair. They reminded me of a pair of doves, close and cozy, and Lander's gaze finally flickered over to me at one point. When our eyes met, the side of my mouth curled up into a mischievous smirk. He shot back a glare, knowing I would be teasing the mess out of him later, and turned back to his romantic endeavors as I shook my head. *That's what he gets for entertaining the attention of another girl. He'll never hear the end of this from me. Not if I can help it.*

The schoolyard was abuzz after this; nothing better than some puppy-love to break up the monotony of the day. The pair practically floated into the schoolhouse, Lander gallantly pulling out her chair, and things settled down as Mrs. Fenter returned to her place. The lecture went on, boring as usual, the sound of her pencil scratching against the slate board near the podium. I'd almost fallen asleep, my eyelids growing heavy, when a loud *thump* rang out from the other side of the classroom. Figuring someone dropped their book, I lazily peeked over to see who it was, shocked to find that one of my classmates had collapsed.

Cyntha had fallen limp in the aisle between the desks, white hair splayed out gracefully on the floor around her head. Shouts rang out from my classmates, and Lander rushed to her side.

His voice shook. "Cyntha! Cyntha, can you hear me? Wake up!"

Mrs. Fenter, skirts gripped in her hands as not to trip over them, hastily pattered over toward the commotion, ordering the students to stand down and get out of the way.

"Move, children, move!"

She swatted at the stragglers with a ruler, her stinging slaps great motivation for everyone to give her space. But Lander didn't budge, still kneeling next to her, and he and Mrs. Fenter locked eyes as she softly touched the girl's face. Cyntha didn't even flinch, and for a brief moment, I wondered if she were dead.

A worry that was quickly quelled by the visible, yet laborious rise and fall of her chest.

"Get in your seats," Mrs. Fenter said, her voice steady and stern. A few students crept slowly to their assigned places, but apparently not quick enough as she followed her order with a loud, "Move!" This sent the kids scrambling, almost knocking each other over to get out of range of her ruler.

She peered over her glasses at Lander, who hadn't even twitched. "You too, dear."

I was shocked at how kindly she'd said it, unsure if I'd ever heard Mrs. Fenter say anything remotely gentle, and the hair stood up on the back of my neck. Lander hesitated, but obeyed, folding his leather-bound hands tightly on top of the desk when he reached his seat.

Mrs. Fenter straightened up, firmly addressing the class. "Do not move, do not talk, do not leave this room. That is an order."

No one even blinked, terrified for both Cyntha and of our instructor as she whisked her way out of the door, the latch clicking into place as it shut behind her. There wasn't a hint of a whisper, no one daring to speak aloud, as electric fear buzzed through the room. Because deep down we all knew what the truth would likely be—the virus was inside the city. And worse, inside our classroom.

***

Mrs. Fenter didn't return.

Instead, medics flooded the schoolhouse, covered head to toe in large, white suits, a mask with bilateral filters making them resemble a common housefly. Furthering the resemblance, they buzzed around the classroom, ushering us into small groups away from Cyntha. A group of them carried her out on a rudimentary stretcher. While they held the door open, I saw gate guards lined up, preventing the entry of anyone except themselves and medics into the classroom. Not a word was spoken to any of us, yet we all knew where we'd be going.

They separated Lander from the group first, Mrs. Fenter likely having told them of his close contact with Cyntha. He was led out of the door, head down, hair obscuring his eyes. Unnerved by the fact I couldn't see his face or his expression, I unsuccessfully tried to peek around the medics in front of me, desperately needing to know if he was okay. I never got my answer. They ushered us outside into the schoolyard, lined up at a distance, and checked us each for symptoms, one by one. No one spoke, no one moved unless instructed. Fear was thick in the warm air, the welcoming warmth of the sun now hot and heavy and oppressive.

The entire examination was a blur, and I was quickly ushered out to the street with a medic. The road was lined with gate guards, curious onlookers peeping, but at a safe distance, for fear of contact with a suspected case. It was strange being on the other side of the crowd, as if they'd forgotten who we were—what we were. People. Children. One of them. Whenever contagion was involved, humanity was thrown to the wayside in exchange for madness. I avoided their glares and jeers, but the words were not as easily ignored. We'd become their biggest threat. And they wanted us dead.

A group of men chanted over and over, "Kill them! Burn them! Kill them! Burn them!"

Another berated the Guards. "What's taking you so long? Get them out of here!"

"The littles are right across the street, evacuate them!" a woman's voice rang out over the gathering crowd, trying to force her way over to their building.

One of my classmate's parents exploded through the crowd exactly as I'd seen that man do the night before. To my horror, the guards beat him down into the street before he could breach the line of medics, his cries of pain slamming into me as hard as each blow he was dealt.

I covered my ears, trying to block it all out, as we walked for a good thirty minutes to the large isolation building. I was no longer Sadie—I was a public spectacle. A hazard. The springtime sun was warm, yet I couldn't shake off a bitter, dreadful chill that pierced me to my bones. Cyntha was going to die. Lander had been the closest one to her. And . . . how could I become a musician for my father if I was killed before even having the chance? How could Lander's mother live without him—the last surviving member of her family?

At one point I was pelted by handfuls of pebbles, the gate guards apprehending the perpetrators far slower than they should've.

I knew where we were going before the building even came into view. I had a brief and fragmented memory of this place, from when we'd first arrived—the isolation dungeon where Ancthia had kept newcomers to make sure there weren't any signs or symptoms of the virus. Sometimes for a month or more. Thankfully, isolation for Ancthians only lasted about two weeks, and I braced myself for the possibility of being stuck here alone for such an extended period. I was no stranger to solitude. However, since Lander came along, loneliness and I had become rather estranged.

The building was tall and made of white stone, melting into the wall of mountains behind it. Strategically placed beyond the edge of the city, the location was meant to keep possible infection at a safe distance from others. It had a large, rectangular shape to it, windows peppered unevenly throughout its surface. The mortar holding together the stones was clearly haphazardly applied, the strokes between each piece uneven and rushed. Yet, it appeared sturdy and solid, with an impenetrable air about it, resembling a prison embedded into the fortress of a mountainside.

"Are we going to be burned?" I asked, nervously eyeing the smoke puffing up from a jagged metal chimney on the side of the building. As expected, my question was unanswered. The city denied ever having burned affected citizens, but based on the amount of rumors, most feared it as truth. Mama told me it was simply ridiculous, that no one with a lick of common sense would burn someone who was infected, lest the viral particles become airborne in the smoke. Still, I worried.

Mama said the preferred method was to let them go naturally. When the fever ended, the force of gravity was no longer applicable, and one would simply float up never to be seen again. Exactly the way the tree from our hometown did.

Exactly as the entire original city of Ancthia did.

Mama.

I was still angry. Still upset that she'd kept secrets from me for so long. But guilt nudged its way into my chest. Was that turbulent argument the last thing we'd ever say to one another? Was she going to live the rest of her life with the fact that I'd died before resolving our fight?

I didn't have time to dwell on it, for I was led through a pair of heavy metal doors. The medic ushered me around a corner to a set of frigid marble stairs.

Chilly was the air, the building's location chronically blocked by the peaks, and as I shivered, goosebumps rose on my arms in a feeble attempt to create warmth. Despite the cold, my palms wouldn't stop sweating.

I counted seven flights of stairs before we reached a door the medic deemed acceptable, and they pushed me into a long hallway lined with various metal doors. The doors were expertly fitted into the stone and mortar entryways, cleanly sealing each room. Another medic stood at the end of the hall leading one of my classmates, a boy named Caven. Our eyes met, and I caught a glimpse of his pure and utter fright before he was ushered in, the door slamming with finality behind him.

I was halted at the ninth door, the medic pulling out a ring of keys as his colleague brushed past us toward the stairs. The medic fumbled endlessly with the keys; the large gloves complicating the process. I rapidly grew impatient, wanting to get on with it already. We'd been standing there forever.

"Need any help?" I offered, only to be waved away with a sharp grunt. Whoever was under there hadn't uttered a word, even to themselves. Not unusual, due to the rumors about the virus spreading across conversation. I was calmed by the knowledge I hadn't spoken to Cyntha today. My words were safe. Yet the calm was short-lived, fear surging again when I remembered Lander and Inala . . . and strict Mrs. Fenter . . .

Distracted by my thoughts, I hadn't noticed the medic had found the correct key. I was pushed hard into the room, stumbling, nearly falling flat on my face. He latched the lock into place faster than I could regain my footing, and I turned and banged on the metal door, thinking again of Mama. Did she know? She'd be worried sick to find that I'd never returned without a single explanation.

"Wait!" I yelled through the door, the pain in my fists intensifying with each blow I dealt the metal. A small window—outfitted with crisscrossing metal wires—was embedded in the top. I jumped again and again, in an attempt to see who was out there. My search came up empty, but that didn't mean the hallway was deserted. "My mom! She knows where I am, right? Hello? Please! Anyone!"

Unsurprisingly, there was no answer, and I resigned to exploring the room, with nothing else left to do. A bed sat in the middle covered in smooth, starched white sheets. Only a single flat and unwelcoming pillow was placed at the head of the bed. I reached out, touching the mattress I'd been sentenced to. It was incredibly hard.

There was a wooden nightstand, a candle atop it, and I noticed it was bolted into the stone floor, leading me to see the bed had undergone the same treatment. A small table stood opposite the bed, with a slate and chalk pencil, I guessed for entertainment. I almost rolled my eyes. Near the table was a doorway with a small bathroom, the stone bath rising out of the floor. It was cramped and chilly, with only one window—one that I knew wouldn't give me the honor of direct sunlight.

Similar to the window on the door, this one had crisscrossing wires from top to bottom, except behind it were thick metal bars. I was perplexed until I realized its wooden frame could be lifted—after a ridiculous amount of effort, of course. Couldn't have the exposed jumping out of the window. Fresh air flooded into the cold room, a sliver of warmth coming with it. I inhaled deeply, resting my forehead against the metal bars to see out as a damp, mossy scent tinged my nostrils.

The sight below left me reeling and dizzy, as I was much too high in the air for my comfort. I stepped back to a reasonable distance, heart roaring in my ears. *If I ever contract this virus, I'll surely die of fear before even being released.*

I sat in the center of the room, placing my head between my knees until the dizziness subsided, allowing the reality of the situation to settle in. There was no doubt about it. It had to be the fever. Normal sicknesses didn't cause someone to collapse out of nowhere. Where had it even come from, and why my classmate? Tears prickled at my eyes as I thought again about Cyntha. The city could let her survive the virus, only to be released into the sky after recovering. Some people didn't even survive the infection, succumbing to the fever early on. Or, the city would kill her outright. I believed the latter avenue to be the most humane, as staring out this high window was torture enough, let alone having to float off into the sky to certain death. She didn't deserve this. She didn't deserve any of it. And she had finally managed to snag the attention of Lander much to my dismay ...

My head snapped up as I thought of him, thick, cold dread filling my stomach. *Lander. He'd found a way out of the city.*

I stood, pacing the room as thoughts ravaged my mind, faster and faster.

Lander had been in contact with Cyntha that morning. *Close* contact. For it to happen right after him telling me about the pathway couldn't have been a coincidence. Maybe he was trying to warn me about something. Or, maybe it wasn't Lander who'd found the path.

It could've been Cyntha.

I shook my head, trying to organize the thoughts. I wasn't sure how many hours I'd spent turning the possibilities over and over, but as the sun disappeared from the peaks, I came to a conclusion. It had to have been Cyntha. Cyntha found the path and told Lander—she was smitten with him, after all. What better way to get his attention than a damning, adventurous secret? Lander obviously returned the affection, I mean, which teenage boy couldn't deny attention from the most beautiful girl in the school? I found myself unexpectedly angry. She'd put Lander of all people at risk, with his kind, selfless heart, simply to explore something that should be left alone. The outside world was chaos and disease, something everyone in the city wanted to escape. How selfish of her. How cruel. The entire class and who knew who else were now exposed. I assumed they were likely rounding up Cyntha's family, and anyone who'd interacted with her within the last two weeks.

I couldn't hear anything through the thick door, try as I might, and I was beyond bored. I drew on the slate, stared out of the window from a distance, and ran in circles to have something to do. A temporary reprieve of boredom arrived when someone slid a plate of food through the doorway, a folded letter alongside it. Before the door could slam behind it, I ran to it, screaming, "Wait! Wait, please stop! How long will I be in here?" I was too late, and the metal clicked shut. I banged on the door, knowing my efforts would be fruitless, but at least I could pretend to be connected to someone else. Even if my pleas fell on deaf ears.

Tiring of banging, I carried the plate of cold food over to the table, slumping into the hard chair they'd provided. I'd been given asparagus, overcooked nearly to mush, mixed in with nothing other than a potato. They'd failed to supply me with any water, so I resigned to chugging handfuls out of the bathroom sink.

I read the letter while I chewed what turned out to be a horrendously undercooked potato. It said I'd be here two weeks for observation. If no symptoms were present, I'd be returned home. *Home*. Reading this word choked me up, the dry potato not helping any as usual, and I cried myself to sleep on the hard bed.

The morning wasn't any better, and each day fell into a routine of breakfast, lunch, and dinner. No other letters were slipped under the door, no other entertainment provided, and I even attempted to sabotage whomever was bringing the food by trying to wrench the door wider as it opened. This ended up being an awful idea, as my fingers were slammed between the door and the wall, bruising them spectacularly. I was thankful they didn't break, but they were purple and swollen for days.

The medics didn't consider the need for clean laundry, and I spent many hours trying to wash my skirts in the bathtub using a bar of soap. My swollen fingers made it difficult to maneuver heavy soaked fabric, freezing cold air and water furthering the difficulties. I realized too late that there was nothing to hang them on after washing. The first time I did it, I laid them on the floor, flipping them here and there, shivering under the thin quilt as I waited. The second time, I attempted to hang them out the window by sliding the fabric between the bars. It worked great until a large gust of wind took hold of one of my underskirts, the white fabric breaking loose and fluttering off into nothingness. I screamed curses out the window at it until I accidentally glanced down, becoming lightheaded from the heights to the point I nearly fainted right there. I returned to laying them on the floor after that, using my singular candle for heat. The risk of losing my undergarments proved to be a far greater danger than slow drying clothes.

Despite my troubles with heights, I kept the window open, wishing to hear the bustling city or any signs of other people. Even when the winds shifted in, the isolation building was too far from the general population for any noise to carry. The effort to connect to the outside world wasn't entirely fruitless, as various types of birds visited, using the windowsill as a perch. I attempted to communicate with feeble attempts at whistling, which typically resulted in scaring the bird off, particularly if they witnessed even a twitch of my nose. Free as they were, their presence kept me company and kept me hoping it wouldn't be much longer before we were on the same side of the bars.

Talking to myself, pretending Mama and Lander were there became another activity of which I partook. I resolved the argument with my mother through manufactured conversations, wishing I could beg for forgiveness for how I'd treated her, if I could see her one last time and make amends. She was all I had left. I couldn't lose her. I bargained with the heavens to let me make it out alive, pleading that I'd even tolerate Thamus if it only meant I could be free.

Inala and I had discussions on books that I wasn't sure even existed, and I found myself rolling around in fits of demented laughter. I'd stop and think about it after a particularly loud peal shocked me back into awareness and then return to laughing at the absurdity of it all. There were various moments where I wished I'd contracted the virus if only to make the isolation end, wondering if my grip on reality was weakening. But perhaps the worst part of it all was the constant, never-ending worry that Lander wouldn't make it out of this alive, one that sobered me out of whatever temporary insanity my mind concocted.

The days had slipped through my sense of perception with such ease that when a medic entered the room for the first time since my stay, I jumped to my feet in shock. The hooded figure stared me down, eyes hidden behind the mesh cover. I cleared my throat, having not spoken to an actual person in so long I was trying to deduce if this was real or if I was face-to-face with an apparition.

"Hi," I managed, squinting to see if the figure would dissolve into a puff of smoke after the words left my lips.

"Sadie Cleamont?" a gruff voice rumbled from underneath the hood. I almost leaped for joy at being spoken to by a real person after two weeks.

"Yes!" I eagerly replied, "I'm Sadie."

"Come with me," the medic indicated to follow. I went without hesitation, the taste of freedom in my grasp.

The warmth of the sun, the sight of large clouds passing by, the brush of wind on my skin, was liberating. I skipped after the medic down the streets, a group of five gate guards on our tail. I couldn't wait to see Mama and reunite with my violin. Had my instrument missed me as much as I missed it? Had Mama been lonely, without her only daughter there to keep her company and get into trouble at school?

That thought was immediately squashed when I remembered Thamus. He'd likely been there, pretending to be her knight in shining armor, sweeping her up out of loneliness. The vision of them together made me cringe. I hated to see anyone other than Papa in that spot. But if it kept her sane in isolation, I grudgingly welcomed it. Being alone for two weeks was no walk in the park, as I'd recently experienced.

Mama was in the kitchen window as we trudged up the path, washing dishes. She was clearly exhausted, purple bags thick under her eyes. I wondered if she'd even slept the last few weeks. Though, despite her disheveled appearance, I could hear her humming softly through the open glass. She must've caught the flicker of movement as we approached because she suddenly looked up, eyes growing wide as the saucer she was cleaning. The dish clattered into the sink, and she raced out of the front door, immediately pulling me into a tight embrace. We wept together, reassured that for now, it was okay, I was alive and untouched by the monster that had run from so many years ago. And that our fight from before was resolved, the threat of separation more than enough to push aside what was a petty disagreement.

"Oh Sadie, I was so scared, I'm sorry, please forgive me, I'm sorry," she sobbed, her grip so tight I could scarcely breathe. "I thought I'd lost you. I rushed to the school to see you in case it was the last time but I was too late."

"It's okay, Mama, I'm sorry too. I forgive you," I cried, her familiar rosy scent tickling my nose. My relief to be home trumped the anger I'd held in my heart toward her. I'd made my peace with her, bargained with the heavens during those long, dreadful hours locked up in those stone and concrete walls.

"I hope it wasn't too miserable. You're a wreck," Mama released me from her embrace, taking in my stiff, dirty skirts, disheveled hair, and bags under my eyes. She swept away my tears with her thumbs.

"The worst part was the incredible boredom. I thought I would end up dead from insanity before succumbing to that stupid fever," I said with a shaky laugh. *Like Cyntha had.*

A bolt of fear struck me. *Lander.*

"Did my other classmates make it out?"

She nodded, a knowing smile on her face. "They did. They made the announcement earlier today." She paused before adding, "Yes, even Lander."

A sigh of relief left me. Lander had made it. He was all right.

"Let's get you cleaned up." Mama ushered me to the house, and I briefly peeked over my shoulder, the gate guards and medic disappearing into the distance. The white of the medic's garb glared against the black guard uniform.

Mama stopped to whisper in my ear the instant she opened the door, suddenly going stiff. "I want you to be aware, Thamus is out back in the garden. He's been helping financially and around the house since you've been gone." Her eyes flickered back and forth between mine, trying to read my thoughts.

I instinctually wanted to rebel. I wanted to dredge up the argument we'd resolved only moments ago. But, I'd missed her far too much. I couldn't do it. I needed her. She needed me. And I wasn't going to let some irritating man get between us. I sighed heavily, resigning myself to the fate of acceptance, also recalling the bargain I'd made with the heavens during my time in isolation. One that had apparently been honored. It was my turn to uphold my end of it. "It's fine. I already figured he would be," I grumped.

She teared up again. "Thank you," she whispered and placed a kiss on my forehead, taking my hand to lead me back into our home.

3

I'd never in my life experienced such joy to have an outfit that was properly cleaned. My skirts were no longer stiff and board-like from the abrasive soap at isolation, fresh as a spring breeze. Every part of me was light and free, relieved of the heaviness and grime from the last two weeks, and I sat out in the garden with Mama, sipping warm floral tea from the flowerbed. Thamus was weeding diligently across the yard, and I hated to admit it, but he was doing great.

I peered up into the sky, large puffy clouds strolling by, the rich deep blue inspiring a song to bubble up from within me. I was tapping out the rhythm when Mama spoke, matching my gaze.

"It's beautiful from here, but it terrifies me to think of everyone who got stuck up there."

I squinted against the bright light, the song fading off into my mind as I imagined floating off into oblivion. A fate I'd only narrowly avoided for a second time in my life.

"I've spent the past two weeks worrying that I'd stare up into the sky and see you, for the last time."

She gripped her cup tightly, knuckles turning white.

The fear in her words tore at me. She'd come closer than ever to losing the only family she had left. "I'm certainly glad that my fate doesn't involve heights." I shuddered, remembering the view from my window. "How long were we in isolation when we first came?"

"Almost a month. But we weren't alone. There were a handful of others that we shared the room with, since they were low on space."

Thamus yanked on a particularly large weed, the muscles contracting under his white linen shirt. Dirt and sweat stained the fabric, a testament to his hard work. I frowned as visions rippled through my mind, faint flashes of old muddled memories flitting around with such speed I could hardly make them out. Some were of the journey here, others of the first few weeks in the city. I remembered the isolation building, but nothing of our first stay there. A misty image of Lander popped up, leading me to revisit the words he shared the night before Cyntha collapsed. *I found an exit.*

"How did we even get in, Mama? I don't even remember. I thought there was no way in or out of the city?"

"You were so young, I'm not surprised. They'd built a bridge atop the gate. When the second city was built in the valley after Old Ancthia lifted off into the sky, the gate had no entryway or exit. During the period of acceptance, there was discourse over whether creating an opening in the gate would cause serious security issues should the virus re-emerge. Little did they know it already had."

The virus had mysteriously appeared for the first time half a century ago, sending what was once a civilized, united world into chaos and madness. Society as a whole broke apart as people fell—or rather, floated—one by one into the sky after being afflicted with a mysterious fever. It didn't matter who you were, what your status was in society. Kings lost their thrones as they succumbed to the sickness, either dying from the sweltering heat of the fever, or floating off once it finished ripping through them. Entire villages collapsed as it spread, a means that was still a mystery to this day. Suspicion ran rampant, causing ruthless, unnecessary murders and death. No one trusted one another. No one was safe. Except for those in Ancthia.

The city stayed strong, keeping its residents as safe as it could amid the chaos, striving for a cure that would never come. A great gate was erected, and all folks screened for signs of sickness or weights before entering. The affected were executed on the spot, and the survived were released into the sky. The rates of death and infection here were the lowest in the world, and millions fought to come here, believing it to be the last safe stronghold from the virus. The city of Ancthia succeeded despite all odds, and it was attributed to the strict vetting policies upheld by authorities. It worked great. Until it didn't. These measures were no match to what the ground had in store.

Being startled awake one night by the sound of cracking rock and trembling earth, the residents found the city splitting in half, not by the infection of its people but by the ground beneath their feet. It took roughly twelve hours for the vast miles of land to fully separate from its base and lift into the sky. Thousands fled, jumping off the rising city into the ruins below. The people descended into madness as their homes ascended upward, exactly like the tree I'd seen in the square in our hometown.

Deaths that night were numerous, from both falls and warfare, leaving a few survivors behind in a massive, newly created valley. Separated from the world by the newly created natural landscape, a new, cautionary gate was created over the peaks to further discourage movement between this world and the outside. Ancthia closed itself off completely. Those left rebuilt the city within the safety of the valley, using rubble that plummeted from the now floating monuments and leftover homes. All the while they watched their old territory drift up into the air over a period of days. After almost a week, it finally vanished, having gone high enough that it would never be seen again, the fate of any infected person or object. A spring bubbled up from the gaping hole in the earth creating a large lake in the center and buildings grew around it over the years.

Eventually, the virus sort of died off, disappearing as suddenly as it had appeared.

Decades passed before they opened their gates to any outsiders at all, and shortly after Mama and I arrived, things were quickly closed down again at the resurgence of the virus. An event as mysterious as the virus itself.

Mama peered across the peaks, pointing to a steep valley nestled in between two of them. The gate was pitifully small from here, but I knew it was taller than Ancthia's main hall. "That's where it was built, in between those two points that resemble cat ears, do you see?" Her eyes darted between me and the peaks until she was sure that's what I saw.

"It was high up in the air, and they had a platform on the top to screen folks for symptoms. Then they'd usher you down a terribly long staircase which led to the descent off the mountains. That was almost worse than climbing up from the outside." Mama wrinkled her nose. "And taking a seven-year-old who's terrified of heights with you? Quite the challenge."

I was incredibly glad I couldn't remember the heights part.

"They tore it down when they heard word of infection?"

"Yes, and quickly. It was gone before we even left isolation." She sat quiet for a moment, a distant stare in her eyes as she brought up more old memories. "There were a lot of people who didn't make it. And not only over the platform."

I observed her curiously, wondering why she'd never told me about it. But when she finally finished rubbing the goosebumps off her skin long enough to tell me what happened, I understood.

"I saw eighteen people get released after isolation. One was a baby."

Mama bit back tears, taking a long sip of tea to keep her voice from shaking as she conjured the memories.

"I still remember the mother's screams. She ended up bound and gagged, but it did nothing to silence her. When the medic let her go, the bundle floated up and up, peacefully asleep, rocked by the winds. Some of the others being released tried to grab her, but they couldn't control their movements enough to reach her."

Visions of the woman and her son I'd seen the night before isolation flashed violently behind my eyes. I gripped my skirts tightly. "How could anyone ever do that, Mama?"

She sighed, shaking her head. "If they didn't, everyone would die the same way. Sacrifice a few for the sake of everyone else."

Thamus apparently finished his duties and joined us then, giving me a small friendly wave as he settled into the wicker. I couldn't stop myself from raking my eyes across the garden. Someone had to make sure he'd done things correctly. He was clearly unaware of the darkness regarding what he'd interrupted, which irrationally irritated me. "Hello there, Sadie." His voice rumbled a deep bass, a contrast to the higher pitch of mine and Mama's voices. "Welcome back. It's nice to formally meet you."

I was pained to even think of accepting any kindness from him, but Mama's wide eyes silently begged me for a peaceful interaction. I was going to give her one, but I wasn't going to enjoy it.

"You too," I gritted out, crafting a fake smile from deep within the darkest depths of my mind. "Did you manage the garden okay?"

He nodded sagely. "No one can tend a plant the way I can."

Thamus rubbed his scruffy beard, and I figured he was imagining his time out of the city. As much as it annoyed me, I wanted to find out more about his past, if not to know for myself, to make sure Mama would be taken care of. Seeing him in something other than candlelight had me noticing his rather unusual contrasting features. The hair on top of his head was a silky dark, stuck all over his forehead from sweat. Despite the darkness of his hair, his beard sported a burnt orange hue, giving his face a unique characteristic, further accentuated by the light sky blue in his squinty eyes. He had laugh lines and crow's feet, from years of laughter or years of frowning, I wasn't yet sure. I hoped it was the former, for Mama's sake.

"You're not from here?"

He shook his head, hand dropping to the arm of the chair. "No, I'm from a large town called Juneai. Entered around the same time you and your mom did, once things became unstable. I lost everything and came here to start anew."

Something about the way he said *everything* piqued my curiosity, furthering my suspicion of him, but I wasn't going to pry it out in front of Mama. I would find out more about this man, to make sure he was good for her, and I might need to enlist Lander to help.

"I'm sorry to hear that, Thamus," I told him, lacing as much sincerity as I could manage, even though it pained me, "but I'm glad you've found a good place."

"Thank you, as am I."

I stood up then, stretching my arms theatrically, giving in to the desire to get as far away from him as possible. "I'm going to go practice. I've got to perform tonight, and it's been a few weeks," I said to Mama, turning to the house.

"Can't wait to hear how beautiful it is, even out of practice," she smiled warmly, and I bent down to hug her before leaving the pair out in the garden, alone.

***

How Lander knew where I'd be every night, I never understood, but he was concealed in the shadows of a nearby building the entire time I played my violin. I found out in an unfortunate manner, nearly jumping out of my skin when he rushed out screeching "Boo!" at the top of his lungs. I swiftly slammed my violin case into the perpetrator's arm, the scare triggering my reflex to hit before realizing who it was.

Lander cried out in pain.

"You absolute jerk!" I huffed, hand shooting to my chest to quell my thundering heart.

"Ouch! Why did you hit me? That freaking hurt!"

Lander rubbed his arm gingerly, scowling, his nose wrinkling upward and piggish.

"Why did you scare me?" I raised an eyebrow, walking past him to the street, knowing he'd follow. The adrenaline receded, giving way to a stark flood of relief. Hearing that he was safe and sound was one thing, but seeing it for myself eased a knot in my stomach I hadn't even realized was there.

"I didn't think you'd attack me," he seethed, sulking along. "Slow the heck down! You always have to walk too damn fast!"

I sighed dramatically, but slowed my pace.

"Buy me a pretzel," he demanded, "since you saw fit to injure me terribly."

"Sorry, I don't feed criminals," I retorted, knowing full well I would absolutely feed him when asked.

"You're no better than those medics at isolation. I'm convinced they didn't even attempt to cook those potatoes. And they refused to say even one word no matter what sort of exciting conversations I tried!"

"I'm plenty better than them. Although, I doubt I would've talked to you either if you were my prisoner, as annoying as you are. Probably would release you before the virus even finished its job."

I was trying to be sarcastic, as we usually were with one another, but I realized too late that I had gone too far. The instant the words slipped from my lips there was a blur of motion from Lander, who was usually slower than a turtle. He whipped around, grabbing me tightly by the shoulders to give me a harsh shake. "Take that back," he spat through gritted teeth, "Take it back!"

Eyes widening in shock, I noticed the dark circles and swollen eyelids, telltale signs of hours of crying. His cheeks were chapped from wiping away tears, and his face had a new sunken appearance to it—one I hadn't seen since he was young and starving. My heart sank.

"I-I'm sorry. I didn't mean—"

Lander released my shoulders with a jerk, turning to walk away, the spot where his hands had tightly gripped me throbbing in protest. As he walked off, he swept the hood of his jacket over his head in an attempt to hide his face.

I stared for a moment, unsure if I should follow or give him space. But I knew how Lander was. He craved warmth and company, not solitude. I immediately shook the hesitation off to run after him, reaching out to grab his coat. I should've kept my mouth shut.

"Lander wait! I'm sorry, I really am! Please—"

He shrugged me off, speeding up, but I grabbed at him again.

"Lander, you idiot! Listen to me, it was a joke! A bad one, I realize, and I'm sorry, I am!"

He smacked at my arm and swirled around, tears running freely down his face. His body shuddered, a sob coming from deep within his throat and he pulled me into a tight and unexpected hug, his lumpy handmade jacket pressing tightly against my chest. I stiffened, thrown off by the whiplash of his emotions, but returned the hug as he wept uncontrollably over my shoulder. I gently patted his back as he cried, shushing softly as my mama always did. He was warm and solid against my body, fitting perfectly against me, and I melted into him, trying to keep his shaky knees from buckling.

My heart fluttered with regret and that other sensation that had been popping up a bunch lately when I saw him. One that I couldn't yet find a name for. I wanted to stay this way forever, nestled against his firm, sturdy form. I shook that thought off, trying to shift my focus back to being comforting as I rested my head against his thick hood. What I'd said was cruel, especially after everything that had happened. If I could've smacked myself for it, I would've. I was supposed to be Lander's best friend, and yet here I was, kicking him in the gut when he was already down.

People veered around us awkwardly, as we were still standing in the middle of the dim, candlelit street. Someone almost ran into us, shouting rudely, and I stared them down, contorting my features to appear as menacing as possible. Apparently, it worked because they skittered off like a rat racing through the gutters the instant they saw my watery eyes.

I wasn't sure how long we stood there, but eventually Lander's sobs turned into quiet hiccups. He awkwardly pulled away from me, sniffling heavily. He couldn't meet my eyes. "Sorry," he quietly mumbled at the ground.

"Don't mention it," I replied softly. "Let's sit down for a minute."

We moved over to the edge of the street, and he almost collapsed onto the cold ground, leaning against one of the buildings. I joined him in front of what appeared to be a candle shop, various colored candles shining brightly inside the sheet of glass, casting soft light onto the streets. Our shadows stretched long before us, flickering with the flames. I watched, briefly fascinated. Lander and I appeared as if we were in a dance together, moving left and right, up and down, then left again.

I lowered myself into a comfortable squat, leaning on my knees to peer over at my ailing friend. A few stray leftover tears spilled over, but he ignored them to swipe unceremoniously at the snot threatening to escape his nose. I lifted my overskirt to dab at his tears, his cheeks already chapped enough from his rubbing, but he instantly batted me away. His hair was matted to his forehead, from tears or sweat, I wasn't entirely sure.

Normally boys his age would be mortified to be in the position of a young man crying in front of a girl. But Lander and I, we'd been here countless times before. Even if it was slightly awkward, this territory wasn't entirely unfamiliar. I was going to let him lead the conversation—to speak when he was ready, but he was taking way too long and the need to apologize was overwhelming me.

"I took it back," I blurted.

"I know," he said hoarsely, trying to clear the lump in his throat to no avail. "Thanks."

"I'm sorry, Lander. I'm sorry for saying that, and for what happened to Cyntha."

He flinched at her name, staring off into the dark street at people passing by. "It's not like we were together or anything. But she was innocent. And kind. I've known her for a while. And she's had her eye on me for quite some time."

"She always was sweet on you. Imagine, having caught the eye of the prettiest girl in school." I gently nudged his arm, trying to lighten the heaviness weighing on our shoulders.

The side of his mouth twitched once, but he remained solemn. "I just want it to stop. I've seen too many people die already from this stupid virus."

"I haven't experienced the level of tragedy that you have. I've only lost my papa." I swallowed hard, my heart aching for him and my father. "But I understand."

"I'm glad you haven't had to suffer any more than you already have." He touched my arm with his gloved hand, giving it a brief squeeze before letting it slide back into his lap. It had only been there for a moment, but I missed his touch the instant it was gone.

"Cyntha was a wonderful person, and beautiful from the inside and out. She didn't deserve any of it. I wish she'd had more time. That I could've gotten to know her better. That's my job as your best friend, to vet any potential love interests, after all." As much as I hated to admit it, Cyntha would've been perfect for him, too.

"It would've only made the pain worse," Lander shivered, a new line of tears threatening to spill over. I went to dab at his eyes again, but he pushed me away.

"Stop moving," I commanded, annoyed that he wouldn't let me help. I needed to do something, anything other than apologize to make up for hurting him.

"You stop!" he huffed, smacking my hand one last time before I gave up. "She's gone," he said, choking on the word. "I only hope it was quick."

"Me too," I told him, my voice thick as my own tears wanted to escape. "Poor Cyntha." I imagined her blonde hair drifting off into the sky, eyes darting around in fear as she screamed. If that was even how she went. The fever might've taken her before the city or the sky ever could've. I blinked hard, trying to erase the images from my head.

Lander picked at the dirt between the stones, lifting up small pebbles and chunking them across the street. He was quiet, gathering his thoughts, and I waited patiently for him to speak.

"Remember where we planned to meet? The night before it happened?" he said quietly, peeping around as he had that night. I saw it fit to answer when I was sure no one was nearby.

"How could I forget that?"

"You forget everything, Sadie."

"No I don't!"

"Yes, you do! Either way, tomorrow. Meet me tomorrow. I'm too tired right now."

I watched him closely, the exhaustion clear on his face, and wondered what he wanted to show me so badly. If there was an exit, surely, after seeing what happened to Cyntha, he wouldn't want to revisit the possibility of another infection? Surely?

There must be something else to his eagerness, another reason for this. I thought back again to my theory that it might involve my safety, something Lander believed was his personal duty.

He finally sighed and stood, movements slow and heavy, reaching out to help me up. I refused the gesture, seeing that he needed his strength more than I did, and stood unassisted. Lander halfheartedly rolled his eyes.

His hand dropped to his side. "Let's take you home," he muttered, turning to the direction of my house.

"No, let's take you home first," I argued, violin case patting against my skirts lightly with each step.

"And what if you get lost? Or someone attacks you in the street? There's been people calling for the murder of our entire class, even though we made it past isolation. You're absolutely not going alone," he growled, continuing in the same direction.

I popped my hands on my hips. I was more than capable of fending for myself. "Excuse me! I know my way home! Before you came along, I was able to find my way fine through these streets, and I was much younger than I am now! I even thwarted people who were suspicious of me being a new arrival."

"Stop arguing with me! It's nonnegotiable."

"You need to go home and rest first, you're exhausted. I'll be fine, I promise," I reassured him. "You can barely even walk straight." I put a hand on his arm to steady him, truly worried by the way he was swaying. It appeared as if he hadn't eaten the entirety of the last two weeks, and I hoped he wasn't about to faint. There was no way I could drag him home. Lander was way too heavy.

"I said I'm taking you home," he insisted.

For some reason, I could never take a hint. I opened my mouth to argue again. He clapped his hand over my mouth, eyes frantic as he stared into mine.

"Can't you ever listen without arguing, damn it, Sadie! You're not going home alone, not now, not ever! Do you understand? I will not lose you the way we lost Cyntha! Or my sisters!"

Ice cold regret and grief rushed through my veins. Strangely enough, I found it was tinged with something unusually warm. I slid my hand into his, moving it away from my face, interlacing our fingers and squeezing tightly once. The familiar leather of his gloves was rough and worn under my touch. Our eyes met, holding each other's gaze as firmly as we had held each other earlier.

"I get it. I'm sorry again, Lander. Please, won't you stay with me tonight? That way I don't have to worry about you, either?"

He hesitated before nodding slowly, pulling his hand out of mine. Thank goodness. Lander gripped the collar of my dress and pushed me forward down the road, stumbling over wayward stones. He didn't let go, keeping me from falling flat on my face, and we continued home in silence. The tapping of our footsteps rang out against the stones, a steady beat that echoed in time to the beat of my heart. A mournful melody swelled up and out of me, and I found myself bobbing along to it, almost vibrating along with the music. Not wanting to forget it, I ran through each note repeatedly in my head, quickening my pace to get home and play it before it disappeared from existence. After a good ten minutes of this, Lander sighed heavily and came to an abrupt stop.

"Play your damn song before you explode."

I scowled at him in wonder. "How did—"

"You're ridiculously obvious. Please hurry up, I'm tired." He sat down in the middle of the street, crossing his legs and arms with a heavy frown. He gestured expectantly toward the violin case I carried. Knowing he wouldn't get up until he got his way, I pulled out the instrument, the cool, aged wood comforting as Lander's hood under my chin. The scent of my father filled the air. Spruce and maple and a soft summer breeze.

I played this new melody, the mournful sound pouring out painfully, and I mean painfully as I messed up so many times it was ridiculous. But after I finally picked out where each note was on the strings and smoothed it out some, the song was perfect. I gave life to the turmoil encompassing Lander's heart, the devastation of having lost a friend, the difficulties of isolation. Despite the melody's overall sadness, I ended it on a note of hope and of love. And a touch of the fluttering that Lander's gaze evoked in my heart.

I paused, eyes closed, until the trembling strings stilled, the song cemented in my mind now that it had been released. The fresh night chill filled my lungs as I reveled in the freedom from the weight now lifted off my shoulders. I could've stayed this way forever had Lander's muted clapping not snapped me out of it.

My eyes flew open, and I packed the instrument up as fast as I could, somewhat embarrassed at the rawness of what the song's ending had displayed. *You're ridiculous,* I thought. *As if he could ever tell what it meant.*

"You won't forget it now?" he asked, red-rimmed eyes searching mine.

"I won't forget it," I answered, reaching out to help him stand.

"Good. It was beautiful."

My heart skipped at least three beats, and I flushed delicately, glad it was too dark to see. Lander ignored my outstretched hand as I'd done to him earlier, and we finished the walk to my house. He was growing increasingly unsteady, and worry grew in the pit of my stomach as we approached the front door. He needed rest, and soon.

No one was awake. I set my violin on the kitchen table, closing the door behind Lander as quietly as possible. Mama had left a large pillar candle on the table, the flame flickering as our presence disturbed the still air.

"Sit down. You can sleep in your usual spot; I'll pull out some quilts," I whispered to Lander, knowing Mama wouldn't mind having him as a guest. He'd stayed here many times over the years. When I returned, having satisfactorily crafted his bed on my floor, I emerged from the bedroom to fetch him. I found him obediently sitting at the table, one arm resting on its top, his olive skin ridiculously pale.

"When was the last time you ate?" I opened the cupboards without waiting for an answer.

"I asked you for a pretzel, earlier," he said with a weak smile. One that didn't quite reach his swollen eyes.

He had asked, hadn't he? Some friend I was. I found a loaf of fresh bread and smeared a thick pat of butter on a slice. "I'll buy you two next time we're in town, and that's a promise," I said, placing the bread in front of him on a cloth napkin.

By the time I brought him a cup of water, he'd already devoured almost every crumb. He gulped the water down just as fast, and I pulled out the loaf for a second time, handing him another slice.

"You haven't eaten much of anything since it happened," I observed, as he greedily tore into the second piece.

Lander chewed silently as his eyes drifted up and down my body, lingering at my waistline with a raised eyebrow. I immediately wrapped my arms around my abdomen, concealing it from his prying gaze. He muttered, "You're one to talk," with a mouth full of chewed up bread.

"You're gross," I scoffed, and turned on my heel to the dark bedroom. "I'm going to sleep. There's plenty more bread in the cabinet if you're still hungry."

I didn't think he was going to respond, likely sore from being called gross, so I left to my room, shutting the door. But I didn't miss the sound of his soft whisper the instant the latch clicked.

"Thank you, Sadie."

4

Lander left sometime in the early morning. I woke up to find the quilts folded up neatly on the rocking chair in my room, and the violin case that I'd forgotten in the kitchen back in its rightful spot at the foot of my bed.

The house was silent, indicating Mama was already gone for the day. She'd left out three boiled eggs and some warm biscuits for breakfast. I wolfed them down as greedily as Lander had eaten the bread the night before, our appetites returning after last night. Sharing the weights on our shoulders always made them easier to carry. I only hoped Lander was okay—I hadn't seen him weep that deeply in a long time. Maybe letting it all out could help him come to terms with Cyntha's death.

I spent the day doing odd jobs and chores around the house, taking a few breaks to rehearse some new songs. Mindlessly humming a novel melody while scrubbing the kitchen table, the door suddenly flew open. I screamed and jumped, terrified the gate guards were storming the house, only to find Thamus standing in the doorway.

"I'm sorry!" Thamus apologized, throwing his hands up to signal that he meant no harm.

Hands to my chest, my heart thundering beneath them, I fought the urge to wrinkle my nose at him.

"Can you knock?" I huffed, far ruder than I intended. He had no right to come barging into my home in such a way. Hopefully Mama wouldn't be hearing about my less than adequate manners later, though I wouldn't regret them even if she did. I reached down with trembling hands to smooth out my apron which had become askew when I'd jumped.

"Again, I'm sorry, I'll be sure to knock next time," he said, awkwardly shuffling his feet.

I narrowed my eyes at his taut jaw, my vision pulsing along with my pounding heart. What had he come here for?

"Mama's working. Which I'm sure you know." I turned back to my task of scrubbing, keeping a close watch on him from the corner of my eye.

Thamus reached behind him, pulling the door shut with barely a sound. "I decided now would be the best time to tend the garden since I won't be able to come this evening."

"Why can't you?" I scrubbed the table harder, aggressively, wishing it was his face beneath this rough old rag.

"A meeting. For work." Thamus's eyes darted from the ceiling to the floor, to his arms which he folded across his chest, before finally coming to a dead stop on me. The silence in the room was deafening. I could practically feel his stare piercing through me.

I paused and stared back. Was he going to stand there and watch me all day? I lifted my rag in the air, motioning toward the back door.

"Get to it, then."

He nodded, speedily maneuvering around the chairs to leave without another word. Why did this man believe barging into my house with no warning was okay? Especially knowing my mother wasn't home? I'd only been in isolation for two weeks. With how comfortably he'd let himself in, I couldn't help but wonder if this had been going on for far longer without my knowledge.

After a solid ten minutes, I slapped the washcloth onto the table and haphazardly dried my hands on the apron. I was determined to make sure he wasn't up to no good. Peering through the screen at the top end of the door, I spied Thamus watering some plants, whistling a light tune. He appeared to be acting normal. Too normal. Gritting my teeth, I pushed the door open and stepped into the garden, skirt tangling in the door. I yanked it free and quietly walked up to the man. I had questions, and I wanted answers. I popped my fists on my hips.

"Do you live by yourself?" I asked loudly and bluntly, satisfactorily startling him.

"Good heavens, Sadie, you scared the daylights out of me," he gasped hand on his chest.

"Payback for earlier," I grumped, waiting for him to answer the question. I loomed over him, hoping he was at least slightly intimidated, though I knew he could easily take me down, as burly as he was. Thamus's panting steadied, and he squinted up at me.

"Yes, I live alone. Anything else you want to know?" he grouched, clearly upset that I'd snuck up on him so easily. I had to fight back a pleased grin.

"I know nothing about you and you're dating my mother. So tell me, how did you get here? And why her?"

He rolled back onto his heels, running a hand through his sweaty, messy hair.

"I-um. It's not the most pleasant story."

"I can assure you, I've probably heard worse."

No one who'd come to Ancthia came with a pleasant story. He wasn't going to get out of this that easily.

I plopped down in one of the wicker chairs, the reeds groaning under my weight, and crossed my legs. He reluctantly joined me, and leaned forward, hands clasped tightly together. A weary sigh left his lips and I watched him closely, waiting for him to speak.

"I don't like to think about it, let alone talk about it. But I guess you have a right to know, being as I'm part of the family now."

I inwardly cringed at this blatantly false statement, but allowed him to continue without interruption. I'd address that subject later.

"Juneai was a large town, almost great enough to be called a city. It paled in comparison to Ancthia. My wife, a fiery, beautiful woman with hair the color of jasper and eyes a deep green, bore three children. The oldest was a girl your age, a month shy of being thirteen. The youngest were twins, the age of four, a girl and a boy." Thamus rested his chin on his folded hands. "Cato was pregnant with our fourth when the virus first struck. At first, it was believed to be a normal sickness, but as the man recovered, his limbs began to float. Starting in his fingers, it rapidly spread down his arms all the way to his toes. He was killed the moment it was clear what was happening. As expected, people reacted badly, but after a month, no one else was affected, and the town returned to normal.

"They called it a fluke, that it was a one-off event. After all, the virus hadn't been seen in almost half a century. Trade and travel continued. My family was excited for our future, for the baby."

Thamus scratched his beard, then let his hand drop.

"People started dropping like flies. One by one, it spread through the town. I begged my wife to leave with me, to go to the famous fortress of Ancthia. Far along in the pregnancy as she was, she was hesitant to travel, afraid to suffer complications or a birth away from home. And then, it hit Mae."

Thamus's voice choked up at the mention of his youngest daughter's name. "Sweet little Mae, with her round cheeks and cheerful laugh. The fever had her for a week before . . ."

He couldn't say the words. Thamus shakily continued. "I took care of her for my wife, to try and spare the baby and the other children. But they, too, came down with the fever. My wife included."

He bit his lip. "I left the town as soon as it was apparent that I was somehow spared. I'd taken the necessary precautions, avoiding skin contact and verbal communication, breathing through fabric to filter any viral particles. Whatever I did, it worked. I escaped here, the day the city shut down, confused and heartbroken. My entire life changed in an instant—my future wiped away. Everything I'd built was gone."

Thamus fell silent. My eyes burned. As much as I hated to admit it, I found myself saddened for this man and these people I'd never met. I gripped the thick fabric of my skirts.

"I'm sorry, Thamus. Truly. I hope that their ascent into the sky wasn't painful."

He shook his head with a dark laugh. "They didn't even make it to the sky. They were smothered before the fever could finish burning."

His words were a punch to the gut, and shame crept into my face at how I'd been treating him. My thoughts jumped to Lander, when he'd told me about his sisters. His town had at least let them go naturally instead of outright murder. I cringed, unable to even imagine the horrors of what this man had witnessed.

"I-I don't know what to say. That's terrible."

Thamus nodded slowly, eyes glued to the fresh spring grass budding up at our feet. "I want you to know that my intentions for your mother aren't meant to be harmful. I've seen my entire family go up in flames once before. I don't want to see it again. I didn't even get to say goodbye."

I felt sick, wishing I'd never even asked, deciding maybe I should've trusted Mama's judgment in her choice of men. A long, heavy silence passed between us. I rubbed my thumbs together.

"Thank you," I finally said. "I'm sorry for being cold to you before. It's ... it's not easy seeing someone in Papa's place."

"It's okay. I was a teenager once too." Thamus grinned, and I managed a small smile in return. His grin was sweet enough. I could see why Mama liked it, as much as the thought frustrated me.

"I guess I'll let you finish up here," I said awkwardly, rising from the chair. "If you need anything, I'll be cleaning up inside."

"See you, Sadie." Thamus waved, returning to his duties in the garden.

With a nod, I made off into the house, his story's darkness drowning out the brightness of the sun. Lander's words echoed in my mind: *I've seen too many people die from this stupid virus.* No one was safe. No one was exempt from the suffering pushed on the world by this sickness.

I shut the door, leaning against it as a chill rolled through me. Thamus told me that his entire town went down from one person. Did that mean it was about to happen here, in the city? Surely not, what with the extreme measures of safety Ancthia was famous for.

Yet again, my conversation with Lander flooded back, the night before Cyntha collapsed. I'd asked him if the city was compromised, his strange answer being that he wasn't sure if it ever was. I was thoroughly confused, but thankful there'd be answers as soon as the sun traded places with the moon.

***

When Mama came home, I had dinner ready: greens and potatoes from the garden along with a new loaf of bread to replace the one Lander had destroyed. I didn't mention my conversation with Thamus but did inform her of his unexpected visit. She smiled dreamily at the mention of him taking care of things and went on to gush about how grateful she was for his continued assistance around our garden after my return.

After cleaning everything up, Mama went to mend some clothes in our small sitting room, and I casually told her I was heading out. She luckily didn't ask where I was going, assuming I meant to play music as I usually did. Little did she know, I was actually heading into the streets to meet my best friend, who was expected to reveal some crazy secret.

It took two or three tries to lace my shoes due to nerves, but I managed to finally slip out the front door without attracting any unwanted attention.

The moon was high over the peaks, accentuated by an arrangement of bright stars and silvery puffs of clouds. I was glad for the brightness of the sky. These streets were sorely lacking in torches, and I wasn't in the mood to trip over an errant rat. The air was chilly, but comfortable and light, a contrast to my heavy, anxious footsteps. I headed south toward the apothecary, hoping my trek appeared inconspicuous.

I encountered stifling crowds when I neared the markets. Shoving through the sea of people, I pressed myself tight against the buildings to make my way through. Finally, I left the chaos behind for serene quiet once again, the dark south side looming up ahead. The relief from escaping the crowds was short-lived, the hair standing up on the back of my neck as I crept down a dismal, lonely road. Scarcely able to see where I was going, I trailed my fingers across the bumpy stone buildings to stay on the path. I thought the bright moon would've made this journey easier, but it cast contrasting shadows instead, complicating my ability to see further ahead.

Eventually, I reached a small, squat wooden structure with thick, coarse mortar slathered between the slats. It wasn't easy to see at night—a fact I was grateful for—but the sea-nymph carved above the door stared menacingly down at me. Not the most welcoming artwork for a shop selling medicinal tinctures. I almost died of fright when a cat jumped off the roof next to me. A light purr vibrated through my thick skirts as it rubbed against my legs.

"I'm sorry," I whispered. "I haven't got any spare food."

As if the cat could understand, it quickly leaped up onto the apothecary's awning, and promptly disappeared off into the darkness.

"So you didn't get me a pretzel then?"

Lander's voice pierced the silence of the night, sending a hot wave of adrenaline through my core. I impulsively thrust a punch in his direction. His palm caught my fist, knuckles thudding against his leather gloves, and he pushed me against the wall of the wooden building. The jolt from the impact rattled my teeth, and we froze, faces only inches apart. His breath was hot on my face, rolling across my cheeks in a gentle caress as our eyes locked. I could barely make out his features in the dull glow of the moon, but the light glittered in his eyes as they flickered between mine.

"Don't freaking punch me." Lander's voice was low and quiet, a deep purr. My heart was on the verge of exploding, from either him or the adrenaline, I wasn't sure. The grip of his fingers on my fist relaxed. My arm flopped down to my side as Lander pushed off the wall, standing straight. I was suddenly hot and winded, thankful for the coolness of the spring night air. He'd gotten so close. And oh, how I yearned for him to lean in even closer.

"Sorry," I squeaked. "You scared the daylights out of me."

"At least I know you can fend for yourself. That's the second time you've hit me in the last twenty-four hours. That hurt," Lander whined, rubbing his palm.

I knew he wasn't being serious. What I didn't know was whether he was trying to compliment my punch or tease me. Probably the latter.

"You've got to be kidding me. Your hand is fine."

I could almost hear him roll his eyes. "Can't get even an ounce of sympathy, huh?"

Definitely a tease.

"Oh my heavens, Lander, stop being so dramatic or else I really will punch you. Get on with it. Why did you bring me here?"

He glanced around, and gently took my arm, guiding me to the left. The apothecary stood at a fork in the road, two pathways heading to who knows where. Apparently tonight I'd find out. A bolt of excitement tickled my limbs, curiosity sparking it forward.

"Is it far?" I eagerly whispered. He shook his head.

"It's not far, but once the road turns to dirt you can't utter a peep, got it?"

"Got it."

Lander gave my arm a gentle squeeze, pulling me closer to him as the street grew narrow. In true Lander fashion, he stumbled frequently, tripping over invisible obstacles that always managed to avoid me. I was about to tease him for it when the street abruptly ended, giving way to soft dirt. Our steps became hushed, the soles of our shoes sinking into the fresh dirt. And as we continued, the houses grew sparse, and the road morphed into a pathway lined by tall grass. Tall enough to reach my chest. The grass stretched out past the row of houses into a large field, dancing fluidly in the light nighttime breeze. Moonbeams glinted off the moving blades, giving them a mystic and blue appearance. We weren't far from the peaks here, having left the limits of the city. I could see the snow atop some of the tallest mountains shimmering as if covered in diamonds.

The closer we got, the more we encountered large, lonely boulders, displaced from when the original city lifted off into the heavens above. Seeing them up close triggered a faint memory of the old oak tree I saw as a young child, the rocks levitating alongside its twisted roots. I wondered why these rocks in particular had been spared from the infection.

We continued on, the city shrinking behind us. Hadn't he said it wasn't far? Uneasiness rose in my throat as we traveled further and further away. Logically, I figured that if there were an exit, it would likely have to be in the mountain range. But Lander and I had never traveled this far on any of our escapades. Plus, he'd told me next to nothing about what we were doing.

My thoughts raced, eyes darting around for any signs of the gate guards. I'd heard that sometimes people were killed on sight who tried to escape the city. And I'd heard many reports over the years of outsiders being murdered for attempting to scale the gates. It wasn't safe out there, and Ancthia was the only stronghold left with the virus under control. The measures they took were exercised for a reason, and it was the only way the city had survived this long without collapse.

Having reached the wall of mountains, Lander climbed over the boulders and jagged rocks, following a small footpath up the incline. The footpath lacked any sort of cover, the tall grasses ending where it touched the stone. Exposed by the bright moonlight, I worried the entire city could see us climbing up here. To make things worse, I struggled in my heavy skirts, having to hoist them up to climb without slipping. If someone was watching, they'd surely be entertained. Looking down didn't help any, as the higher we went, the more the heights made my head spin. Lander didn't mind my sluggish pace, used to always being the slow one. He waited patiently for me to reach his side each time we got too far for comfort, well aware of my reservations regarding heights.

I wasn't sure how long we climbed, our ascent slow and steady, but we finally reached a wide landing, littered with craggy boulders and sharp bushes. Scraggly trees littered the rocky area wherever they found access to soil, providing some much-needed cover. Lander waved me forward and dropped to his knees, crawling through the underbrush. I sighed to myself, lifted my skirts, and tied them in a sturdy knot out of the way. The ground was damp and chilly, dirt caking underneath my nails as I followed him. Sharp branches scratched against any bit of exposed skin, and I was pretty sure I lost a few chunks of hair. I cursed myself for not tying it back before leaving the house.

The crawl wasn't long, taking a total of maybe thirty seconds, but it was thirty seconds too many. Lander waited at a small opening near the ledge, and I was thankful the darkness concealed the mess I'd become and the distance we were from the ground. Should I see the bottom, I'd be out faster than Lander could utter the word "heights."

We laid there on our bellies, shoulder to shoulder, staring over the edge of the landing into a dark void. Nothing happened. I silently glanced over at Lander for an answer, even more confused than before. What were we even supposed to be looking at? I guess I was squirming too much because he leaned over my shoulder, his whisper tickling my ear.

"Watch and wait. It may be awhile."

I nodded, resting my chin on my fists, already bored out of my mind. My eyelids grew heavy as I watched the moon slowly trek across the sky. At one point I dozed off, and my head lolled over to the side, slamming right into Lander's shoulder. He pushed me off him so forcefully I swore a vertebra in my neck cracked. I dished out a solid punch in response, but his thick jacket had the unfortunate ability to blunt such a blow, my knuckles receiving the brunt of it. Perhaps that was why he never took it off—it was a solid defense against my increasingly frequent attacks.

"It'll happen, I swear. It's happened every time I've come out here so far," his hushed voice cut through the still air.

"What if tonight is the one night it doesn't?" I hissed back.

"Then we'll come back tomorrow."

"Heck no," I grouched, adamant that I wasn't going to waste another ounce of effort on a wild-goose chase. "What are we even supposed to be looking for? And how did you even discover whatever this is?"

Lander sighed, obviously bored out of his mind too if he was willing to risk talking after making such a fuss about being quiet.

"You have to see it for yourself, first. You won't believe me otherwise."

What was all this about trust? I'd always trusted him, the same way he'd always trusted me. "Lander, I would trust you with my life. I even believed you that time you thought you saw fairies."

He stifled a chuckle. "Yet you still say I 'thought' I saw them. Point proven. I know what I saw."

"Fairies or not, something better happen soon, because I'm about to fall asleep." I yawned deeply, wondering how late it was. We'd been gone for at least two hours, if not longer. Lander was about to say something, but hesitated, picking at the dirt as he gathered his thoughts.

"Cat get your tongue?" I quipped.

"No." He paused, rubbing the dirt between his fingertips. "You . . . You could lean on me for a bit. Rest your eyes. I'll wake you when it happens," he said softly.

I detected a hint of shyness in his tone, stirring up a cozy warmth in my chest. Lander was never shy. Even with Cyntha. A smile pulled at the corners of my lips, but I bit it back, even though there was no way he could see it in the dark. I obliged his request, gently nestling my head against his steady, solid shoulder. His earthy scent tickled my nose, overpowering that of the surrounding pines.

"Don't forget to wake me," I yawned, and closed my eyes, comfortable and content to lay here forever.

I instantly floated off to sleep, almost too fast to catch his quiet reply, "I couldn't forget if I tried."

***

I was confused at first, irritated by the pesky, nonstop tapping on my arm. I tried brushing it away, enticed by the promise of comforting sleep, but the tapping continued. Finally annoyed enough to give up, my eyes shot open. The chilly reality of waking up on lumpy dirt and beneath sharp bushes jarred me into awareness. I found the incessant tapping to be Lander, smacking my arm hard with his leather-bound hands, as subtly as he could manage. The recollection of how I got here flooded back so fast it almost hurt. At first, I was unable to discern why he'd woken me. But as his deep brown eyes came into focus, a finger pressed to his lips, I realized something was quite different.

He was bathed in dim light.

The branches around us cast zigzagging shadows along his face. I blinked, briefly wondering if I'd slept through the entire night when he pointed downward to the source of the light. I slowly turned my head, cautiously peering down the ledge, too shocked by what I was seeing to even be afraid of how high up we were.

A massive hole had opened up in the side of the mountain, where two doors covered in a thick layer of dirt had been concealed. Light poured out of what appeared to be a large, tile-lined tunnel. I couldn't see how far in the mountain it stretched, but judging by the line of horse-drawn carts emerging from the tunnel, it had to be unfathomably deep, if not all the way through. Gate guards gathered around them, inspecting the contents of the oddly sized wooden crates they carried. But the strangest part was the carts themselves. The only ones I had ever seen here were crafted from scraggly pine, trees quick to grow in mass quantities for an overcrowded city.

These carts were not made of pine, nor of the less commonly seen hardwood. They were shiny and metallic, made from a material harder to come by here than wood. Metal could be mined from the mountains of Ancthia, but the resources were scarce and nearly depleted, since it couldn't be grown the same way as trees. It simply wasn't possible that the city would have enough to create such elaborate carriages, complete with designs and ornamentations past the basic functions of structure.

I also noticed that the drivers weren't gate guards but instead normal people, lacking the shields and heavy armor characteristic of the city's protectors. Gate guards didn't tend to interact with the public unless there was a threat, so seeing them speak casually to each carriage driver was almost jarring. We were too far to make out any words, but their garbled voices floated up to us as the guards addressed the drivers. Once inspected, the fancy carts were waved toward a line of wooden ones that clearly came from within the city. As each driver reached their designated carriage, the goods on the back were unloaded crate by crate.

I glanced toward Lander, wide-eyed and entirely shocked at the sight. He nodded, smirking at my amazement, and gestured for me to continue watching. I stared, fascinated. There were eight carts that went through, the guards unloading the heavy packages one by one, significantly weighing down the wooden carriages. When the last crate had been unloaded, the metal carriage drivers expertly turned their horses around and headed back through the tunnel, hoofbeats fading away as they returned to which they came.

The city's carriages followed a dirt pathway through the field into the city, proceeding onwards until the night swallowed them up, led by nothing other than moonlight. I supposed it was to stay inconspicuous, so that they would remain unseen, but I wondered how they could find their way without even a single lantern on their carts.

Once the carriages had satisfactorily disappeared, I watched, bewildered as the gate guards shoved a key into a rock jutting out of the mountain. The mountainside rumbled and two doors erupted from the sides of the tunnel to meet in the middle. They latched together with a loud clank, and Lander and I were once again surrounded in pitch black and silence.

I was frozen to my spot, in absolute disbelief at what I'd witnessed. I couldn't make sense of the questions ripping through my head, the wonder erasing the sleepiness I'd been struggling with before. Quite frankly, I wondered if I'd ever be able to fall asleep again, I was in such a state of amazement.

Lander tapped on my shoulder, indicating that it was time to turn around, and I followed, the sharp bushes ripping at my hair and skin nothing more than a minor annoyance. I wasn't sure if I was hopelessly preoccupied or if the way back was genuinely shorter, because our trek back passed in only an instant.

As soon as we safely returned to the city limits, our vow of silence shattered.

"I can't believe it!" I squealed, practically jogging down the torch-lit street. "I absolutely cannot believe it! Lander, do you know what this means?"

The dim glow of the fire revealed his smug smirk. I grabbed his shoulders, stopping him in his tracks as I stared up at him, wide-eyed. "Do you know what this means?!"

He laughed, slipping his hands casually into his pockets, pleased that I'd received this information with such excitement. But he said nothing, continuing past me down the street, a note of sadness in his watery eyes. My enthusiasm faded. Cyntha. He was thinking of her again.

"There's obviously a lot more to this story," I said, calmer this time, walking alongside him. "Now that I have proof your 'fairies' exist, are you going to spill?"

"I will, I promise, but let's get somewhere more private," Lander said, keeping the volume of his voice low.

I threw my head back in exasperation. Hadn't I waited long enough? "There's no one here! What is it, one in the morning?"

Lander placed a steady hand on my back to push me along, walking faster than he typically did. "Yes, and I agree, most people are probably sleeping. However, if you think about what you and I just did, sometimes people can be waiting and watching in the most inconspicuous of places."

He peered around us, eyes flickering toward the cloaked alleyways where the dim torches couldn't penetrate the darkness. The kind of alleyways Lander waited in while I played my music.

"Oh," I said, instantly seeing the point, and let him guide me without resistance in the direction of his modest home.

This journey didn't take long, despite the way Lander diligently checked our surroundings every few moments to make sure we weren't followed. The anxiety rolling off him crept into my stomach, shoving away much of the excitement from the mystery I'd observed.

Lander let me in to his home, a small cabin similar to mine. Familiar as it was to me, navigating in the dark wasn't even a challenge—not that it was big enough to be one. There were only four small rooms: a kitchen with a table, two bedrooms, and one shared bathroom sandwiched between them. Lander's room was to the left of the kitchen, his mom's to the right. A door off to the side led to a small fenced-in garden similar to ours, where they grew food and herbs to supplement their lack of income.

I swung my skirts around the table, straight to Lander's open bedroom, and he shut the door behind us, lighting a half-melted candle on his nightstand. Plopping down on his bed, I folded my hands in my lap, eagerly waiting for answers. With a deep exhale, he settled down next to me.

"All right. I guess I'll need to start from the top."

"Please do, because I'm terribly lost."

Lander scratched the back of his neck and flopped backward; arms folded behind his head as he stared up at the ceiling.

"It all started with her," he said, voice becoming gravely when he said her name, "with Cyntha."

My breath caught in my throat. I knew it. Cyntha really had been involved. He continued.

"Roughly six months ago, you were playing in the market not far from the apothecary. I'd snagged a pretzel, hanging out in one of the drippy alleyways; ugh I hate those alleyways, they're gross and smelly and damp." He curled his lip.

Lander was right, the alleys and roads in that part of town weren't the cleanest.

"You were playing that one song, you know, the one you used to duet with your Papa. That's one of my favorites, by the way."

I blushed hard, knowing exactly which song he spoke of. I hadn't a clue it was one of his favorites, though I should've guessed, as often as he requested me to play it.

"I was trying not to laugh because your face does that weird wrinkly thing when you concentrate, kind of like this." Lander squinted goofily and pulled down his cheeks in a mocking imitation.

I kicked his leg hard, and he fell into a fit of laughter, rubbing at the spot I'd assaulted.

"Shut up! You're going to wake up your mom!" I hissed, snatching one of his pillows. I smashed it into his face, trying to muffle the sound, but I was easily fought off. He eventually got ahold of himself and continued, back to being serious as he tossed the pillow across the room.

"That's when I noticed her. She's hard to miss, pretty as she is. Was. She was slinking around through the crowd, trying to be inconspicuous, white hair piled high above her head in an elegant halo. But even though she stopped at the markets and sifted through the goods, she didn't buy anything. No, she kept looking around, as if someone was watching."

"She wasn't wrong," I chuckled. "You were watching."

"Yes, but I'm obviously no threat," Lander rolled his eyes. "I wondered, who or what was she afraid of? Or, what was she doing that she didn't want to be noticed? I had to find out."

I frowned, trying to work out the details. "I know you took me home that night. Surely there wasn't enough time to go to the mountains and back in one performance."

"You're right. There's not. Cyntha eventually slipped out of the crowd and down one of the side streets toward the apothecary and never came back. I worried that something might be seriously wrong, and after taking you home, I turned around and searched. There was no sign of her anywhere, and I couldn't figure out the exact direction she'd gone. So I stopped by her house."

"Wait. How did you know where she lives?"

As far as I knew, he'd never been to her house. But, then again, I had no clue he and Cyntha had been sneaking around and finding secret tunnels all these months.

He smirked mischievously. "I have my ways. She wasn't home, and I knew she had to still be out there. I went back to my spot. And waited. And waited. Until she finally appeared, covered in dirt and a bit worse for wear. Piqued my interest, so I confronted her. The fact that I'd noticed without her realizing scared her half to death, as it should've. She begged me not to tell anyone I'd seen her, but I wanted answers. It wasn't hard to get them since, as you already know, Cyntha kind of liked me." Lander's smirk grew wider.

"What she saw in you, I have no idea," I joked, trying to ignore the pang of jealousy when I imagined him sitting this close to another girl. Or worse, letting her snooze against his shoulder as I had earlier.

"You know exactly what she saw in me," he retorted. "I'm the best catch in the school!"

My cheeks burned, and I lashed out in defense. "You irritate the daylights out of me! Stop dancing around the story and get to the point already! How did Cyntha find it? And what is going on out there?"

He huffed heavily. "Fine! Cyntha had found a discrepancy. See, she was a genius when it came to math and discovered that Mrs. Fenter's lesson didn't make any sense. The acreage of farmland versus our city's population, that is. Now, yes, most people have gardens in their backyards as we do. But as you know, that's not enough to support a family in its entirety; at least half of our food comes from the markets. According to her calculations, the gardens couldn't offset the production the city produces, particularly in places where people don't have yards. Insane that a twelve-year-old figured out what most adults couldn't."

I could scarcely breathe as my mind quickly went to Thamus. He was a farmer. Did he realize this?

"She said she spent weeks searching for the answer, that maybe there was something she missed. She visited the fields, searching for secret greenhouses or special plants that could overproduce. But what she found was yet another discrepancy. There were crops available for sale in the markets that were not grown in the city's fields. After this breakthrough, it was easy. She staked out the markets that carried the unusual produce and waited for deliveries. The rest is history. They led her right to the passageway I showed you. The doors are camouflaged to blend in with the mountainside, but when she approached them in the day, the difference was obvious enough."

A chill went down my spine. "It was that easy? She found out that easily?"

Did other people know? Was the city lying to us for our own safety, or was something else at play?

Lander nodded, peeking over to read my expression. Instead, his eye caught one of the scratches on my cheek from the underbrush. He reached out, turning my chin to get a better look, running a finger down the length of it. Despite his tenderness, the leather was rough against the raw wound, and I winced.

"Sorry," he mumbled, pulling his hand away. He tucked it back under his head, staring again at the ceiling. The departure of his touch left a strange hole in my chest.

"It doesn't make sense. We're supposed to be a fortress. And if Cyntha figured it out, then surely, anyone with wits even half as decent as hers would realize?"

Lander shook his head, face growing dark. "I agree. And I believe I've figured that part out, too. See, the same way I found out about her so easily, the city found her, too. Which means they weren't entirely ignorant about the possibility of being followed."

I sucked in a breath, putting a hand to my chest, the risk of what we'd done tonight settling in.

"We planned to meet, in a different, less concealed area than we were in tonight. I was too slow that night—"

"No surprise there," I muttered.

He rolled his eyes.

"As I said, I was too slow that night, but it was in my favor. Unfortunately, not hers. One of the gate guards had caught her right when I was arriving. He grabbed her by the arm, twisting it to an unnatural angle. I can still hear her screams." Lander shuddered. "The man demanded to know if there was anyone else with her. She wouldn't break, and he finally threw her to the ground in disgust. He said he couldn't kill her quite yet, at least without knowing how she found out about the gate. She told me later he'd been so impressed with her smarts that instead of death, he'd offered her a job in the future as a gate guard."

I was stunned. None of this made any sense. *They'd offered her a job for breaking who knows how many laws and spying on city officials?*

"But there was a catch. The offer only stood if she revealed who was with her that night. Said he knew for a fact someone was there. She denied it heavily, of course, fully ready to die to keep my identity hidden, but he threatened to take even her family's life. That's when she broke. She lied to him about who it was, and the man released her.

"A few days later, I heard that one of the boys from Mrs. Geni's class disappeared. She came to me, terrified about what she'd done."

"Are you sure it wasn't a coincidence?" I butted in, trying to make sense of it all. Lander shook his head quickly.

"Are you kidding me? There's no way that a few days after Cyntha gives his name that he mysteriously disappears off the face of the city. No way. She was distraught, we kissed and—"

My heart sank. I couldn't help but interrupt again at this blunt admission. "Lander. You kissed her?"

He went pink in the cheeks. "Well, it was more like she kissed me. Suddenly, too, I wasn't even remotely prepared! Thank goodness I didn't have anything in my teeth!"

I squashed down the thought that I wished he did have something in his teeth.

"After that, she said she felt responsible and was going to talk to the city official that had captured her, hoping the boy was still alive and that she could save him. She was determined to tell the truth. Cyntha did, sort of. Her plan was to say she truly was alone, and that she panicked and lied in the moment to save herself and her family. I told her not to, but she wouldn't listen, the guilt eating her alive. I think that's why she wanted her first kiss. In case it was her last."

I choked up at this bit of information knowing now that it came true. And from the hot, boiling jealousy that had suddenly tightened around my throat at the knowledge that she'd kissed him. I pinched my arm with my thumb and forefinger. *What is wrong with you? Cyntha is dead! Can't you feel a little sympathy instead of something selfish?*

"I waited at our meeting spot, terrified she wouldn't come back. To my surprise, she did. I spent hours talking with her, trying to distract her from it all."

"What did they even tell her? What did you guys talk about?"

"The entirety of our discussion is none of your business. That's between me and Cyntha," Lander grumped, a tad stern. His reaction stung in a way I didn't expect. We'd always told each other everything. I'd never had to share my best friend before.

The next words he uttered were difficult for him to say.

"They gave her a deadline to redeem herself, to find out where a possible survived is hiding within the city. But smart as Cyntha was, she said it didn't make sense, the same way the acreage didn't. If the city was concerned that there was a survived possibly spreading sickness, why were they letting possibly contaminated goods and people into the walls almost nightly? Not to mention, why would they send a child they didn't even know, who'd uncovered a damning secret to find them? There must not be an actual risk, or if there was, it wasn't as big as it's made out to be."

I wondered the same thing. It didn't quite make sense. None of this did, honestly.

"What happened to the boy?"

"He's still missing," Lander said quietly. "Cyntha ... Cyntha got sick not long after that. And, well, you know the rest."

I chewed on my lip, turning over the details in my head.

"How do you think she fell ill? Do you believe she found the survived?"

Lander was still, unnaturally so, staring so hard at the ceiling I thought his eyes would pop out of his head. "She would've told me."

"Oh," was all I could muster. I never would've suspected such depth to their relationship. How had I missed it? Was I that caught up in my own daily routine that I'd been completely blind all this time? They'd kissed. They'd actually kissed. And Lander, the best friend I'd ever had, who always told me everything, had failed to even mention it until now. An odd stirring of embarrassment tightened my stomach into a cold, hard knot. Sure, we were friends. But I'd always thought …that maybe, there was something else there. That Lander might've wished we were more than friends, the same way I sometimes did when I saw that sweet little half-smile spread across his face …

Stop it, Sadie! Don't be ridiculous! It's Lander! He's your friend, you're his replacement sister, nothing else!

I grabbed the sides of my head, trying to drown out the screaming thoughts racing through my mind. Lander, oblivious to the turmoil inside of me, had grown unusually quiet. I almost didn't hear him over the mental chaos.

"There's more to the story."

That finally snapped me out of it, and I waited eagerly for him to gather his words, deeply curious as to what else he could be hiding.

"We left the city."

I was so stunned, I could only laugh at how ridiculous it sounded. My hands dropped to the bed. "You're lying."

"I wish I was," he said, solemnly.

I froze as a single tear escaped, running down into his ear as his words sunk in. He really was serious. "Lander. You've left the city? How many times?"

"I've lost count." He still didn't move, as if the weight of guilt was physically pressing on his chest, keeping him in place. A heaviness so tangible it pressed against my own chest. "I …well, I …it's possible she may have come in contact with a contaminant. Maybe if I had convinced her not to instead of going along with it, she would still be alive today."

"Her theory of there not being any true danger wasn't entirely correct, then? The outside can still be dangerous," I whispered gently. I wanted to ask about the outside, about the contaminant, about everything, but Lander wasn't in any kind of state to continue the discussion, as he didn't provide an answer to my query. I turned to console him instead, needing to ease the pain etched into his every perfect feature. "I'm sorry, Truly, I am."

"I do wonder, though," he continued suddenly, brows wrinkled as the wheels turned within his mind. "We hadn't traveled out of the city for nearly three weeks when she fell ill. Which is out of the incubation period."

"What are you thinking?" I probed, yearning to have a glimpse into the inner workings of his thoughts.

"I don't think it was an accident. That guard knew what she was up to. And we never went outside alone. If she'd found a contaminant, encountered anyone else while outside, I would've known. I would've seen it. I think he killed her."

Killed her? She was only a kid! Typically, the city at least allowed them the grace of isolation before immediate death. Unlike the adults. "Surely, he wouldn't have."

"You've seen the things they do to people. He threatened to kill her and her entire family. Do you know what the king of Ancthia would do to him if it was uncovered a kid was sneaking past him out of the city? I wouldn't be surprised if he killed her to protect himself."

He was right. I had seen the things the gate guards did to people. What the king had ordered upon us. The terrible, unforgivable atrocities that were simply an everyday occurrence in our city, a place that was supposed to be the ultimate escape from the dangers of the world and the virus. How ironic that we'd only traded one threat for another. To be threatened by the very people whose purpose was to keep us safe. A moment of silence passed between us we processed this theory. As exhausted as we were, it wasn't easy.

"Maybe we should rest," I suggested, the back and forth of my thoughts only serving to make me weary. "Staying awake worrying won't help anything."

Lander finally broke his stare-off with the ceiling and turned to me, eyelids heavy with sleep. "For once, I think you're right about something."

I narrowed my eyes at him, knowing he was only attempting humor to lighten the mood, and I halfheartedly smacked him with another pillow. We both stood, now part of a routine we'd practiced hundreds of times, and I took the extra quilt from the top shelf of his closet. He tossed back the pillow he'd thrown across the room earlier, which I gracefully caught.

"Your toothbrush is under the sink where it usually is. Try not to wake Mom." Lander ruffled my hair, and we said goodnight as I went to curl up on the floor in his mother's room. It wasn't the most comfortable spot ever, but the wood was soft Ancthian pine, and it was surely better than the bed in isolation. I thought I'd fall asleep instantly, but my eyes shot open as the math Cyntha had discovered raced suddenly through my mind. If the city couldn't keep up with a fast-growing food supply, then how could it possibly keep up with impossibly slow-growing wood?

Maybe the pine I was lying on hadn't come from Ancthia.

Maybe it had come from the outside.

5

Robyn Holland woke me in the same manner as her son had on the ledge, patting me firmly on the arm until I stirred.

"Sadie. You have to get up for school. What in the world did you two get up to last night?"

I yawned, peeling open my swollen eyelids to see Mrs. Robyn bent over my sleeping form. Lander was the spitting image of his mom, with the same olive skin, wavy dark hair, and deep brown eyes. She regarded me curiously, flitting between the scratch on my face and the mess atop my head. I squinted hard against the morning light before pulling the quilt right back over my head, turning over to go right back to sleep. I was way too tired for this. She deftly yanked it from my grasp and stood up straight, hands on her hips as she launched into a scolding.

"I'll be damned if you miss your first day back after being out more than two weeks! I can't believe you and Lander can't stay out of trouble for one night! Get up!"

"Yes, ma'am."

I groaned and got to my feet, heading to the bathroom to freshen up, a task that proved to be an unexpected challenge. My matted hair was tangled with twigs, its typical golden-brown luster muted by the chaos, framing eyes with thick and purple bags. The scratch on my cheek was puckered and red, flecks of dried blood scattered all the way to my chin. Cleaning the blood off was easy, but taming my hair proved to be nearly impossible. I gave up after plucking out most of the twigs, too annoyed and exhausted to deal with it any longer.

Lander knocked on the door right when I swung it open. He whistled at the sight of me. "Have you been battling a tree nymph or something?"

I stuck my tongue out at him. His eyes mirrored mine, purple bags and red-rimmed eyelids, but somehow, he was free of twigs and scratches which deeply irritated me. I let out a few choice words at his insult which prompted Mrs. Robyn to throw a frying pan at both of us. The pan slammed into the wall, and we scattered like cockroaches, tidying the rooms while she lectured us for being irresponsible. Once she decided we'd been properly berated, Lander and I were politely informed that breakfast was ready.

"Thank you for the food, Mrs. Robyn," I said cautiously, testing to see if she'd simmered down enough to communicate casually.

I was relieved to see that she was, in fact, cooled back down to baseline and open to normal conversation.

"You're very welcome, Sadie. I am so glad to see you again; it's been quite a while since Lander's brought you around." Mrs. Robyn cut her eyes at her son, and he scowled back. "I don't have any girls to dote on any longer. Come around whenever you want, even if he's too rude to extend an invitation."

"Thank you, ma'am."

I stifled a chuckle at Mrs. Robyn's subtle dig at her son's politeness, and he kicked my leg hard under the table in response.

We made quick work of our modest breakfast of toast, honey, and sausage, Mrs. Robyn taking the comb to my messy hair once we finished. She raked the tangles out, nearly ripping out my scalp along with them, muttering how I couldn't step out into public resembling a deranged ruffian. Whatever that was. She was surprisingly successful in making my hair presentable, plaiting it down my back with a spread of shiny oil. We were booted out the door with a jam sandwich and some carrots, something Mama and I could never seem to grow with success in our garden.

Lander and I were quieter than usual on the way to school, even though I was brimming with questions. It wasn't safe to ask them here, on busy streets during the day. There were too many people who could listen in—too many nooks and crannies for someone to spy from. I kicked a few rocks down the road to have something to channel my irritation into, Lander joining in at one point, until the middle's building finally appeared. I took to the steps, scaling them two at a time, believing Lander was right behind me. About halfway up, I noticed he hadn't followed.

"Lander," I called, turning around. "Come on."

He stood at the bottom of the stairs, staring at the wooden doors with trepidation, wearily shaking his head.

"I can't do it."

The defeat in his voice was unlike him. I hopped back down the stairs to his side. I couldn't stand to see him this way. Not Lander. My goofy, resilient best friend.

"This is where it happened. It's the last place I saw her. I can't do it. I can't."

His words were a knife in my chest. And not solely because of how mournful his tone was. "Yes, you can. You will. And you won't be alone."

I gently wrapped my arm around his, pulling him in close. Well, as close as his thick jacket allowed. He met my eyes, bleary and worn from stress and sleepless nights. "If you need to escape, I'll fling some spitballs your way."

This elicited a smile at last to my utmost relief, and he ruffled the top of my hair. "You better make good on that offer, Sadie."

"You can count on me."

I led him into class, both of us gripping each other's arm as a lifeline. That's what we were to each other, anyway. The one thing that kept the other grounded. We received a handful of dirty looks and heard a few odd whispers as we entered, referencing our unusual proximity to one another so soon after Cyntha and Lander's semi-debut. But they could go kick rocks. They didn't understand anything about her, Lander, or me. The only look that bothered me was the glare from Inala when she caught sight of us. The instant she was sure I'd seen her expression, she turned away, nose in the air, as if she'd smelled something terrible. My heart sank. In her eyes, I'd betrayed her best friend, swooping in to steal Cyntha's man the instant she died. Though she should've known that was the furthest thing from the truth. Lander and I always stuck together, through the hardest moments in our lives. There was nothing romantic about it. At least, from our perspective. *Unfortunately*.

I sat by my usual window, longingly staring out at the sky, wishing I could be anywhere but here. The clouds today were small and numerous, never colliding, moving along slowly but steadily across the vast blue plane. A fleeting thought crossed my mind, wondering how soft it would be to sleep within one, rocking slowly with the wind instead of on a scratchy straw mattress. A thought born out of peace that was immediately marred when I remembered that's where thousands of people—my father likely included—had met their demise, floating high against their will among the clouds. I shuddered, goosebumps erupting atop my skin, and turned my attention away from the sky and back to the ground, where things were safe.

Mrs. Fenter hadn't yet appeared, and after half an hour, the class buzzed with worry and curiosity. She was never late. And to be tardy the first day back since quarantine? Something had to be up. I heard a few students spinning elaborate tales that she'd contracted the virus and they saw her floating away last week. I turned toward Lander only to find him waiting for my gaze. I could tell what he was thinking. It was written all over him. When Cyntha collapsed, she'd touched her—bare handed. There was no way Mrs. Fenter survived. No way. It hadn't even dawned on us until this moment.

We found out, to our disappointment, that we were correct about ten minutes later, when a young woman who was not Mrs. Fenter entered the class. The instant she stepped through the doorway, the class fell silent, the realization of our teacher's fate settling over us—a dark cloud.

"H-hello everyone," the young woman said, hands shaking as she stood before countless pairs of scrutinizing eyes. Her shiny black braid trembled in time with her hands, and her skin was so pale I couldn't tell if it was nerves or her typical pallor. The girl had eyes opposite her dark hair; they were such a light shade of blue they were almost white. She couldn't have been a day over seventeen, likely one of last year's graduates from the nearlies building.

"My name is Miss Poe. I'm going to be your new teacher for the year." She pushed up her glasses, as they'd slipped forward when she'd glanced down at her shuffling feet. "I know this is a difficult time for everyone, and if you need support or assistance, please don't hesitate to let me know. Now, since it's been over two weeks, I think it's best to jump right back into learning, that way we don't miss anything. Can anyone help me get up to speed on where you left off?"

One of the motherly girls who had at least eight little siblings raised her hand, offering guidance to our new, struggling instructor. Seeing she was taken care of, I gazed back out the window, wondering if the world beyond the peaks was as bleak as it was within them. How many people were still out there? How much had it changed? The original city of Ancthia had already broken apart and lifted away, leaving behind this ten-mile-wide crater and mountains. Had the rest of the world done the same? Were the once flat fields and woods of my old village now covered in valley after brand-new valley, jagged mountains and bumpy terrain? Maybe Lander could tell me, if we could ever get a moment alone to discuss what he and Cyntha had seen on the outside.

***

Lander sat next to me during lunch.

I was fortunate to have someone to sit next to since everyone was avoiding us as if we'd been stricken with the virus. What was unfortunate was when Inala decided to approach us, her eyes glued to one small detail: Lander and I had identical lunches, both crafted and wrapped with the same cloth. Inala stared in disbelief, even though the two of us often shared the same food from his mom.

"I can't believe you," she hissed, crossing her arms firmly over her chest.

I met her scrutinizing gaze. "Inala. Come on. This isn't unusual."

"No. This isn't. But walking in together, clinging to each other tighter than Cyntha ever had the opportunity to? That is. And only *two weeks* after she left us? I-I can't believe you'd betray her this way." Inala's voice cracked.

I bit my lip, devastated to be on the receiving end of Inala's completely misguided scorn. This meant nothing. We were friends, I was Lander's replacement sister. That's how it was and that's all it ever would be. *But why does that make me so…sad?* Luckily, it was Lander who spoke up then, as I was currently finding it difficult to form these thoughts into words.

"Look, I know you're upset by Cyntha's death. We all are. But Sadie's the only sister I have left. We're not betraying anyone by being there for each other."

"Being there for each other and being together are two different things. And I know the difference." Inala pointed accusingly at us before curling her hands into tight fists at her side.

"Inala—" I began, reaching fruitlessly toward my friend.

But she ignored me, turning on her heel to storm off without another word.

"Wait! Inala!"

I went to stand, to chase after her, but Lander grabbed my skirts, yanking me back down on my bottom.

"Give her some time," he said softly, picking at the grass beneath us. "I think we all need it."

***

My performance that night wasn't one of my best. The fatigue and sadness that had become normal lately made for difficulty concentrating, and I ended things early, funds almost as lacking as my music. The sting of Inala's anger, the knowledge of my mother's lies, the permanent loss of my father and a classmate. It was all too much. Lander didn't say anything about my lackluster performance, but eyed me closely as I plodded home, falling into his slow and steady pace much easier than usual. The words we exchanged lacked the usual silliness, our journey mostly silent.

When we arrived home, multiple candles were lit, indicating that Mama was unsurprisingly still awake. She passed by the window not even a moment later, confirming my thoughts. But when a second person passed immediately behind her, Lander unexpectedly grabbed me by the arm, yanking me into the bushes out front to hide. We tumbled to the ground, branches whipping at my face and my arms.

"What are you doing, Lander?" I asked, hot adrenaline surging through my core at his abrupt and sudden reaction.

"There's someone in the house with your mom," he said, panicked.

He peeked out of the bushes, pushing me backward, trying to keep me hidden behind him. I laughed, realizing I'd never told him.

"That's only Thamus, Mama's new boyfriend. In all the chaos, I haven't gotten around to telling you yet. Come on, he's annoying as hell but he's harmless."

I went to escape from the bushes, wanting to avoid gaining any more scratches or twiggy, matted hair, but Lander refused to loosen the grip he had on my skirts. I fell back to the ground, annoyed but confused.

"It's fine. I promise. What's gotten into you?"

"When did you meet him?" he questioned, turning to me with wild, fearful eyes. I frowned, trying to understand what the big deal was and thought back to the night we'd met.

"The night before Cyntha died. What's wrong? Why do you look like that?"

He took a deep, shaky breath. "Because that's the man. The man that caught Cyntha."

6

My entire body went numb. My legs, my arms, and, strangely even, my teeth. The adrenaline rushing through me peaked in a crescendo, and I shivered uncontrollably.

"Are you okay?" Lander asked, noticing how badly I was trembling.

"No! I'm not okay! Are you sure? You only saw him for a moment. The light's dim. Maybe you're seeing things."

I was practically begging him to tell me he was wrong. He had to be. My mom couldn't be associated with him, surely.

"I'd know him anywhere. His beard doesn't match his hair. Nor do his eyes. It makes him stand out."

My breath caught in my throat, and my head spun. There was no doubt about it.

"I hated him the moment I saw him," I gritted out. "Deep down, I must've sensed it."

A deep crease formed between his eyebrows.

"What should we do?"

"He didn't see you, did he? When Cyntha was taken?" I asked.

He paused, throwing my anxiety even higher through the roof.

"Lander! Did he see you or not?" I asked again, shrilly.

He finally shook his head. "No. There's no way he saw me."

I released a breath I hadn't realized I was holding and tried to get ahold of myself.

"Okay. Even if he didn't, that doesn't mean you're safe. There were multiple guards out there."

"Surely if I had been seen, they'd be coming after me already," Lander pointed out. "The city even had me locked up in quarantine."

"Yes, but Cyntha was let go. Twice. And then she ended up dead."

He squeezed his hands into fists and slowly released them with a sigh.

"Yes, she did. What if he does the same to you? It's one thing to show you the secret, which I now regret. But it's another knowing he's in your house!"

"He has a key too," I huffed. "He walked in the other day when I was home alone. Said he had to tend the garden, and—" The memory of our conversation hit me harder than a rock, and I swallowed hard. "And he said he had a meeting that evening. At work. Which doesn't even make sense; what sort of work meeting would a farmer need to have?"

"Apparently one about receiving your crops from shipments instead of your fields," Lander remarked sarcastically, going to stand. "I'm going in with you."

My head whipped around with such speed I thought I might've dislocated my neck. "No, you're not. It's too risky. You're going home," I sternly ordered, pushing him back down. Lander wasn't going to put himself in harm's way on my account.

He fought against me. "Like hell I am! Don't you get it? I can't do this without you! I can't do anything without you! I need you, Sadie!" Lander exploded, teeth clamping down hard on his bottom lip the instant he realized what he'd said.

I froze. That strange fluttering in my chest started back up, replacing the hot adrenaline with something comforting and warm. Had I heard him right? Did he . . . ?

Lander anxiously rubbed the back of his neck and stammered, "I-I mean . . . Oh, forget it. I don't even know what I'm trying to say."

The words flowed out so smoothly that, for a second, I wasn't sure if I'd even spoken them.

"I need you too, Lander."

His lashes flickered as he searched my eyes. For what, I didn't know. I was confused, exhausted, laden down with grief as an uncertain future loomed before me. But here, sitting next to Lander, everything suddenly felt so right. Us, together, against the world, arguing over what to do next while hiding in a bush.

We finally broke our gaze; this strange moment having slipped away as quickly as it arrived, reality wedging its way back in. Mama had been enticed by a possible murderer and liar, and neither of us would let the other go alone. There was no way I'd let her be trapped by a dangerous man. I'd stop at nothing to keep her safe and happy, no matter the cost. She was all I had left. So, we emerged from the bushes, Lander plucking yet another unfortunate twig from my hair, and we walked up to the door, side by side.

I steadied myself, turned the knob, and tossed the door open as casually as I could manage.

"I'm home!" I chirped, obnoxiously plunking the violin case at the end of the kitchen table where Mama and Thamus were sitting.

"Sadie!" Mama exclaimed, jumping up in surprise. "Where have you been? I was worried sick!"

Sure, you were. I'd seen how close she was to Thamus. I pointed at Lander.

"The usual."

"Please let me know when you're not coming home. Thank goodness Thamus stopped by the school for me to make sure you were there."

I frowned at him over Mama's shoulder, the man sitting casually in one of the chairs at the table as if he owned the place. What, did she have him following me now?

"I didn't see you there," I remarked, trying to keep the suspicion out of my words to no avail.

"I peeked in the window," Thamus said smoothly, fidgeting with the cloth napkin beside his cup of tea. "Is this the famous Lander I keep hearing about?" He motioned toward my friend, who was still in the doorway, jaw tightly clenched.

"That's me," Lander replied. "Nice to meet you, Mr. . . . ?"

"Thamus. You can call me Thamus."

Lander nodded, practically squirming where he stood.

"The pleasure is mine," Thamus said, and performed the city's handshake as a greeting, Lander tersely following his lead.

Mama interrupted them, reaching out to touch my scratch. "What happened to your face?"

I swatted her away, rolling my eyes at the unwanted attention.

"She got in a fight with a bush," Lander cut in, rapidly creating a cover story with unexpected ease. "You know how she is—if anything gives off even a hint of sound, she's got to chase down a potential song."

"And you found it in a bush?" Mama asked, flabbergasted. "Was it even any good?"

"I have no clue," I heaved an exaggerated sigh. "The shrubbery took me out before I could even get it down! You should've seen the mess Mrs. Robyn helped me comb from my hair."

"She tried taking the whole thing with her," Lander quipped, his smile growing smug as the cover story proved successful.

"Whatever. I was so angry I lost the song that I couldn't get things to flow. And, here we are." I flung my hands up in mock exasperation.

"Sounds like an adventure, if anything," said Mama, eyebrows raised. "Are you two hungry? I've put on some potato chicken soup."

The pot bubbled gently on the woodstove, the divine scent of chicken and thyme in the air. It wasn't often we had enough chicken for soup.

"Stay, Lander. You haven't had much to eat today," I said, knowing that was his plan all along.

Lander stiffly nodded and took the seat across from Thamus. I sat by my friend, and we made some small talk about school and my songs while Thamus discussed how the drought affected his crops. The latter discussion led my friend to grow restless, but luckily the soup finished right around that time, shifting the focus. It tasted as good as it smelled and was the best food I'd had in weeks. It even managed to relax Lander some.

"Where do you come from?" Thamus questioned, wiping bits of soup out of his beard.

"A small town near the sea. Entes is what it was called. Moved here for safety during the resurgence," Lander replied. I glanced at him sideways. Yes, his town was near the sea, but it wasn't called Entes.

Thamus scratched his chin, frowning. "I've never heard of that town. How old were you when you left?"

Lander shrugged, glaring at Thamus for daring to ask. "It was small. I was small. It's not like the outside matters in here."

Thamus scowled, thrown off by the rudeness of his response. I decided to jump in and change the subject, sensing the tension and suspicion that Lander was practically oozing.

I smacked my hand on the table to grab their attention. "You know, I found a new stand that sells pretzels in the market square."

This distracted Lander a little too well, and he instantly turned to me. "And you're telling me this now?"

Mama chuckled, knowing Lander's passion for a pretzel. "Next time you're there, I'm sure Sadie will treat you."

"She'd better!"

Lander and I gathered the plates and silverware when dinner ended, taking on the job of washing up while Mama and Thamus had tea in the garden. Lander removed his leather gloves, a rarity for my oddball friend even on a sweltering summer day, and we went to work. I couldn't stop staring at his strong, pale fingers, a contrast to his olive skin elsewhere.

"What are you looking at?" he grumbled, knowing the answer already.

"Why don't you ever let your hands get some sun? They're so pale."

As expected, he deflected my question.

"The color of my hands is the least of our problems right now, unless you want to end up like Cyntha," Lander said darkly. "Besides, I enjoy having smoother skin than you."

"As if! Boys can't compete against girls when it comes to the skin department. See?" I reached for his hand, but he yanked it away.

"Quit worrying about stupid things right now. We have to finish so we can eavesdrop!" Lander ordered. I huffed, stomping my foot, but went back to work.

"What are we going to do about him?" I asked, peeking at the back door to make sure we weren't the ones being listened in on.

"I don't know yet. But we've got to come up with something, and fast."

"I think we should tell Mama." I handed Lander a soapy plate and set to work on the next one. He rinsed it under the tap, the cool water spattering the countertop and the front of his jacket.

"A good idea but what proof will we give her? Surely, she's not going to believe a couple of kids with such an outlandish story."

"We'll have to find some. We could tell her about Cyntha's math."

There was no way I'd let my mother be trapped by someone who'd been lying to her all this time. I'd stop at nothing to make sure she was safe and happy, no matter the cost. She was all I had left. No man was going to ruin that, not if I could help it.

"Again, how would we prove that without bringing her there? She'd have to see the fields for herself," he argued.

I sighed heavily. Was he going to shoot down every one of my ideas?

"Then what would you have us do, Lander? It would be easy enough to bring her to the fields."

"We'd have to find some way to convince her, then bring her to witness every acre of crops to compare with the markets. There's also the slight complication, being that her boyfriend works the fields during the day. Who's to say he won't realize what we're doing and stop her?"

I finished washing a fork and tossed it into Lander's sink, wood clattering against porcelain.

"What if we brought her to the gate?" I suggested.

"I highly doubt we'll be able to drag your mom all the way across a mountain in the middle of the night on, for all she knows, a wild-goose chase," pondered Lander, working his jaw as he thought. "We need something quick and simple, on her end, anyway. I do have an idea."

"Tell me," I begged.

I finished the last dish, dropping it in the sink for Lander to rinse, and used my skirts to dry my hands. He deftly ran the cold water over the platter, setting it carefully in the dish rack. Instead of being his typical uncivilized self by using clothing as a towel, he used the one hanging near the pantry to dry off. And then, one by one, he replaced his stifling gloves despite the warm spring air.

"It's not going to be easy, but I think it'll be fun."

I raised an eyebrow, hands on my hips. "Fun?"

"Have you ever seen the ocean, Sadie?"

***

We went over the details at least a hundred times, but I still quaked in my boots about what Lander had proposed. He and Cyntha had risked everything to investigate the mountains, wondering if it truly led outside. What they found was a series of tunnels that snaked throughout the mountains, leading to various exits all around the city and to the sea. The original city of Ancthia had a booming seaport, which was common knowledge taught in school.

Despite living most of my life near the sprawling, endless mass of salty water, I'd only ever seen it in paintings. Even if I had passed by on my journey here, I surely didn't remember.

Lander sketched the pathways he and Cyntha traveled in the dirt, patiently rehearsing the journey again and again to ease my nerves. It did help, but the effect was minimal.

The plan was simple enough. We were to wait behind one of the large boulders by the entrance, in a hideout that Cyntha and Lander had crafted with various sticks and transplanted bushes. After the shipments were received and the gate guards escorted the carriages back through, we'd slip between the doors right before they shut. Once inside, we'd race to a tunnel off on the right that was seldom frequented. Lander said that most of the gate guards would be preoccupied with leading the carriages after unloading, leaving behind only one as a lookout. As long as we stayed swift and silent, avoiding detection would be easy.

The night Cyntha was caught, Thamus was the one who'd been left behind. I'd made my reservations clear about this whole situation, but Lander emphasized Cyntha wasn't the sneakiest of people—one of the main reasons Lander had insisted on accompanying her on each expedition. His reassurance that they'd been passing through successfully for months was enough to quell my anxieties, and the darker fact that Cyntha was gone. Meaning they wouldn't be expecting her any longer. He'd originally planned to go alone, but I vehemently refused. He reluctantly agreed, since two sets of eyes were better than one.

Whether he was trying to convince me or himself, I wasn't sure.

Lander said that sneaking inside was the most frightening part, but after that, it was smooth sailing. The tunnel only took about five minutes to travel before arriving at the door to the outside. It was equipped with four locks, but luckily Lander was equipped with the knowledge of how to pick them, remnants from the days when he was a poor and starving newcomer. And that was it. We'd be out.

The way out was an entirely different strategy, but Lander said we didn't need to rehearse that part. I couldn't shake the feeling that something had to be missing, that it was way too simple, but Lander assured me that was all there was to it.

"The knowledge the city denies us is greater protection than any lock," he'd said. "My father always told me that knowledge is power. And that could've made Cyntha either a threat or an asset to them. I think that's why initially they offered her a job. After she wouldn't meet their demands, they chose *threat*."

I'd asked him multiple times how he could be sure we wouldn't get in contact with contaminants while on the outside. But Lander insisted he knew for a fact they hadn't.

"Sadie, Cyntha and I never left each other's side. We both touched the same things," he explained.

It dawned on me then what he was trying to say.

"You would've been sick too."

"Exactly. And use your brain here. How do you know if the virus is affecting something?"

I glared in response to his unsolicited rudeness. "It becomes immune to gravity."

"Good job! Ten points to Sadie."

I threw a handful of dirt at him, the only item within reach that could be a projectile.

"Cyntha didn't get sick from any of our trips we took together. There's no way. Hence why I think Thamus did something to her," Lander insisted, swiping at the dirt stuck to his face. "You'll be safe if you pay attention. Trust me."

I did trust him. I always had. And as far as I was concerned, I always would.

***

Making it through school was almost painful, as the butterflies in my stomach raged. I was extremely excited to see the outside, yet horrendously terrified that we might not see the sun rise the next morning. But I was willing to risk it all to keep Mama safe.

When class was finally over, I was the first one out of the room, Lander being the last as usual. I fled to my house, weaving through the passersby on the street, eager to get this over with. The only way to make the anticipation stop was to get on with it, and I was beyond ready. I imagined Mama's face when we showed her the evidence from the outside, the shock and the anger at Thamus's betrayal. I hoped she'd be thankful for my efforts and for trying to protect her from a murderer and a liar. It would be a good way to pay her back for everything she'd done for me over the years.

Mama was home already, thankfully, and I burst through the front door, startling her as she sat knitting quietly in the sitting room.

"Oh, Sadie, please be easy on those hinges. They've gotten rusty, and I'm not sure if we'll be able to replace them anytime soon."

"Sorry, I'll be more careful." I gave her a hug and a kiss on the cheek and raced to my room to change into my boots.

"Where are you headed? You just got home!" Mama shouted.

"The square! There's a sale on the pretzels, and I planned to get a few extra for Lander while they're still hot," I shouted back, out of breath from running the entire way home.

It wasn't exactly a lie. There *was* a sale advertised earlier in the week, and I *did* plan to grab him some extras. After tying my boots, I made sure to put my hair up, wrapping the braid into a tight bun at the nape of my neck. After deciding that I had everything together, I washed my face, hoping the cool water would calm my nerves. My reflection stared back at me in the mirror, those pesky purple bags still underneath my eyes. I hadn't realized my cheeks had become so gaunt, from the stress and lack of proper eating, no doubt.

Despite this, there was something different in my eyes: Hope. I was hopeful that we could save Mama from Thamus, hopeful that we could figure out what the city was hiding. There was plenty to uncover, and Lander and I were on the verge of possibly reaching that goal. What if the virus wasn't as risky as they said? Surely it wasn't, given that we receive goods from the outside.

And the world. Oh, to see the world beyond the peaks. Lander said it was unlike anything you could ever imagine, that the paintings and descriptions didn't do it justice. Young as I was when we came to Ancthia, I barely remembered anything other than the small town in the woods where I was born. But Lander, he lived by the sea, a force that gave a lasting impression, no matter how young.

Lander said that standing by water so vast made everything appear ridiculously small in comparison, its undulating movements giving the impression that the water itself was alive. It sent wave after wave crashing against soft sand, pushing and pulling with a strength that even the largest ships couldn't resist. He'd learned to swim with his sisters before he could even walk, diving in and out of the waves, saying it was the freest he'd ever been floating in the salty water. I once dared him to jump into Ancthia's lake, but swimming there was banned, and Lander was far too terrified of his mother's wrath should she have to bail him out of jail.

I was ready to see what Lander spoke of, to experience the world that I'd only ever traveled to in Inala's books. I patted my face dry with a towel.

Mama appeared in the doorway of the bathroom, arms crossed. "What's given you such a pep in your step?" she asked, a sly smile playing at her lips.

I immediately grew suspicious. She knew something was up. Panic surged in my chest, and I played dumb, trying to sound as innocent as possible.

"Huh? What are you talking about?"

"You seem awfully eager to leave the house for a simple sale on pretzels," she said in a singsong voice.

"You know how obsessed Lander is with them—he'd be awful upset if I missed it," I laughed nervously.

I hung up the towel, cornered in the tiny bathroom without a way out. At this point, I'd stand a better chance with a gate guard instead of her. Gate guards at least couldn't smell fear.

"I know you and Lander have been best friends since we came to the city," she said, giving me that knowing smile exclusive to mothers. "The older you've gotten, the closer you two have become."

"Obviously, we see each other every day." I rolled my eyes, going to step around her. "We're best friends. That's kind of how it works."

She sidestepped, blocking the way out.

"I've seen the way he looks at you, Sadie."

The relief that she wasn't on to me was replaced by embarrassment as I realized what she was insinuating. And annoyingly, a small hint of happiness. If she'd noticed, perhaps it was true.

"No! It's not anything like that!" I shrieked, face burning. "He's my friend, nothing else! I can't believe you'd even say that!"

She stifled a giggle with her hand as I shoved her aside to escape the bathroom. I grabbed my violin and raced out the front door.

"I'm not coming back tonight!" I screeched. I could've fried an egg on my cheeks right now.

"Enjoy your pretzels!" she called out behind me, and I stomped my way down the street.

7

We did, in fact, enjoy our pretzels.

Especially Lander. He ate three, spouting some nonsense that they would be sufficient fuel for our upcoming journey as we sat in our usual spot by the fountain.

"It's not even healthy," I told him, frowning in disgust as he practically inhaled the last one.

"It's healthy enough to pull us through a secret mission," he stated, talking with his mouth full. I scrunched my nose.

"Eww, Lander, you're so gross."

"Good," he said, ripping off a piece of my first and only pretzel, which I hadn't even eaten half of yet. I sighed, handing over the rest.

"I'm not even hungry anymore after witnessing your lack of manners," I grumbled, my stomach doing some precarious flip-flops.

"Nah, that's not why. It's because you're too nervous to eat. My grossness never actually bothers you. You only say it does."

He smashed the last of my pretzel into his mouth, and I shook my head, trying to continue my façade even though he was spot on. As always.

"Whatever. We still have about thirty minutes until the sunlight's completely gone." I squinted up at the fading gold light splashed against the eastern peaks.

"We need to get moving, then."

Lander held out his canteen of water in a silent offer. I gratefully accepted, pretzels rather dry for my taste. Once I handed it back, he stood, holding out a hand to help me up. I wiped my sweaty palms on my skirts before accepting, even though he wouldn't have felt them through his leather gloves. Crumbs fell off my lap as I stood, evidence that I'd been picking at the pretzel more than eating it. A brief flash of guilt for wasting even a morsel of food struck me.

"Quit worrying so much," Lander said softly, messy dark hair brushing across his forehead in the fountain's breeze. His lip curled up in a small, reassuring half-smile. "I'm not going to let anything happen to you."

I went weak in the knees as Mama's words flowed through my mind. "*I've seen the way he looks at you.*"

"Th-thanks," I stammered, barely able to hear him over how loud my heart pounded in my ears.

Lander led me in the direction of the apothecary, weaving through the crowds to hushed streets. I closely eyed the people we passed, going about their lives as I had previously, blissfully unaware of what was going on in the mountains. *How can everyone be so blind? Surely, some people must have suspicions.*

Daylight faded rapidly as we crossed the city, cooler air replacing the warmth of the sun. A thick fog rolled off the lake in the city's center, as if sensing our need for secrecy. The air was heavy and damp, cloaking not only our bodies, but our footsteps. I was grateful for its help, sending out a silent thank you to the water even though I knew it wasn't sentient. Lander's words about the ocean appearing alive must've gotten to me.

Now that I'd traveled this pathway before, I moved faster than last time, surprised that even Lander was keeping a speedy pace. The excitement of seeing the sea again was almost radiating off him, encouraging me to push through the nerves to match his energy. The climb up the mountainside was slightly more difficult due to the half-moon that sat low in the sky, but we made quick work of it. Before long, Lander had guided me off the ledge—with a lot of coaxing due to my absurd fear of heights—and to the small hideout behind the boulder that he and Cyntha had created. The space was incredibly tight, and we sat side by side, close enough that each inhale was saturated with Lander's sweet, woodsy scent. What had he and Cyntha talked about, stuck in such proximity? I tried swatting the thought away. It wasn't my business. However, I was curious, and bored, and we weren't exactly short on time.

I finally blurted, "Was Cyntha your first kiss?"

"Where did that come from?" Lander replied, taken aback.

"I was thinking about how you and Cyntha used to sit here exactly the same way," I admitted quietly.

Lander was silent for a moment. A small flash of worry that I'd struck a nerve pierced through me.

Then he said, "Why do you want to know? Jealous or something?"

Judging by the tone of his voice, he had that stupid grin plastered on his face, and my cheeks burned hotter than when Mama cornered me earlier. I hadn't struck a nerve, but he sure had. I was beyond glad for the cover of night.

"No! Never! I've seen how you eat a pretzel." I made a fake gagging noise.

He choked back a laugh. "If you must know, yes, it was." Lander grew solemn now, the ever-present heaviness of Cyntha's death absorbing the humor he'd tried to cover it with.

An earnest question, a curiosity of what I might've experienced should I have been in Cyntha's place came tumbling off my tongue. "What was it like?"

I could feel his head move on instinct to search my face, even though he'd see nothing.

"Um. It was a bit squishy. I didn't expect that. But it was nice," he said, after thinking for a moment.

"Squishy isn't the description I'd expect, either," I replied, curling my nose up at the thought. But when I thought about Lander's lips, as soft as they appeared, the crinkle in my nose rapidly smoothed itself out.

He took a deep breath, and I could tell by the way it sounded he was about to say something stupid. "Who was your first kiss?"

I huffed, more than irritated. "I don't know why you're even asking me this when you already know the answer."

"Was it Brandon? I saw you talking to him at least thrice. You two seemed pretty cozy."

I scowled over at him in the darkness. "Never," I hissed. "The only things his parents grow are onions. I wouldn't get within ten feet of those lips."

Lander snorted and slapped a hand over his mouth to muffle the noise. "Stop making me laugh!"

"It's not my fault you can't be serious for longer than five seconds!"

"Sorry! I'm trying my best," he said, smothering yet another snort. "It's hard not to laugh when you're not supposed to laugh."

"That's fine, but right now is not the time to struggle with that," I said. *I swear, if he gets us caught...*

"Okay, okay. You're right. I was kidding. I know you've never kissed anyone. I couldn't help it." He finally got ahold of himself, his giggles squashed. "Whew. That was funny."

"Glad you think so," I grumbled, beyond ready to be far, far away from him right now.

I briefly considered leaving him here and going through the mountains alone when the deafening rumbling began. We both froze, the seriousness of our situation settling back in. Light erupted from around the boulder, filtering between the various twigs surrounding us, and I knew then that the gate had opened. We were much closer this time, which unnerved me. Up on the ledge, the voices were garbled and faint, the light much less penetrating. Here, I could understand every word spoken, and my eyes almost hurt from how bright it was.

"Line up! The receivers are on their way."

The deep, booming voice was so close I thought my heart would explode. I couldn't even look at Lander for reassurance, for fear that the movement would somehow be detected. After what seemed like hours, the thumping of hoofbeats on dirt emerged from the direction of the city, mirrored by the ringing of horseshoes on tile from the tunnel.

"Produce: to the left for inspection. Metals and wood: to the right."

I couldn't exactly pinpoint what the noises were, but I heard a cacophony of clanging and thudding. I imagined what each sound could possibly be, trying to shove the horrific fears down deep where they couldn't be found. Was it a box or a body falling to the ground? Metal clanging, or the sound of a guard unsheathing his sword? Orders for the carts to line up, or a shout that someone was found spying? My chest galloped faster than a horse ever could, and I was wondering if I might pass out when a hand wrapped in leather gently squeezed my wrist. Lander. It was okay. We were fine. No one knew we were here but us. He wouldn't let anything happen to me.

Slowly, my heart settled down, and I focused hard on what was about to happen.

"Jonas, Anil, and Thamus, join me on escort. Mauney, take the guard."

I nearly gasped at hearing his name but quickly quelled the rising panic. I already knew he was involved. This was no surprise.

I knew the time had come when the rumbling started up again, and Lander peeked out behind the brush to confirm our exact placement of action.

He hadn't let go of my wrist, which was to our advantage since I wasn't as ready as I thought I was when Lander whispered, "Let's go!"

He yanked me away from the safety of the shelter. At first, I wasn't sure where the guard named Mauney was in relation to this path, but I quickly realized we were behind him, jumping from shadow to shadow. A line of boulders effectively concealed the majority of our journey to the doors, the rumbling drowning out our frantic footsteps. Terror flooded me when the cover ended, Lander nearly dragging me at this point toward the rapidly closing doors. I'd never seen him move with such haste, and I caught a brief glimpse of the guard's back right as we slipped between the massive, foreboding pieces of metal.

As suddenly as it started, the sound ceased with a solid, trembling clank, and I found myself clinging to Lander's arm, peering down a long tunnel.

The tunnel that led to the outside.

***

How this tunnel was created, I couldn't fathom. It was carved through solid rock, the walls smooth and gray as if someone had spent years sanding it down to perfection. Rivulets of water rolled down into various shimmering puddles. The air was heavy and damp, the scent of mold and stagnant water stinging my nostrils as frigid air swept across my face. It was drafty and hollow, and a low and eerie howl carried along the wind that wouldn't abate. I didn't know where it came from—perhaps erupting from the mountain itself. Honestly, I wasn't sure I even wanted to know, unnerving as it sounded. The hair on the back of my neck prickled, prompting me to grip Lander even tighter.

The end of the tunnel wasn't visible, and not simply due to the carriages inching into its gaping maw. It extended forever, the torches becoming closer and closer together as it stretched deep through the belly of the mountain. I glanced up at Lander, eyes wide. My shoulders quivered as I attempted to breathe quietly, horrified that any noise I'd make would be amplified in the echoey chamber.

Lander tilted his head to the right, and the map he'd created in the dirt flashed through my mind in time with the flickering torches. I nodded almost imperceptibly, and together we tiptoed to the edge of the tunnel, pushing our backs against the wall. We crept along in silence, the frigid drops of water soaking into the back of my dress and atop our heads. It was as if the mountain was trying to figure out what we were, tapping us to elicit a response that would reveal our identities. The carriages had gained a significant amount of distance at this point, and with each torch they passed, the fright eased some. If their massive Clydesdales and fancy metal carriages were difficult for us to see, surely our small, creeping forms were a greater challenge to make out.

Lander and I slipped out of the main tunnel into the small side one. The constant eerie howl was hushed here, though the tunnel was dark and wet. I missed the soft light of the torches, but I supposed the darkness was safer for cover. The further we trudged, the heavier my boots became, soaked through with cold, gritty water. My socks squished grossly with each step, and I couldn't wait to get out of this disgusting, cramped excuse for a tunnel. Neither of us dared utter even a whisper, as though it were a scream to every gate guard in the nearby vicinity.

After a lifetime of splashing our way through the tunnel, Lander slammed into a hunk of metal. I sucked in a gasp, terrified that alarms would sound, indicating our presence after such a jarring noise. When nothing happened, I released my gasp, temporary relief taking off the edge of anticipation.

"We made it," Lander told me.

I almost didn't hear him, hushed as he was. I knew what came next. Lander set to work on the four locks, expertly picking them despite the solid wall of thick velvet dark that enveloped us.

"How do you even know what you're doing?" I asked, voice as hushed as his.

"I can see fine," he replied, soft sounds of metal working against metal whispering against the stone walls.

"You're crazy if you think you can see in here."

"I've been called worse," he retorted, and the first lock clicked open.

I'd be lying if I said I wasn't impressed, as even with optimal light and the best tools, I never would have managed. He went to work on the second, the third, and finally, the fourth.

When the final lock clicked, I froze, in utter disbelief that we'd made it. The next move would bring us to the outside, a place I believed I'd never again set eyes on as long as I lived. The entire world lay right in front of us, separated only by a few inches of metal. I hadn't seen it since I was seven, when everything collapsed for a second time in history. Would we get captured? Hunted down? Lander said he and Cyntha never saw another soul out here, but the carriages had to go somewhere, right? I wiped sweaty palms on the skirts of my dress, willing myself to shake off the nerves in exchange for excitement. This place was only a distant memory, and I'd spent hours staring out the classroom window, wondering what could possibly be left behind the towering peaks.

I was about to find out.

I shivered when I heard the wheel in the center of the door clanking. Lander grunted with the effort, the gears within turning, groaning, and finally coming to a stop. He panted, spent from fighting the wheel, which I assumed was as damp and slippery as the floor.

"Are you ready, Sadie?" he asked, excitement tumbling out of each word.

"I'm ready," I said. "Let's do this."

His hand searched through the darkness for mine, and we laced our fingers together, ready to face the world. His other hand went to the door and pushed.

A gust of wind whipped into the tunnel as the door opened up, taking my breath away. We had stepped out into a rolling, grassy field, conifers scattered about, illuminated by the dim light of a crescent moon. The sky was not only above us, but around us, meeting the ground in a dark half dome. The stars were vivid and endless, forming unique patterns I'd never laid eyes on, the majority of the sky in Ancthia enclosed by the peaks. We were even more exposed here than on our climb up the side of the mountains. Mountains which towered behind us, albeit a tad shorter than I was accustomed to. Because Ancthia was nestled in a giant hole, the peaks appeared much taller on the inside than the outside. I understood now why a fence atop them was necessary, as the trek up some of the shorter tips would be a lot more manageable from this direction.

The song of insects was like nothing I'd never heard before, a wild, disjointed tune that rattled my core with intrigue and inspiration. There was a beat in the background, a steady, rhythmic pounding that resembled the whoosh of wind. I tried to find where it was coming from, afraid that someone or something was near.

"What's that sound? Is someone coming?" I panicked, tugging on Lander's jacket yet again.

To my surprise he chuckled, patting the top of my head.

"That, Sadie, is the heartbeat of the ocean. The waves, to be exact."

I swept my eyes left and right, but found nothing resembling a sea. The small hills around us were all I found, a gentle, steady wind rippling across a lively field of grass.

"Where is it?" I asked, still in awe of the sky.

"Follow me," Lander grinned, thrilled with how entranced I was by our surroundings.

We trudged through the plush grass, Lander laughing at how often I tripped or stumbled over rocks and sticks, too distracted by the sights to focus. The peaks shrank as we grew further away, yet another thing I couldn't stop staring at. I didn't even realize when we had arrived, too focused on the oddity of leaving the mountains that were ever constant until Lander came to a sudden stop. I crashed into him, smashing my nose into his hard, thick jacket.

"Ouch! A little warning next time!" I grumped, rubbing my throbbing nares.

"Sadie. Look," Lander murmured, pushing me around to the front so I'd have a clear view of whatever he was trying to show me.

My feet sunk; the ground having become loose and soft. I stared at it in wonder, intrigued by the white hue the dirt had taken. I was about to ask what it was when Lander gingerly tilted my head, redirecting my gaze to the most breathtaking scene I'd ever witnessed.

A sprawling, vast expanse of rippling water spread out as far as I could see, the two deep blues of the sea and sky almost melting into one another. I had difficulty discerning where one ended and the other began, the glittering moonlight on the water resembling the spread of stars above. I understood what Lander meant when he said the ocean was sentient. Its crashing waves and constant thrashing resembled a creature caught in a trap, struggling and roaring to rip free. Its breath was the wind, endless and swirling, yanking loose strands of hair from the carefully placed braid wrapped around my head. The wind was tangy with salt, a delicious aroma that tickled the back of my nose and my tongue. I couldn't get enough of it. I inhaled deeply, yearning for the flavor to grace my tongue again and again.

"I-I've never seen anything so beautiful," I gasped, in complete awe.

"Neither have I," Lander murmured.

At first I thought he was referring to the sparkling ocean. But when he spoke, his breath tickled the side of my face, and I realized he hadn't taken his eyes off me since we'd crested the top of the hill. I ripped my gaze away from the water, staring at him in shock, mouth agape. He curled his finger under my chin, slowly lifting it upward. My pulse thundered in my ears, loud as the crashing waves. What was he doing? He surely wasn't about to kiss me. There was no way. But . . . oh, there was. I was being pulled blissfully underwater, riding on a smooth, warm current. My eyes fluttered shut as our lips grew so close I could feel the heat of his skin.

And then he froze.

I opened my eyes back up, peering into his. Moonlight reflected off his brown irises, as if the sea was trapped inside of them. We were incredibly still for what seemed an eternity, but it was only a matter of seconds before Lander suddenly pulled back, hand dropping to his side in a tight fist. We both turned away from each other in tandem, the odd moment having crested and dissipated as quickly as the waves we stood by.

"I-uh. Sorry," Lander muttered, kicking the soft, gritty ground beneath us that I now realized was sand. "I thought you, you know, had some dirt on your face or something."

I chuckled nervously, gripping my skirts tightly in awkwardness. "You know me, always getting into some kind of mess."

My thoughts were reeling. *Had he been about to kiss me? Why did he freeze up? He hadn't done that with Cyntha. Was something wrong with me?*

We both turned, going to speak at the same time.

"We need—"

"There's a—"

I stopped right when he did, each going to let the other continue. We stared, at a stalemate, the wind making his hair stand up in a distinctly adorable way. He nodded in my direction, indicating for me to speak first. I obliged, wanting to crawl out of my skin with how uncomfortable this was.

"Seashells. Where can we find some good ones?" I blurted.

Lander pointed to the water. "Usually right along the edge. That's where the waves leave all sorts of gifts from the deepest parts of the water."

I rapidly tried to change the subject, to shift our conversation out of this rift of uneasiness. "What's the most interesting thing you've ever come across?" I questioned, observing how the sand became flatter and firm as it neared the water. Walking was much easier here, my feet no longer sinking.

"I found a dead shark once," he replied, scratching his chin in thought. "I wanted to rip out a tooth to make a necklace, but I'm sure you can picture the earful I'd get from Mom."

I laughed, glad for the conversation to shift to normal, knowing exactly how Mrs. Robyn would react. I started toward the water's edge.

"Wait. You might want to take your boots off," Lander cautioned. "The water carries sand with it. It's not the most comfortable thing, walking in wet, gritty shoes."

"Good point." I bent down, undoing the laces. Lander stepped back, reaching a safe and comfortable distance from the water. I scowled over at him. "You're not going to join me?"

He shook his head, peering wistfully at the horizon. "Maybe another night. Someone has to stand lookout, anyway," he said, scanning the surrounding area. He shoved both hands in the pockets of his jacket, going back to kicking at the sand. "Not to mention, this stuff gets everywhere. And by that, I mean *everywhere.*"

After draping my socks over the top of my boots, I plunged my feet into the sand. It was chilly on the top layer, but deep down it still held the warmth of the sun.

"I should search the edge, then? You're sure there'll be shells?"

Lander nodded. "You'll find a treasure trove."

"Okay, I'll be right back!"

I hopped across the beach, racing to the waves with childlike glee with my skirts bunched up to keep them dry. The water collided with my feet, sending a warm spray of foamy droplets up my shins. I shrieked, jumping backward, freely laughing. As quickly as the wave reached out, it yanked back, sending another splash up my calves. A small pile of sand settled over my feet, burying them.

Splashing down the coastline, I noticed that along with the sand, the water carried hundreds of small hard objects that I initially thought were rocks. They tumbled along with the push and pull of the waves, and after close inspection, I realized they were shells. Some were flat and smooth on the inside, the outside sporting ripples mirroring those of the ocean. Others were smooth all around, curling withing themselves into a grand spiral. I sifted through endless shapes and sizes, each one as unique as the next until I finally found the one.

It was a swirling, twisting shell the size of my hand. I couldn't tell what color it was in the night, but I knew I held a work of art. I stumbled back up the shore to Lander, my skirts soaked at the fringe.

"I got it!" I panted.

I held up the large shell, placing it in Lander's outstretched palm.

He whistled. "Ooh, you found a good one. This is called a conch."

I plopped down into the sand next to him, watching intently as he brushed away the grains caked into the conch shell's folds and knobs.

"Conch," I repeated, letting the word roll around on my tongue the same way the shell had in the current. "What an interesting word."

"That's not the most interesting thing about it," Lander said, handing it back to me. "Put the opening to your ear."

I gingerly lifted it to my ear, salty drops of water dripping onto my shoulder. And as I listened, I was amazed for the hundredth time that night. A gentle whooshing noise, matching that of the ocean's wind and waves echoed from its core.

"That's amazing! How does it do that?" I wondered, turning the shell over and over to try and find the answer.

"Mom says it's because they hold the breath of the ocean. No matter where it goes, it'll always sing its song."

"How remarkable," I said, entranced. "If this doesn't convince Mama, nothing will."

"She'll be convinced," Lander asserted. "I'm sure of it."

We sat in peaceful silence for some time, enjoying the view and the breeze. I shoved my feet down into the sand, moving them around in all directions.

"It's so soft!" I squealed, wiggling my toes, reveling in the unique grainy sensation between them.

"Mom used to spend half the day sweeping it out of the floorboards," Lander reflected. "My sisters would always forget to take their shoes off. I know she'd give anything to have that mess back, even though she still complains about it."

He peered up into the sky, the last place he ever saw his siblings. I joined in, the vast expanse of stars stretching endlessly in the heavens.

"I wonder what happens to them," I wondered aloud, "when they float away."

"They probably suffocate," Lander replied in an almost scientific manner. "I've heard that the higher you go, like on tall mountains and stuff, the air gets thinner with less oxygen. And without oxygen, you can't breathe."

"That's not dark at all," I snorted.

"It's only facts," Lander huffed.

"You don't know for sure, though. You've never been up there."

"You're right, I haven't. And judging by how much the city's lied about our supply chain, it wouldn't surprise me if they lied about the lack of oxygen."

I pulled my knees to my chest, resting my chin atop them. "I like to think that they don't suffocate. That once they pass the clouds, they become another star."

Lander laughed, leaning back to get a better view of the sky. "That's a nice sentiment, but that's silly. The stars don't change."

"Oh yeah? Have you ever counted them?" I gave him a sly smirk.

He tilted his head, mulling it over. "You have a good point there, Sadie. Can't say I ever have."

"There's too many to count," I added, referring to both the stars and the people lost.

"Most definitely."

I'm not sure how long we stayed on the beach, laughing and chatting in endless conversation, but the end to it all came much too soon. We had to get back before the sun graced the horizon, and before it was too late to get any sleep. After all, we did have school in the morning, and the last few nights had been sorely lacking in anything resembling rest.

The journey back was even easier than the journey out, and I understood why Lander had previously told me not to worry about it. As I'd noticed earlier, the peaks weren't as tall and steep on the outside. We scaled one of the shorter peaks with little effort, the incline gradual and sloping instead of jagged and cliff-like.

Lander was much more aware of our surroundings the closer we got, scanning the approaching gates with bright, wide eyes. He said the gate guards patrolled through each area roughly every thirty minutes, with the entire platoon circling the mountains once every night. He parked us behind a massive, cracked rock and peered around it, watching and waiting for one to cross. I sat impatiently, hoping they'd pass soon, growing incredibly sleepy. The excitement of the trip was wearing thin now that the best part was over. Eventually, Lander gave the signal, and we raced toward the fence, the guard now out of view. He twisted a few wires before yanking the chain links upward, revealing a carefully crafted and hidden hole near a support pole. I slipped through, Lander following behind me, and I waited as he retwisted the wires holding the flap shut.

Once secured, I kept close behind my friend, as he skidded and slid down the steep mountainside. Rocks and dirt tumbled down with us, in a rough and speedy descent. Much of the sliding was uncontrolled, given how steep the decline was. We eventually reached a point where the decline tapered off to a gradual slope, and we regained our footing. Lander led me around boulders and dead trees until we came to a familiar area. I recognized it as the road leading to the ledge we'd spied off, and once we arrived there, the rest of the trip was easy.

"Did you make that hole?" I asked Lander.

He nodded, glancing around to make sure no one was nearby, even though the streets were deserted at this hour.

"I cut it with a pair of wire cutters I found on the road a long time ago," he explained, "and took out a few pieces from the fence buried under the dirt to use as ties."

"Aren't you crafty," I said, impressed. "I understand why that's the way in and not the way out. Might as well be a dirt slide."

"When it rains, it's more like a mud slide."

We continued on, finally ending our journey at his house. I was beyond ready to lie down and sleep, but that dream was promptly shattered when we entered to find Mrs. Robyn waiting for us at the kitchen table.

Lander muttered a curse under his breath, which led his mom to slam her knitting down hard onto the table's surface. We both jumped.

"If I ever hear that disgusting language spew from your lips again, I'll smack you 'til your ears bleed!" she shouted.

"Yes, ma'am." Lander sighed, knowing what was next.

"Where have you two been?"

Our eyes shot to our feet, the presence of the conch shell suddenly heavy in my pocket.

"Do I need to ask again?"

She rose from her chair, standing stiffly in front of her son. They stared each other down as she slowly inspected him, even pausing to sniff the collar of his jacket. That's where she found the answer she sought, as Mrs. Robyn suddenly straightened up, crossing her arms while glaring down at him. Of course she'd been the one to catch us. She was the only person who could sniff out our mischief quicker than any gate guard ever could.

"I'd know that smell anywhere, son," she rumbled.

"Mom, it's not—"

"Yes it is! Don't lie to me, Lander! You've been to the sea, and worse, you've dragged an innocent girl into your ridiculous escapades. Do you realize what could happen to you? To her?"

Her voice was shrill, and it almost sounded as if she was on the verge of explosion. A fact that unnerved me. Mrs. Robyn hardly ever lost her cool.

"It wasn't his fault, I insisted," I protested, trying to take some of the blame off Lander. If it wasn't for me, he would've never been in this situation in the first place.

"Sure, but it was my idea," Lander said calmly, much to my annoyance.

"Sadie dear, why don't you go clean up and get some rest? Lander and I need to have a talk."

She managed a smile, one that didn't quite reach her eyes, and patted me softly on the shoulder. I nodded and reluctantly obeyed. I knew better than to argue with her.

I attempted to eavesdrop, pressing my ear against the bedroom door. But no matter how hard I strained, the words were too hushed, resembling the breath of the ocean inside my conch shell. As quiet as they were, I could still tell it was a heated conversation, whispers shifting from soft to harsh, again and again. Eventually, they grew silent, and I raced to hide under my blanket, not wanting to get caught listening in. Mrs. Robyn came to her room, pausing to cover me with an extra quilt. I tried to keep still, to appear deeply asleep, but sharp as she was, I knew Mrs. Robyn knew better.

She settled in, and I was calmed by the fact Lander was no longer getting chewed out. Though I must say, I was thoroughly disappointed I'd missed out on the details of their conversation. As sleep became heavy in my chest, I let it pull me under, welcoming the peaceful stillness as visions of crashing waves illuminated by moonlight took over my dreams.

8

When I woke up, bright light filtered in from a sun already high in the sky. I gasped, jumping up, realizing we were late for school. Right before I blasted through the shared bathroom to beat on Lander's door, I noticed Mrs. Robyn's bed was neatly made, not even a wrinkle visible on the smooth quilt. Confused, I changed my route to the kitchen, which was also empty. The house was quiet, the only noise a lonely, steady ticking from the old windup clock above the mantle, of which pointed to twelve sharp. I wondered if school had possibly been canceled and quietly cracked open Lander's bedroom door to find his room deserted.

No sooner had I shut it, I heard voices out back, and peeked outside to find Lander and Mrs. Robyn working in the garden together. Seeing them outside together, laughing and getting along, was a relief after the heated discussion they'd shared last night.

I pushed the door open, the hinges giving a delicate squeak, and stepped out into the warm, spring sun. Lander peered over his mom's shoulder, a smile exploding across his face at my presence. His teeth glinted white, hair tousled and sweaty, and I suddenly found myself weak in the knees.

"We're almost done now, Sadie. You can sit and watch if you'd like," he offered, using his wrist to swipe some loose hair off his forehead but smearing dirt across it instead.

"I don't mind helping," I told him, picking up a small trowel to pull the weeds, "but you've got a little something there."

I motioned toward his messy face, moving to use my skirts to wipe it, but Mrs. Robyn wiped it clean with a hand towel before I could even get close.

"Was school canceled today?" I probed, trying to figure out why Mrs. Robyn hadn't forced us out the door before the sun could even think about rising as she usually did.

"I swung by on my way to market to tell Miss Poe you two were suffering from afflictions of the bowel. With the lack of sleep you've been getting, I figured you might need it."

"That sounds gross," Lander said, yanking a fistful of weeds from behind a row of carrots. I gave him a dirty look for being unappreciative to his mom's kindness.

"Thank you Mrs. Robyn. I'm grateful," I said, meaning every word.

"Don't get used to it," she sternly replied. "You're not getting away with it next time I catch you hooligans, sneaking in at three in the morning. And there better not be a next time, either!"

"Yes, ma'am," Lander and I replied in unison, though all three of us were well aware there would be a next time.

The garden truly was almost finished, because not even ten minutes after I joined in, we were done. Mrs. Robyn headed inside to grab a snack and something to drink, and Lander and I sat on one of the benches under a small willow tree. The instant his mom was out of sight, Lander leaned over to me.

"She gave me quite the earful last night," he explained, eyeing the door for her return.

"I know, I heard," I said, revealing my attempt at eavesdropping.

He immediately tensed up. "What did you hear?"

My eyes went to the sudden tautness to his shoulders. What was it about their conversation that he didn't want me to know about? Clearly, he was uncomfortable with the thought that I'd overheard. I said, cautiously, carefully observing his reaction, "Nothing of meaning, only a bunch of hissing and spitting, like a pair of cats in an alley."

The tension in his shoulders immediately dissolved. He chuckled at the visual. "Oh. I told her everything, about Cyntha and Thamus. She said she understood our intentions were good, but that we're complete and utter idiots for even considering what we did. She's not mad anymore, but I'm grounded for the next year. Save for escorting you home from your performances."

Deep down in the pit of my stomach, I knew he was leaving something out. Something important. But I already knew he would brush me off if I asked—we'd been down this road plenty of times before. Instead of asking questions, I whistled.

"An entire year, huh? Hopefully we got everything we needed, then, since it'll be a year before we can even think about going back."

I wiggled my toes, nestled in the blades of grass and brown dirt, a sharp contrast to the light and airy ground of the beach. We'd only been there once, for an insignificant amount of time in the grand scheme of things, but I already missed it with every ounce of my being. I wondered briefly if this was how Lander always felt, since it had once been his home. It was as if the waves had torn out a piece of my essence and sucked it out to sea. The peaks, instead of being a shield against a dangerous outside world, were now stifling, akin to the door that had sealed behind me during isolation. The need to go witness the beauty of the sea again tugged at my core, begging me to go back, taking up every thought in my mind. Every thought except one, that is. The memory hit me like a jolt of lightning, face heating up all the way to the tips of my ears as I remembered what Lander had said to me atop the hill.

How we'd almost kissed.

Lander tilted his head, regarding me curiously. "What are you thinking?" he asked.

"Nothing," I grumped, turning away.

"You're thinking about something. You're the same color as these beets right here."

I yanked my hair down, hiding behind the makeshift golden-brown veil. "I am not!" I huffed, crossing my arms.

He smirked. "Whatever, keep your secrets. You'll tell me soon enough, anyway."

"I'm not telling you a thing!"

Lander leaned against the back of the bench, stretching his arms out above his head. "You will. Tonight, to be exact. When you pull out your violin."

I whipped back around. Spitting out a clump of hair that slipped between my lips, I raked the strands out of my face to glare at Lander in utter disbelief. His smirk widened.

"What's that supposed to mean?"

"You might be closed off when it comes to your words," he remarked, "but everything spills out when you pick up that instrument. Trust me, I know it all."

I shifted uneasily in my seat. He was bluffing. Had to be. I'd poured some seriously personal emotions into my music, but it simply wasn't possible for someone to read their exact meaning. Right? The more uncomfortable I grew, the more pleased Lander appeared, stoking my sudden doubts. I worried my face might burst into flames, but luckily at that moment, Mrs. Robyn came bustling out of the back door, a most welcome interruption.

"Here you go, some homemade chicken sandwiches with fresh squeezed lemonade. I worked extra last week to afford the lemons." Mrs. Robyn set the platter down on the small table between the benches, doing a double take when she noticed my face. "Sadie dear, have you got sunburn already?" She clicked her tongue, leaning in to get a closer look. "I have a spare hat in the closet, should I go get it for you?"

I aggressively shook my head and said through gritted teeth, "I'm fine, thank you."

Lander reached for the platter, already digging in, choking back a laugh. His mom glanced back and forth between us before deciding she'd rather not get involved and turned her attention to her sandwich.

Our afternoon was relaxing despite endless chores, but the three of us always enjoyed the time we spent together, no matter what we did. Time moved quickly, and before I knew it, the sun was ready to set. I'd stashed my violin under Lander's bed the night before, and we prepared to head to the square for my nightly performance.

"Do you want something to eat before you go?" his mom asked as I laced up my boots.

I shook my head, knowing that Lander would be begging for a pretzel. "Don't worry, Mrs. Robyn, we'll figure something out."

She watched Lander carefully, narrowing her eyes at him. "You're still grounded, by the way. You're only going to watch over my seventh daughter."

"I know, I know," Lander grumbled, shoving his hands in his pockets.

As we were heading out the door, she stopped him once more with a hard grip on his shoulder, voice a low warning.

"Don't you dare forget."

Lander nodded tersely, and she let go, almost pushing him forward. I didn't dare ask what Mrs. Robyn meant, as she could be rather scary at times. We went straight to the market square, Lander hiding in his usual alleyway, and I went to work.

My music was a tad different from usual, full of life and excitement as I detailed the journey we'd taken through sound. I played the song of crickets and wind, of stars and rolling fields. I played of the lively waves and endless horizons, the entire experience erupting out of my fingers raw and unfiltered. I could see the music in my head, swirling around me in a chaotic dance with each sweep of the bow. The movements left me weightless as I swayed with the rhythm. People stopped and stared, but I ignored them, engulfed in the story I was spinning. Toward the end, my music changed somewhat, as the strange stirring in my heart that Lander created manifested itself. The tune was heavy and warm, with an irresistible tang resembling the salty air of the ocean. I eventually wrapped it up, ending on a long, drawn-out swing of the bow. The final note rang out across the square, echoing off the stone buildings.

Sensing the end, Lander emerged, a smirk on his face as I packed up my instrument, the bag of coins almost spilling over. "I must say, that was an exquisite performance. I don't think I even heard a single squeak."

"Let's be real, you were probably napping with the rats back there," I retorted.

"No way I was going to miss hearing your thoughts tonight."

His reference to our earlier conversation had my face even redder than before. I slammed the violin case shut, embarrassed that he might've understood what my music meant, but I talked myself down, knowing it was completely unrealistic. He was only trying to mess with me, as usual, and I couldn't help but egg him on.

"What did my thoughts say, then, if it was that obvious?"

Lander chewed on his lip, mulling over the question for a moment. "I don't know if I can explain it. Doesn't really translate to words."

I narrowed my eyes at him.

"Either way, it doesn't matter. Whatever your music was saying was exceptional."

His compliment left me more than flustered. Muttering a bashful thank you to my friend, I quickly redirected his attention to his favorite pretzel stand. A few minutes later, he was contentedly gnawing on his treat, and we sat at our favorite spot by the fountain.

"Thamus isn't supposed to be there tonight," I said, brushing the crumbs off my lap for the pair of doves pecking at the pebbles. They wouldn't go to waste this time, much to my relief. "It should be fairly smooth sailing."

"Good. And then I won't have to worry as much," said Lander through a mouthful of pretzel. "Having you near the jaws of a murderer stresses me out."

"Me too," I told him, a shiver rippling down my spine. "If it weren't for him, Cyntha would still be here right now."

Lander's face dropped as it tended to when I mentioned our lost friend, neglecting to take another bite of his pretzel. "Yeah. If it weren't for him," he said solemnly.

I patted him on the back. "In only a few hours, he'll be out of our lives forever."

"Let's get on with it then." Lander stood, grabbing my violin to help carry it home. "I can't wait."

I was nervous to tell Mama, because I'd also be telling her we broke the law. If Mrs. Robyn could understand why we did it, then Mama surely would come around. I'd done it for her. She had to understand that, even if she'd be devastated at the betrayal of someone she thought she loved. We would save her from a future of lies and heartbreak before it got out of hand.

I reached the front door before Lander—as always—and held it open since he was carrying the bulky violin case. He managed to smash it against the doorway in at least three different angles prompting me to punch him in the arm.

"Break my instrument and I'll break you!" I threatened, grateful for the thick case that my father had crafted for it.

The violin luckily managed to make it to the foot of my bed, unscathed, and hearing the commotion, Mama emerged from the garden.

"Sadie! Welcome home, I'm so glad you're here!" She pulled me into a tight hug.

"Me too, I—"

"Lander! Great to see you, too!"

She went to give him a hug, but he deflected it as always. In true Lander fashion, he pretended that he was searching for something under a kitchen chair.

"Good evening, Mrs. Cleamont, you look well. Seem to have dropped my key again," he said in a singsong voice, clearly using the chair as defense from her affections. Lander reminded me of an overstimulated cat that never wanted to be touched, that is, unless it was on his terms.

"You are always dropping something," Mama laughed, oblivious to the truth behind his butterfingers. "I've put on a roast," she said, swinging her skirts joyfully around the table to peer into the oven.

"A roast?" I asked, aghast. We hadn't had a roast in at least a year. My mouth instantly watered at the promise of something so rare. "How?"

"You've been pulling in a lot of extra money lately in the square," she explained, poking the slab of meat with a long fork to see how done it was. Finding it less than satisfactory, she shut it back in to cook longer. "Plus, I have something exciting to tell you and figured it would be the perfect treat to celebrate."

Dread filled my chest, settling in like the ache of a lingering cough. *She's not going to tell me they're getting married, right?* I glanced over at Lander for reassurance, who was also panic-stricken. I took a step toward Mama.

"That's great, but first I have something important to talk to you about."

Mama bustled around the kitchen, grabbing plates and utensils to set up around the table.

"Do you? How wonderful! Go make the table for me, please." She thrust the plates into my arms, setting a handful of forks on top. I plunked them down on the wooden surface, desperate to get her attention.

"Mama, it's serious. I need you to listen," I pleaded, but she continued to prepare for dinner, filling up a kettle for tea.

"I can imagine it is, but first things first, please set the table. I don't care to repeat myself."

I huffed, reluctantly obeying.

"What's it about?" Mama questioned halfheartedly, distracted by her kitchen preparations and whatever stupid news she was about to share.

"It's about Thamus and Cyntha, I—"

The door swung open without warning, Lander practically leaping across the kitchen as Thamus stepped into the doorway. That's when I noticed, albeit far too late, that Mama had handed me four plates for dinner. Which meant *he* would be joining us. The hair on the back of my neck bristled, as I watched her kiss him on the cheek in a greeting. Lander moved to my side, trying to provide both silent support and protection. I'm sure Mama and Thamus could sense how hard I was glaring, because they both stopped awkwardly in the middle of their kiss to stare in our direction. She didn't pay it too much mind, though, because her face was positively beaming despite my disapproval.

"Thamus, darling, I wanted to tell them over dinner, but you know what, I can't wait another minute!" she squealed, with childish delight, the enthusiasm setting off alarm bells in every part of my brain.

Thamus pulled her in close, hand around her waist, and the grossly happy couple stood over Lander and me. We might've been standing in the same room, but it was as if I were standing a world away, Mama and Thamus enveloped in a bubble of some sort of deranged bliss.

"Okay, Lauren."

I watched in horror as Mama placed her hands delicately over her abdomen, the smile on her face so big I feared it would drown out her eyes. Thamus matched her expression, beard twitching with the pull of his muscles. I almost didn't hear her, as loudly as my pulse roared in my ears. I wished I hadn't, as each syllable slapped me in the face with such force I thought I was seeing stars.

"Sadie, we're having a baby!"

9

A baby.
A baby.

How much worse could things get? I couldn't move. Couldn't think. I was frozen to the spot, speechless, all rational thoughts having abandoned me. Mama was having *his* baby. I was going to be a big sister to the child of a possible murderer. The room spun as my mind swirled, and I'm pretty sure I was about to hyperventilate. Lander placed a hand on my back, grounding me, and I steadied my breathing, trying to process this.

"Are you—are you sure?" I sputtered.

Mama nodded, and she and Thamus locked eyes for a moment, her eyes dreamy and heavy-lidded as they gazed upon one another. The unnerving smile stuck to Thamus's face had me squirming. How could she ever fall for someone like him?

"Your little brother or sister will be here right around the first snow," she declared proudly. "We might have to expand, or move into Thamus's house to accommodate two more feet, but we'll manage."

I took back my previous thought about how things couldn't get worse, because it had. It was bad enough having him visit constantly, but to live under the same roof? If he ever found out that I'd left the peaks, that I knew he was the reason Cyntha wasn't with us any longer, I'd be even more at his mercy in his own home. I wanted to scream, to rage and throw the food she'd worked tirelessly on into the floor at how ridiculous this all was. In all honesty, I was only a heartbeat away from it when Lander spoke up, extinguishing my fuse.

"Congratulations," he said in an almost professional manner. "I'm sure you two are excited."

He tapped my back, urging me to say something, anything, to act in some semblance of normalcy. I peered at him in disbelief, but knew he was right. He raised his eyebrows and tapped me again. I swallowed hard, throat so dry I almost choked.

"That's great, Mama," I mumbled, unable to even manage a fake smile.

She laughed nervously, acutely aware that I wasn't remotely happy, her and Thamus exchanging an anxious glance.

"We'll talk more about it later," she said calmly, gliding over to the oven. "Food's ready! Let's sit down and eat together, as a family for the first time."

I was given a plate piled high with the tastiest appearing roast I'd ever seen, but couldn't bring myself to even try it. When Mama and Thamus were too distracted by each other to notice, Lander would swipe some of my food, desperately shoving it in his cheeks as though he were a chipmunk. I didn't mind, glad it wouldn't go to waste. I was relieved when dinner ended, but instead of Lander helping clean up and spend the evening with us, Mama hinted in a not-so-subtle way that she wanted to talk to me, alone. She ushered Thamus out the door to my relief, and when she came back inside, nodded in Lander's direction, indicating he should do the same.

"Thank you for the meal, Mrs. Cleamont," he told her. "I haven't had anything that delicious in a while. And congratulations again."

"You're welcome, Lander. Be safe walking home," she replied, going to give him a hug, but he skittered out the door before she could even get close.

I said my goodbyes to Lander, pulling the door shut behind me. Mama stood in the kitchen, hugging her chest with her arms, regarding me cautiously.

"Sadie. I know this was somewhat of a shock for you. For that, I'm sorry. But please, please, can you find it in your heart to be happy for me? I haven't had any real joy since moving here, and I've finally found it. You were doing great for a while there, in accepting Thamus. What happened?"

I gave her a vacant stare, wishing badly for this to be as simple as she made it out to be. But there was far too much going on behind the scenes that she didn't know.

"Mama. I need you to listen. Really listen," I said, my voice low and shaky. "Please, let me finish the entire story before you interrupt."

She nodded, and we sat down at the kitchen table as the events of the last two weeks came pouring out. I fought back tears of anger and frustration, as I explained everything, what we found Thamus doing, how Cyntha most likely died, and the most damning part, our venture out of the city. Mama didn't move a muscle or eyelash the entire time I spoke, which unnerved me to the core. She folded her hands on the table, fingers tightly laced together to the point her knuckles were white as Lander's.

When I concluded the story, I fished into the deep pocket of my outer skirt and pulled it out. The conch. I sat it on the table in front of her hands, presenting the final piece, the evidence, to the case I'd argued. Mama's eyes flickered down to the pink and white piece of the ocean with an unreadable expression. She didn't reach out or attempt to even touch it, instead pulling her hands off the table and into her lap. She bit her bottom lip, hard, working her jaw as she stared. And stared. The silence was deafening. I was almost glad for the pounding of my heart. For a moment, I was genuinely concerned that she might be in shock.

"Mama?" I probed gently. "Are you—"

"Stop. Just stop it," she said harshly. I shut up immediately. I braced myself for the impact, knowing she'd be angry that I snuck out of the city. "I figured you'd have some apprehensions about such a big change in your life, but Sadie. This? You come up with some … ridiculous, over-the-top story to try to get my attention? You want me to believe you've left the city?"

I flinched against the stinging bite of her words. "Mama, it's true! I swear! That's why I brought you this, because I knew you wouldn't believe me otherwise!" I grabbed the conch, thrusting it in her direction.

She glared at the shell, scrutinizing it.

"I don't know how much you paid for that, but I must give my compliments to its sculptor," she said tersely, abruptly pushing her chair back to stand.

"No, it's not a sculpture! Pick it up, you'll be able to tell if you hold it!" I motioned for her to take it again, prompting her to take a step back.

"I don't need to." Mama continued backing away, bumping against the countertop, one hand protectively on her abdomen.

My eyes darted between her and the shell, briefly confused at her adamant refusal when understanding flooded me, cold and unforgiving.

"You know."

She didn't move, gaze glued to the shell.

"Am I right?" I demanded. "You won't touch it because you know it's real?"

I wanted to step forward, to test the waters should she not reply but hesitated when I received an icy stare.

"I didn't think I'd have to worry about my own daughter putting all of our lives in danger."

"You don't understand, there is no real danger! As I explained, it's—"

She interrupted me with a wave of her hand. "You're the one who doesn't understand!" she shouted, and I flinched, not accustomed to hearing Mama raise her voice. "Putting Thamus's career on the line and for what? For some thrills? To try to break apart the life I'm trying to build? You're reckless and brazen! I knew something was up, what with the amount of time you and Lander have been spending together, but I never expected this! I was too blinded by my own budding romance to see that's not what was happening here."

She'd known. She'd known all along he wasn't a farmer. I'd caught her in another lie. What else was she hiding and lying to my face about? "That's not what I was trying to do! I was trying to save you!" I argued, throwing my hands out to my sides.

"From what? From what, Sadie? From some half-assed theory that my boyfriend murdered your classmate? You are right about one thing, Thamus does work for the city as a gate guard, and that is privileged, top secret information! But my heavens, Sadie, he's not part of some secret conspiracy! I've been there, I've seen where he guards! There's nothing there!" She was practically screaming at this point, her words charged. "And you! Slipping past him to bring back dangerous items, possible contamination to prove what, exactly? That he made a mistake on the job and didn't notice that kids were pulling one over on him? Do you know what that will do to him, to me, to you? To the baby? He will lose everything! *You* will lose everything! Yes, the money you make is a great help but it's not nearly enough. I lost my job a few months back, and if it wasn't for him, we'd be back on the streets."

She took a deep, shuddering breath, tears threatening to spill over as she continued. "Telling these kinds of stories, putting all of us in such a precarious situation, it's . . . I don't even know what it is! Absurd? Insanity?"

My own tears spilled over at this point. "I'm sorry. That's not what I was trying to do at all. I'm sorry! Please, listen, I wasn't trying to hurt you or us! Lander—"

She threw a hand up for me to stop. "*Lander*. It's always *Lander*. I don't care what he thought he saw! Cyntha got sick because they did something they shouldn't have. It was Lander and Cyntha's fault, not Thamus, not the city's, no one else's but theirs!"

"He was only trying to help," I said quietly. "I swear on it. I saw the carriages, Mama, I saw it with my own eyes. I'll take you there, that way you can too!"

"All you saw was a figment of your over-the-top imagination. I won't be going back to the mountain. Like I said, I've been there! And I'm not putting the baby at risk by bringing that in here. Have you forgotten why your father is dead? Because of things like this! Because of the outside world! Because of reckless, irresponsible people who can't follow the rules put in place to keep them safe! Cyntha wasn't the only one who died from this, either. She killed your teacher by bringing the virus in!"

She slammed her hand on the countertop, causing me to jump. She eyed the conch shell in my hand as if it were a bomb, ready to explode at any moment. For what it was worth, it might as well have been one, as it was the catalyst of this explosive mess.

I didn't know what else to say. This hadn't gone the way I'd hoped, even by a small amount. The only thing I could mutter was, "I'm sorry."

She paused, wrapping her arms back around herself. "I don't want you near that boy."

My head whipped up, horrified. Lander was as much my family as she was. "Mama, no! He's my best friend. I won't! I can't!"

"You can and you will! He's not right!" she cried. "Never has been, but you're too blind to see that too!"

I blinked, stunned at this revelation. Mama had never given any indication of dislike for Lander, always including him as one of the family. Tonight's expensive and rare dinner was no exception.

"What are you talking about?" I said through gritted teeth.

She sighed heavily, swiping her hand across her forehead in exasperation. "I don't know! I can't lay my finger on it! There's something about him . . . He's . . . Wrong! I mean, look at him!"

Hearing her bring up my father's death was painful enough. Hearing her completely disregard everything about the mountain as a lie, choosing Thamus's story as truth was a slap in the face. But to insult Lander, the one person who had held me up through our years at Ancthia? Sure, he had his odd quirks. He didn't have the best taste in style, either, that much was clear. But he'd risked everything to help me and my family when he didn't have to, and not only in escaping the city. He was the friend who I'd shared every quiet thought, every laugh, every hardship. This was over the line.

I yelled with such force I was sure my teeth rattled. "Shut up! Shut up! You don't know anything! You think I'm the one with a weak, half-assed theory about Thamus, but you! I'd say the same about yours! I have an actual story, even took the time to bring back proof when all you have is a baseless, rude, cruel theory! I won't deny that he's odd, but losing everything the way he did tends to mess you up! He cares, he's kind, and he's never let me down, always trusting me as much as I trust him. Unlike you. The only thing that matters to you anymore is Thamus. Not me, not Papa, not the life we built together. It doesn't even matter that I wanted the best for you, that I risked my life for you, all you care about are the consequences to you and him! You're nothing but selfish!"

I spat the last sentence with as much malice as I could muster. I wanted them to sting; for her to hurt as much as I did. It appeared to be successful, as she finally broke down, sobbing. I'd wanted to do the same when I knew she'd never believe me until she'd mentioned Lander. Now, the only thing burning inside my belly was rage, a fire that had grown out of control, whipping around to consume everything in its path. A small flicker of satisfaction about her reaction flashed through the anger, and I was immediately disgusted with myself for it. I had to leave, to get out before things got worse. After all, Mama was pregnant, and I didn't want any actual harm to come to her and the baby should I stress her any greater.

I snatched up the conch shell, shoving it back in my pocket.

"I won't be back," I mumbled, stomping across the kitchen.

Her sobs echoed across the house in a haunting rhythm, as she slumped against the countertop, face in her knees, sending an eerie shiver down my spine. One part of me wanted to apologize, to comfort her and say that it was all a lie, that she was right. The other part, the one currently taking control, demanded I storm out, and give no other thought about the hinges on the door as I slammed them. The latter part was the unfortunate winner, and the entire house vibrated as the door collided with the frame, hinges squealing in violent protest at the abuse.

10

When I woke up, my entire body was stiff and aching, from both stress and the hard surface on which I'd slept. A cobblestone alleyway wasn't the most welcoming bed, but exhausted as I was, the uneven ground was more than tempting. We'd never raised our voices at each other that way before, and I supposed I was in a state of shock. I didn't even consider going to Lander's house, angry and heated to the point I couldn't bear the thought of being near someone else, lest I lash out and cause more hurt.

Now, under the carefree and cheery light of an early morning sun, the only thing left of the raging fire I'd stoked the night before was ash. The heat of the anger left me raw and burnt, an aching soreness in my belly that wouldn't stop throbbing. Or maybe it was hunger, I wasn't sure. No matter the cause, it hurt, and not a small amount, either.

School would've been starting right about then, but I couldn't bring myself to care. Miss Poe would send me home anyway, disheveled and covered in dirt, matching the stray animals staggering the streets. Not that I'd learn anything in such a state. I rolled over on my back, staring up at the sliver of bright blue sky peeking through the buildings.

Puffy white clouds rolled along as usual, racing to wherever it was clouds went. As they moved, their shapes shifted, and I imagined I was watching a story unfold sans words. A tree blowing in the wind until it dissolved, leaves scattering the ground to form a wood nymph. The wood nymph collided with a ship, traveling aimlessly upon a raging sea, merging with the ship to grow it larger. I giggled hysterically to myself, wondering if I'd truly lost my mind, the nonsensical clouds providing a sort of delirious entertainment to my over-whelmed thoughts. It reminded me of the theater that Mama had taken me to as a small child, where actors in unusual costumes performed humorous dances while in precarious situations.

Eventually, the sun passed directly above, indicating the arrival of high noon, and I squinted angrily into the blinding light, upset at the disturbance of my show. Right when it had finally traveled low enough for my natural theater to resume, a large, familiar head popped over me, blocking it yet again.

"There you are," Lander declared, "I've been searching everywhere!"

I turned on my side away from his view, curling in on myself to hide my swollen eyes. "Go away," I mumbled.

"Hey now, roly-poly bug, quit that." Lander squatted next to me, prying my knees from my chest with his leather-bound hand.

I fought him, stiffening up.

"What do you want?" I groaned, wanting nothing more than to be left alone. I knew better than to expect him to leave, though, and braced myself for the onslaught of conversation.

"I want you to come with me, get cleaned up, and get a bite to eat. You look absolutely terrible. And then you're going to tell me what happened," he said firmly.

"Aren't you supposed to be at school?" I snapped. I didn't want to be bothered or helped. I didn't deserve it—not after what I'd done to my family.

"Hypocrite, much?" Lander retorted. "I told them you were still suffering from 'afflictions of the bowel' when you never showed up. And then had to embarrass myself, pretending I wasn't fully recovered either to come find you. Wasn't my proudest moment." He sucked on his teeth.

A brief flash of curiosity struck me, wondering what exactly he did, but it slipped away as fast as it bubbled up.

"You're not going to let my public embarrassment be for nothing, are you Sadie? Up you go," he continued, taking my hand.

I didn't fight him this time, and reluctantly stood, more than unsteady from lack of food and lying in a cold, hard street. Everything was heavy, as if I were underwater, and I dragged uncharacteristically behind Lander. He eventually tired of having to wait every few feet and sighed, popping the hood of his jacket up over his head. I frowned at him quizzically, confused as to what he was doing.

"Hop on," he instructed, motioning for me to get on his back.

"I can walk," I insisted, plodding past him defiantly.

"You're taking too long. I'm supposed to be at school right now, and you're supposed to be sick. We can't be dawdling. What if Mom sees us?"

I scowled at his utterly ridiculous appearance. Not to mention it was a relatively muggy day.

"What's the hood for?"

"How else am I supposed to hide my identity? I'll be much more noticeable carrying a deranged ruffian on my back. Hurry up," he urged, making a show of searching around for witnesses.

I rolled my eyes but did as I was told, climbing up on his sturdy back. I nestled my cheek into the back of his hood, clinging to the thick material of his jacket as he carried me through the city. It wasn't effortless, I could tell that much, but he brushed me off every time I insisted I was perfectly capable of walking. Despite my protests, I was grateful for his help, though I'd never admit it.

Lander's forehead was drenched with sweat from the physical strain when we finally arrived at his house. I knew better than to suggest he take off his jacket, having been down that road before, and I went straight inside to take a warm shower. Scrubbing off the crusted tears and collection of dirt in my hair made me feel somewhat better, and I soon joined Lander in the kitchen.

He prepared us each a bowl of vegetable soup, piping hot, and sat across from me. No sooner had he sat down, everything that happened poured out in a jumbled mess of pathetic blubbering. I tried to eat while talking, so that his work on the food wouldn't be wasted, but I only managed to eat about half, crying uncontrollably into the soup as I finished the story.

Lander looked at me, then at the food, then back at me, twirling his spoon in his fingers.

"I have salt, you know. Using tears is unnecessary," he remarked, motioning toward my soup, completely off subject as usual.

I laughed and laughed until I couldn't breathe, then laughed some more. Lander sat and watched, still playing with his spoon, a smile twitching at the corner of his lips as I got it all out. When the giggles turned into hiccups, I found myself wiping away tears of laughter instead of sadness.

"Feel any better?" he asked.

I nodded, less raw and aching on the inside now that I'd shared both a good cry and a good laugh with him. He set the spoon down on the table, his bowl already empty before I'd taken my first bite.

"I'll talk to Mom. You can stay here until you're ready to go back."

Lander gathered up the bowls and utensils, placing them in the sink.

"Thanks," I mumbled, glad for the escape. Lander and Mrs. Robyn were always here when I needed them, and for that, I forever vowed to one day pay them back for their kindness. There was one other problem, though, and it hit me with leaden dread. "Wait. I don't have my violin. I left in such a hurry I didn't stop to grab it."

"We'll swing by to get it," he assured me, leaning on the edge of the table.

"Preferably when no one's home," I added, not wanting to see Mama or Thamus in any capacity at that moment. Especially not Thamus.

"How about tomorrow, after you get some proper rest?" Lander suggested, scrutinizing the bags under my eyes.

I gladly agreed, the matter settled.

We spent the evening doing chores and getting into whatever games we could think of in the garden. Lander got an earful from his mom for skipping school again, but she welcomed me warmly, assuring that things would straighten out before long. My heart was still heavy, but the weight had lightened some with the hopes that Mama and I would mend things.

I figured she'd never accept what I'd learned about Thamus, especially with his baby on the way. Her abrupt denial and blind trust in him were alarming but not entirely unexpected. I'd wrongly assumed that as her child she'd believe me first. Yet, despite being the best of friends, Lander had chosen to show me the tunnel before telling the entire story. He was under the impression that without proof, I wouldn't have believed him. Had he told me first, would I have thought he was spinning a tale, or would I have blindly believed him the way I expected Mama to?

That was part of the issue, though. I didn't expect her to believe blindly, hence the reason for the shell. But it wasn't enough. The only way to make her see would be to make her *see*. Bringing her there in person was likely impossible, particularly with the baby. She wouldn't physically be able to, especially being pregnant, and as afraid as she was of the conch, being near the gates was out of the question.

I spent hours mulling it over, tossing and turning through the night, as I replayed the argument in my head over and over. I thought of all the ways it could've gone if I'd tried something different, or if it had been any night other than the one where she announced her pregnancy. But none of them ended the way I wanted them to. Not after what had happened.

The next day, Mrs. Robyn made sure Lander and I went to school. Class went on as usual, but Lander's hasty exit from the day before made him the subject of a few rude and embarrassing jokes. He took it like a champ, laughing along with each jab and letting them roll off his shoulders.

During lunch, I watched the boys continue their teasing from a shadowy corner by the fence. Lander peered over with a cheesy grin and a thumbs up here and there to make sure I was still okay. Inala continued avoiding me, which hurt, but the issue with Mama was at the forefront of my mind. Worrying about both was much too taxing, so I took solace in the fact that quiet Inala had found another friend to talk to. *Once Mama and I get things sorted out, I'll work on figuring out my friendship with Inala,* I decided, the thought easing my sadness by a hair.

The day came to a rapid end. I slept much easier that night, the burning sting in my core having reduced to a dull ache. I finally had enough of an appetite to eat a full meal, one that wasn't seasoned by tears, and the sleepy warmth of a full stomach also aided in lulling me to nothingness. Being around the lighthearted banter of Lander and Mrs. Robyn always set things right, and by morning's arrival, my mind was no longer restless. I was ready.

Lander and I crafted our plan to get things moving. We'd attend school in the morning, tell Miss Poe that we had to run to market on lunch, swipe the violin, and head back. No one would notice, no one would be the wiser.

When lunchtime came, we approached our instructor.

"Miss Poe," he said, pulling her attention from the papers on her desk.

She set down her pencil, squinting at Lander over her glasses. "What is it, Lander? Are you feeling better?"

"Yes, ma'am, thank you. I wanted to ask, would it be okay if Sadie and I stopped by the market? We're nearly out of food, and since Mom is working late, she asked us to grab a few groceries on lunch."

He wasn't outright lying, but I raised an eyebrow at how smoothly he wove deception into truth. Mrs. Robyn did task Lander with acquiring something for dinner. The only difference was, she wanted us to get it after school.

"You two have missed more school than any of the other students as of late," Miss Poe stated, clearly doubting Lander's story despite his convincing tone. "Can't you go on your way home?"

I shuffled my feet, trying to appear as hungry as possible. Because I was. Sure, we each had a hefty slice of bread, but I was as sick of eating bread as I was potatoes.

"That would've been the original plan, you see, but we hadn't enough at home to bring for lunch, either," Lander replied.

That one was a lie. That is, if a slice of bread could be considered a real lunch.

Miss Poe stared at our pitiful, hungry faces, Lander jutting his bottom lip out in a subtle pout. Our claim to starvation was accentuated by our gaunt figures, more pronounced than usual due to grief and isolation. With a heavy sigh, our young teacher begrudgingly granted us permission to leave on the promise that we'd be returning as soon as possible. As we rushed out of the schoolyard, Inala's suspicious glare threw painful daggers at our backs. Guilt took my chest into an iron hold, but I couldn't let myself dwell on it. Not yet.

I raced down the street as fast as I could, ready to get this over with.

"Slow down, Sadie!" Lander panted from behind, slow as usual.

"We have to hurry," I insisted. "You heard Miss Poe! She was not happy. Pick up your feet and come on!" I waved him forward, as if the swing of my hand would somehow speed him up.

"Easy for you to say," he muttered, but he managed to pick up the pace.

Not long after, we approached my vacant house. Each window was sealed shut, not even one propped open to a minuscule crack. Mama typically left them open on fresh, warm days such as today, even when she wasn't home. I hesitated at the bottom of the step, eyes darting around anxiously. I couldn't shake the feeling that something was off.

"Should we check that no one's home first?" I asked, almost a whisper, stopping Lander when his boot heavily landed on the first step. "I want to make sure."

He paused, scanning over the front of the house.

"Good idea," he finally said, and took to checking around for any signs of life.

Since Lander was tall enough to reach the windows, he did the majority of the work. I peeked through the slats in the garden fence while he tiptoed around the house, sneakily peering into each window. After a few minutes of close observation, we came to the conclusion that the house was indeed vacant.

I pulled out the key to the front door, fumbling with the lock as my hands trembled. My shoulders went slack when the latch opened without incident, the door creaking open on its overused hinges. I was careful not to put any undue stress on them this time around, guilty for how I'd treated my trusty door during our last heated encounter. I would've apologized to it had Lander not been there. Not that it was alive to hear me.

The light scent of woodsmoke hung in the stuffy kitchen. Not a dish was in the sink, the counter spotless, and the silence was heavy, restlessness creeping into my bones. I eyed the cabinet Mama had slumped against during our last heated encounter. Her despair haunted me. Facing where it happened again deepened the urge to apologize. Lander noticed me eyeing the spot, resting a reassuring hand on my shoulder as he stood behind me.

"It'll all work out. We can come see her as soon as you're ready," he whispered, his words tickling my ear as he leaned over my shoulder. "You don't have to be alone, either."

"After what she said about you?" I wouldn't want to show my face around his home had Mrs. Robyn said such a thing about me.

"I don't care what she thinks about me. I don't care what the kids at school think about me, either. I only care what *you* think." He leaned in closer, his voice becoming low and alluring as he continued, "And with that, I'd like to ask, what is it you think about me, Sadie Cleamont? Do you agree with any of her statements? Am I ... wrong?"

A shudder racked my spine, triggered by his heated whisper or the question at hand, I wasn't sure. I turned my head to find his face inches from mine, earnestly searching my eyes for the answer.

"You're odd, I'll say that," I whispered, cheeks rapidly heating up being in such proximity to his soft lips. He was as close as he'd been that night by the sea. I focused hard on *not* focusing on them, on how soft they'd be against mine, managing to articulate the rest of my response, "But no, I don't think you're wrong."

He paused, parting his mouth slightly with a sharp inhale, as if he were about to say something. But he didn't. Instead, his lips curled into a sad smile, and he pulled his head away, standing up straight. I found myself strangely disappointed that he hadn't gotten any closer, kicking myself internally for even entertaining the thought.

"Right. That's settled then!" he exclaimed, giving the front of his thighs a heavy pat. "We've got work to do. One violin, coming up!"

Flustered, all I could sputter in reply was a "Right."

His abrupt shift in emotion left me reeling. What was all that about? What else had he wanted to say? And why did my response make him sad? I didn't dare ask him now, our current situation being minor house robbery, and resolved to question him extensively later.

I took the lead, propelling myself into my bedroom with Lander close behind. He paused in the doorway, waiting for me to find our bounty. Strangely enough, the violin wasn't in its usual place at the foot of my bed. Nor was it under. I stared, confused, bending down to check again when I heard a scuffing sound from behind. Figuring Lander had gotten himself into another typical clumsy situation, I didn't even spare him a glance, continuing my search.

"What are you doing now?" I asked, feeling around underneath my bed to no avail. Lander never could stay out of trouble, and quite frankly, it got on my nerves. I sneezed, having disturbed a fine layer of dust from my typical hiding spot, and got to my knees to get a better view. High noon had the room cast in shadows, since the sun couldn't shine directly in the windows. Not in the mood to light a candle, I squinted into the darkness under the bed, unable to see even a hint of my violin case. With a sigh, I got back to my feet, wiping the dust on my skirts as I turned back to my friend.

"That's strange, it's not here. I wonder if—"

I froze.

Thamus stood in the doorway, his large, muscular frame holding Lander in a chokehold. Lander's feet struggled to keep contact with the floor, his face reddening as he feebly attempted to push his chin over Thamus's arm for air. He could only draw in shallow gasps. I staggered backward, nearly losing my footing when I slammed into my bedframe. I immediately homed in on Thamus's strange attire—a long-sleeved leather shirt with a hood, and matching gloves. Unusual for somebody simply visiting their significant other's home. He'd planned this. He'd been waiting to attack us.

"Lander!" I screamed.

I frantically grasped at my thoughts, trying to find a way to free him, but my mind came up empty, blank from panic. "Let go of him!" I fiercely demanded, no other thought close enough to grasp.

Lander's eyes desperately searched for mine as he repeatedly mouthed the word *Run!* Even if I'd wanted to, the only way out was the window. I wouldn't have been fast enough. Thamus could've reached out to grab me, even while holding Lander, should I attempt to shatter the glass and flee.

Thamus laughed darkly, creating a thrill of unease in my core. "It took me long enough, but now I've finally got you where I want you, Lander Holland."

Lander wheezed, wincing as he managed to hurl an insult at Thamus. "Raging lunatic," was his excellent choice of words here.

"What do you think you're doing?" I hollered, snatching the candlestick from my nightstand, the only solid object I could find.

Thamus chuckled at my pathetic attempt to defend us and lessened his grip on Lander since he nearly lost consciousness. Lander gasped, finally getting a good amount of air, but Thamus still didn't let him go. I chucked the candlestick at Thamus's arms as hard as I could, but it simply bounced off, leading him to laugh again.

"I'm doing what I should've weeks ago, when I found out there were *children* sneaking past me at the gates," Thamus crinkled his nose, as if the mention of children tasted foul on his tongue. "I should've taken the girl out the instant I found her."

I took in a sharp breath, Thamus smiling in satisfaction at my reaction.

"But I found something . . . unexpected," Thamus drawled, smirking down at his captive.

Lander's eyes widened, and he struggled again, frantic this time.

"Don't you dare," Lander spat.

"Shut the hell up!" Thamus tightened his hold again, eliciting a gasp from my friend, silencing him. Lander feebly clawed at Thamus's arms.

"Not too far from where I found her, there was a jacket lying on the ground, similar to the one you're wearing, Holland. I'm inclined to believe it was the same exact one."

"Leave him alone! He didn't do anything wrong! You did when you killed Cyntha!" I shouted, realizing how useless I was as I tried to pick up my nightstand for a weapon. It was far too heavy, the wood solid and thick, and I was only able to scoot it over a few inches. Thamus stared down at Lander's red face, veins bulging in my friend's neck and forehead.

"Is it heavy, having to carry that much weight, Lander?" Thamus taunted him.

This odd question triggered something animalistic in Lander, and I watched in both awe and utter terror as Lander took action. He gripped Thamus's arm, holding himself up as he lifted both legs off the ground, swinging them backward as hard as he could into his attacker's groin. This was an entirely effective strategy, as Thamus lost his grip on Lander immediately. He doubled over, hands protecting the injured area with a painful howl while Lander slid out of his grasp, rolling across the floor in front of me. He staggered to his feet, holding out his arms protectively, coughing as he cleared his throat.

"That was genius," I said, thoroughly impressed by his quick thinking.

He managed a feeble smirk before refocusing on the reemerging situation in the doorway. Thamus was getting ahold of himself again, his wince easing as his labored gasps dissipated.

"See if you can make any more kids after that," Lander chuckled.

He realized too late that this was the wrong comment. Thamus swung his fist so rapidly I almost didn't see it. He made contact with Lander's nose hard and fast, a sickening crack reverberating in the room. A spray of warm blood splattered me on the face and Lander staggered back with a groan, almost knocking us both flat onto the bed. I grabbed him under his arms, trying to hold him upright as his legs buckled but failed spectacularly under his solid weight, sending us both crashing to the floor.

"Fucking bastard," Thamus grumbled, shaking his hand from the sting of impact. He fell to his knees, eyes closed, panting hard as he leaned against the doorframe.

"Are you okay?" I asked frantically, the blood cooling quickly atop my skin.

We'd both landed on our bottoms, propped upright by the bedframe, Lander leaning heavily into my chest. Dazed, his head lulled to the side, eyes squeezed shut in a tight grimace. I watched in horror as a sea of red ran freely out of his nostrils, bubbling with each shuddering breath. The impact split the skin atop the bridge of his nose in a deep cut. Purple bruising had already formed underneath his eyes, indicating a fractured nose.

"Damn, that hurt," he sputtered, finally getting his bearings.

He leaned forward and spat, choking on the blood that had entered his throat. I wanted to grab Lander and run, but Thamus's crumpled figure was still blocking the doorway, and climbing over him wasn't exactly a feasible way out.

"Here, let me help," I said to Lander, the only thing I could manage to do in this moment while utterly trapped. I yanked a pillowcase off the bed to stanch the flow of blood, but Lander immediately jerked his face away from my reach.

"Sadie, stop," he protested weakly. "You can't."

"I can if I want to!" I asserted, more than offended at his refusal of my help, stretching out my arm to try again.

Lander had certainly helped me often enough. Surely, he could allow me to do at least this. He scooted away. Blood pooled on the floor at an alarming rate as he shook his head in adamant refusal, refusing to face me. I jumped at the sudden sound of Thamus's voice.

"I wouldn't do that if I were you," he bellowed, giving us both a spectacular side eye, as he noticed what was going on.

I rolled my eyes in disgust, going to ignore Thamus and force my patient to comply when Lander's next words made me freeze.

"He's right," he groaned, coughing up another mouthful of blood onto the floorboards. "Damn it all to hell, but he's right."

I blinked. "Wh-what? What do you mean he's right?"

Thamus laughed maniacally, still braced against the doorframe. Lander refused to turn around, refused to reply, leaning further away from my touch still.

"I said, what do you mean he's right?" I repeated, demanding an answer.

"If any of my blood touches your skin, you're toast," Lander cautioned, defeated. My hand shot to my face where the damp spray was already beginning to dry.

"I-I don't . . . I don't get it," I stammered, not wanting to believe the obvious answer, which was dawning on me; something that had been staring me in the face all this time.

"Oh, how delightfully humorous," Thamus crowed, finally straightening up to stare us both down. "Sadie, don't you see? Lander's a survived."

11

*L*ander's a survived.

I suddenly felt sick, and rolled backward from the crouching position I'd assumed, scooting against the wall. Anything to gain distance from him. The words echoed in my head nonstop, as everything that had ever happened between Lander and me clicked into place with a dizzying impact. Mama had been right all along. There really was something wrong with Lander. There was a reason why he never took off his heavy jacket, which I now understood was heavy enough to keep him on the ground. There was a reason he avoided any and all touch unless it was through thick leather gloves—why he pushed me away any time I got close. It was the reason he had no fear of the outside, where the city claimed the virus ran rampant. Why fear a virus you've already gotten? And Cyntha . . . No. There was no way.

"No," I quavered. "It can't be." I didn't know if I wanted to cry, scream, or give him a second punch to the nose. "You lied to me. About everything." No wonder he was such an expert at weaving deception into truth. He spent every waking moment practicing with me.

Lander sat hunched over the floor, holding himself up shakily on his hands. He shook his head, drops of blood splattering in a zigzag pattern below him.

"Not everything. Only what was necessary," he said, ashamed.

"It was you the entire time. *You* were the contaminant. *You* killed Cyntha!" I shrilled.

This triggered him to finally whirl around to face me. "It wasn't my fault! Cyntha chose it! She chose to kiss me that night, knowing I was sick!" he yelled, ready to squabble. But the moment his eyes settled on my blood-streaked features, his anger quickly switched to alarm. "Sadie. No. Please tell me that's not mine."

"Makes my job much easier here," Thamus declared, finally standing up with some difficulty, mostly recovered from the blow to his family jewels. "I'll tell the city, and the contamination will be contained and away from my coming child."

Lander gritted his teeth at Thamus, a pained groan escaping him from the movement.

"You tell them about us, I'll tell them everything about you. How you've been letting us run around, contaminating everyone, sneaking out without notice. What do you think the punishment will be for treason?"

I cringed at his inclusion of the word "*Us.*" I'd come in contact with his blood. I was exposed to the virus I'd spent my entire life hiding from, that apparently had been right next to me for five years, lying in wait inside my best friend. He'd known the risk to my life, yet let me come close to him, betraying my trust. And how close we'd been; he'd almost kissed me on the beach! Even knowing it had killed Cyntha, he still leaned in. I'd always thought Lander was my biggest protector. But I'd had it all wrong. He was my biggest threat. The thought sent a terrible shiver through me, and I hugged my chest, unsuccessfully fighting the involuntary trembling of shock.

"Not if I kill you first," Thamus threatened, pulling out a long, glinting knife from inside his sleeve.

Lander guffawed loudly at the weapon, and Thamus was clearly taken aback at his victim's reaction.

"How do you think you're going to kill both of us with that and not get infected yourself? Someone didn't think this through." Lander waggled a finger at Thamus as if he were a naughty child.

Thamus frowned. "You think it'll soak through this, smart ass?" he boomed, flexing his leather-bound arms. Lander's unexpected playful attitude clearly rubbed him the wrong way.

"All it'll take is one of these in your face"—Lander spat a large wad of bright red blood toward Thamus's feet in demonstration—"and it's game over."

Thamus stepped back to avoid the splatter, warily considering Lander's counterthreat.

"How are you going to hide our bodies? Drag them through the middle of the city? Even at night, that's risky. Have you thought of what you'll tell Sadie's mom when she comes home to find her daughter dead by your hands?"

Thamus faltered at the mention of Mama, his pained expression mirroring mine. Lander deviously grinned, knowing he had Thamus right where he wanted him. Thamus huffed, fidgeting with the knife. He glanced at his weapon, and then at the two blood-soaked children in front of him before sliding it back into its concealed sheath.

He spoke quietly but sternly. "Let's make a deal. I'll tell Lauren you are in quarantine until we find out if Sadie falls ill. If all is well, I'll let you return home, as long as what happened here today doesn't ever come out to your mother. And if you cut all ties with Holland and your ridiculous escapades out of the city."

I couldn't breathe. "And if I get the fever?"

"Keep your end of the bargain and you'll never hear from me again, as long as you can contain yourself. If I hear of a single citizen falling ill, it's over."

I clenched my jaw, biting back tears. *You might never see her again.* "Why? Why are you doing this?" my lower lip trembled.

Thamus stared at me with wide eyes. "Have you forgotten how I lost my family? When I found that girl, and evidence that there was a survived, here, within the one place we should've been safe, I was livid! There hasn't been a true case within the gates since they were closed. Even with receiving shipments from Ancthia's annexes right outside the gates." He scratched his beard, blinking hard. "I couldn't report her without jeopardizing my job, so I took matters into my own hands. I knew she lied about who was with her, even before I captured the boy she'd sold out. That's why I offered her a job, to throw her off, to keep her from suspecting I was following her. It didn't take long before she led me, unknowing, to Holland. I saw them that night, before she told me the truth; I saw their kiss. I planned to kill them immediately for their recklessness, but I overheard something I didn't expect. They mentioned you, Sadie."

I scowled over at my friend, wondering what exactly they'd mentioned me for. He wouldn't look at me, purposefully turning away so I couldn't read him.

"I told her she could have a second chance, to bring him into custody to give me more time to assess the exact risk I was facing. That's where I found out his proximity to my own home, to my new life, to my new child. I knew I'd have to eliminate them both—it was simply a matter of how and when. Cyntha was easy enough. It took longer than expected for her to go down, but I knew with enough certainty she would." Thamus sneered at the memory. "Holland here would've been simple on his own, but he never left your side. Which was another complication. How could I get you two apart? And how could I be sure you weren't exposed at any given time, even if I eliminated him? How could I be sure the city wouldn't come for all of us if I notified them of his presence? Come for me for not realizing I'd been outwitted by two children?"

Lander gagged on another mouthful of blood. My hand twitched, instinctually wanting to assist as the heavy bleeding continued, but I hesitated.

"When you brought home the conch, that was the last straw. I couldn't let this go on any longer. I had to get rid of you both. Putting everyone at risk, putting my career at risk? What were you thinking, Sadie? We could've been happy! But you had to go and be reckless!" He stared up at the ceiling, eyes watery. "I don't want to have to kill my family again!"

"You-you killed them?"

Pure horror churned in my gut. I thought I'd been shocked before, learning what Lander was. But this? This man, who had been in my house, gotten as close to my mother as my father, had *murdered* his entire family? Sure, the effect of surviving the fever was terrifying. And living as a survived meant an eternal risk of spreading contagion while confined to a life of weights. But to outright kill the people you loved and cherished the most? Despicable was an understatement.

"Yes! I admit it! I killed them to spare them their fate! They all came down with the fever together. What else could I have done? I smothered them in their sleep and then burned the house to pieces." Thamus wept openly, pacing in the doorway. "I couldn't bear to hear their screams as they disappeared into the sky to suffer. I wouldn't do it to them. I couldn't."

His sobs were harsh, and I instinctively wanted to feel empathy toward him. But murdering the people he was supposed to love was inexcusable.

"I'll do it again if I must. Don't make me, Sadie," Thamus pleaded. "I love her, with all my heart. All I want is to keep her and the child safe."

A lump formed in my throat. His declaration of love was sincere; that much was obvious. But he'd kill her without hesitation. He'd done it before and could do it again. And now, with Lander's blood on my face, I was the catalyst of a repeat situation.

I had no other choice. My voice cracked as I parted my lips to speak. "If I accept your deal, do you truly promise never to hurt her? To leave me alone if I get sick?"

The pain on Lander's face intensified. From my statement or the broken nose, I wasn't sure. Thamus nodded.

"I'll agree to these terms," I gritted out, fully resolved to make good on it should he go back on his word. "But if you ever, and I mean *ever*, do anything to harm her or Lander, I'll be the one to kill you. I'll ruin your life, your family, your career. That is a promise." I stared him down, letting the meaning of my threat land. "There is one other thing," I added as the tension in Thamus's shoulders dissolved. "If I do get sick, before I disappear forever, will you let me say goodbye to Mama, from a distance, one last time?"

Thamus hesitated, rolling his tongue around his teeth as he considered my plea.

"Please, Thamus. You never got the chance! Don't deny me that."

The reality of the situation sunk in—the possibility that I might never see my mama again. I'd never feel her gentle touch, her warm kisses, or her love. We'd never share any laughs, or hardships, or silly stories. We were a team. She was all I had left. And the last thing I'd said to her was to defend the person who'd upended my entire life. Lander.

"We'll see what happens first," Thamus finally replied, his tone solemn.

I nodded once, sniffling as I tried to hold it together.

"I take it we can go?" Lander grumbled rudely. In typical Lander fashion, he couldn't stop himself from muttering a sarcastic, horribly timed joke. "We're awfully late for class now, thanks to you."

Thamus stepped away from the doorway, indicating that we could pass. "Go straight to your home, no detours," he ordered. "No one is to know about this. Is that clear?"

"Clear," I whispered.

I stood trembling, wondering if I were wading through a dream—no—a nightmare. I faintly heard Lander asking for my violin, the entire reason for the escapade to begin with, but didn't care to even turn around. I didn't want my violin. I wanted to go to school, despite my deep hatred of the place. I wanted to go back to when Lander was simply my quirky best friend, and not a risk to humanity. I wanted things to be normal, to be okay, to see Mama. I needed it. I needed her.

People stared, sharing charged whispers as Lander and I treaded silently to his house. I paid them no mind, lacking the will to stare rudely back, carrying the blood on my face with shame. An eternity passed before we arrived at the small wooden house, a place I'd once called my second home. I now stared at it as if it were my own personal hell, where I'd be spending yet another quarantine. One I might never leave.

Lander held open the front door, and I slid past him, keeping as much space between us as physically possible. He slammed it shut, ripped off his leather gloves, and headed over to the kitchen sink. I was stunned, not knowing what to think or do, unsure of who Lander Holland even was anymore. It still looked like him. It still sounded like him. Yet it was as if a stranger stood in the room with me. I couldn't make my tongue work. The chaotic tremor of unspoken words was stuck deep in my throat as I stood, frozen in the kitchen, staring him down.

He leaned over the sink, splashing the water onto his face, crimson rivulets trickling off. His hair grew damp as he scrubbed, dangling heavily in front of his eyes. I knew he was aware of my scrutinizing line of sight, but he chose not to speak first, giving me the opportunity to break the silence when I was ready. I watched, cringing as Lander took in a sharp breath, sturdily gripping the bridge of his nose. He produced an agonizing, guttural cry as he set the bone in one swift, practiced movement.

"Fucking hell!" he yelled, panting over the sink as a fresh stream of blood poured into the basin.

The door to Mrs. Robyn's room flung open forcefully as the woman came storming into the kitchen.

"What have I told you about using that kind of language?" she hollered, hands already on her hips. Her hair was disheveled, face hot and red with anger as she homed in on her son's back. "And why are you not at school?"

"Where do you think I learned it from? It wasn't from my classmates!" Lander retorted, splashing his face again as the bleeding continued.

"Certainly not, since you're never there!"

Mrs. Robyn jumped, having noticed my silent, stunned presence. She put a hand to her chest at the sight of my bloodied face. "Oh! Sadie! I didn't see you there, dear. You're so quiet! What happened? Are you hurt?" She reached over to pull me in closer, as she always did.

"Stop! You can't touch her, Mom!" Lander warned, turning his face in our direction.

He grabbed a tea towel from the edge of the sink, holding it gingerly under his nose. The stream of blood reduced to a weak drip. Mrs. Robyn yanked her hand back, gasping as she saw the mess Thamus had made of him. The mottled blue and purple bruising had spread out over the tops of his cheekbones. The deep split in the skin atop the bridge of his nose had thankfully stopped bleeding, and the bone was straight and tidy now that he'd set it. But it was red and swollen, having grown nearly three sizes, and the rest of his face had taken on a pale and clammy pallor. He braced himself against the kitchen counter.

"It's not her blood," he said gravely.

Mrs. Robyn's jaw jutted out as her eyes went from Lander's nose back to me, alarmed.

"Lander!" she cried. "I swear on my life, if that's your blood I'll give you something way worse to worry about than a broken nose!"

"What, do you think I did it on purpose?" he shrieked, throwing his hands up in exasperation.

Mrs. Robyn let out a string of curses that proved Lander did not, in fact, get his foul language from his classmates. The pair started bickering intensely, something I wasn't unaccustomed to, but the chaos, the terror, the sudden thought that Mrs. Robyn had also been lying, became too much. I was completely and terribly overwhelmed.

The words stuck in my throat suddenly broke free as I screamed at them both. "Stop it! Shut up! Shut up!" I glared at them both, panting as I finally broke the surface of the despair that had been drowning me.

The pair immediately stopped, sheepishly meeting my glare.

"I want to know the truth," I demanded. "Who are you, really?"

Lander's eyebrows knitted together, visibly distressed by my question. "I'm still me, Sadie. The same Lander you've always known."

I shook my head. "But you're not. The Lander I knew didn't lie to me," I accused.

Mrs. Robyn shuffled her feet, uncomfortable. "Sadie. You have to understand. There was no other way. We couldn't exactly go shouting it out to everyone in the streets. You've seen how people react."

Lander pointed to his smashed nose. "Exhibit A."

"First of all, you kicked Thamus in the balls, and then taunted him," I said flatly.

"After he tried to strangle me!" he protested shrilly.

I stomped my foot. "What I'm trying to say is they react that way with good reason! Cyntha and Mrs. Fenter are *dead*, Lander. Do you know what that means? They're never coming back! This isn't some . . . some game where you can easily start over when you make a mistake. The consequences are dire! These are people's lives. This is *my* life! I might be about to die! And if not? I'll spend the rest of my life suffering alone, hiding away from the entire world. And I haven't even made things right with my mama." I choked on the last words, holding back tears.

Lander's guilt-ridden, distraught face mirrored that of Mrs. Robyn's.

"I never intended for any of this to happen," he insisted. "I only wanted to keep you safe."

I laughed at the irony of it all. "What was your intention then? Keeping me safe meant lying about Cyntha? Putting me at risk of contact every day of my life? I mean, holy shit, Lander, you almost kissed me on the beach!" I shrieked.

"But I didn't!" Lander retorted.

"You almost did!"

"Yet I did not!" he yelled back. "Did I want to kiss you? Yes! I've wanted to kiss you every single minute of every single day since the moment I first heard your beautiful music! I've been starved of genuine human touch since I was *eight years old*. I can't hug my own mother, can't touch anyone unless it's through thick leather gloves! I can't get close to others without taking extreme precautions, monitoring every single movement the both of us make. Do you know what it's like to feel so utterly trapped by your own body?"

If the situation had been different, his confession might've made me blush spectacularly. I'd probably admit that the feeling was mutual, that I'd wanted the same since I saw him stick out his dirty, starving face from behind the alleyway. But not today. Not after what I'd learned.

"I guess I'm about to find out, aren't I?" I hissed. "I finally get it. Why you were so upset about Cyntha. It wasn't because you loved her. It was guilt. Guilt that you caused her death."

Lander grimaced. "She was going to die anyway, and she knew it. Thamus confirmed that much."

He couldn't be serious! "Heavens, Lander, that doesn't make it okay! That doesn't make any of this okay! Cyntha didn't choose this!" I massaged my temples in disbelief.

"That's where you're wrong," he explained cooly. "Like I told you earlier, *she* kissed *me*, knowing what I was. She chose to take the risk."

"You could tell Cyntha, whom you barely knew, but not your lifelong best friend, huh? I deeply appreciate being given the option to choose this, too," I spat, bitter and sarcastic.

"That's not how it happened, Sadie. I didn't tell her."

"Then why don't you go ahead and tell me? I've got nothing but time." I yanked out one of the chairs from the table and sat down, arms crossed against my chest.

Lander pursed his lips, glancing at me warily before slowly joining me. Mrs. Robyn sat as well, taking care to remain a safe distance from the both of us.

"Where do you want me to start?" Lander sighed, slouching in his seat.

"The very beginning," I growled.

He and his mom grimaced, locking eyes as they dredged up whatever horrors lurked in their past. Lander rested one hand on the table, fidgeting with his thumb and forefinger.

"The very beginning, huh? I guess we're starting with my sisters, then."

I nodded, motioning for him to continue.

"It happened to Dad first," he said. "Mom was away that week, assisting one of her close friends with childbirth. When he came through the door, eyes fever-bright, we had no clue what beast had entered our home. After all, it hadn't been seen for many years. Believing it was simply a run-of-the-mill flu, my sisters and I cared for him the way we normally would."

Lander rubbed his chin with a faraway look in his eyes as he gathered his next words.

"As the fever lifted, so did he. He couldn't be held down without a significant amount of weight on his chest. We were terrified at first, having no idea what was happening until my eldest sister recognized it for what it was. The townspeople got wind of his affliction and tore through our house, carrying him away and locking my sisters and me in our home to keep it from spreading. By that point, it was already too late, as we all came down with it a few days later.

"Dad was gone so, being the newly appointed man of the house, I took on the responsibility of caring for my ailing sisters. I cooled their fevers and dribbled water and honey down their throats around the clock, even though I was burning up just as bad. When the weightlessness started, I crafted heavy blankets to keep them from getting stuck on the ceilings."

"You did all that while sick?" I asked, incredulous. Though, as much as I currently hated to admit it, I wasn't surprised. Lander would stop at nothing to keep those he loved safe. I mean, even while being strangled by Thamus, all he'd cared about was telling me to run. And putting himself between us the instant he'd escaped, even though he was no match for a man that size.

"What, do you think I'd lie around and let them die?" he snapped. "Of course I did! And I did a damn fine job of pulling them all through it." Lander sighed. His voice quavered. "Except for Lovena."

Mrs. Robyn wept quietly at the mention of her late daughter's name.

"Lovena's fever didn't burn; it seared. It tore through her little body. I tried everything I could think of to bring it down: using every last bit of ice from the icebox, soaking her in the bath, fanning her until my arms gave out. I even tried absorbing it myself, the way I did when she was a baby, by placing her bare on my chest. But my own skin was too fiery for it to do any good. When I came to on the floor, having fallen unconscious from exhaustion, I . . . I couldn't wake her up. The fever had burned too hot. She was gone."

A thick, painful lump formed in my throat. The only sound in the heavy room was Mrs. Robyn's heart-wrenching sobs, her shoulders shaking, face in her hands. Lander stayed stoic, though his throat bobbed with emotion as he watched his mom.

After a pause to regain his composure, he soldiered on. "Ada expanded upon my idea of a weighted blanket, crafting a jacket heavy enough to keep us on the ground. We made a plan to survive, to escape and hide until Mom came back, and we figured out what to do. I feared she had encountered the virus on her way home, as she was taking longer than expected."

"I made it home, delayed because of a difficult birth. And by then it was too late," whispered Mrs. Robyn.

"The townspeople came back," Lander added bitterly. "Said we brought the virus to the town. By now, many others were coming down with it. If they'd left my father alone, they might not have exposed as many. They couldn't keep from meddling, though. I fought them off for as long as I could, but one by one my sisters were dragged out, their hand-sewn coats from Ada ripped apart. And one by one, they were thrown into the sky. Ada screamed at me to run, to go and keep Mom safe, as she gathered as many of our sisters as she could into her arms. She held them tight as they disappeared upward, screaming repeatedly to save Mom."

Lander glanced at me from the side of his swollen eye. "That kick I gave Thamus earlier? That's the same one I gave to the man trying to rip off my jacket. It's the move that saved my life, allowed me to run and find Mom, and escape. I vowed to honor Ada's dying wish. So here I am. That's how it started."

My stomach ached. I chewed on the inside of my lip, brokenhearted for the loss Lander and Mrs. Robyn had both suffered, at both the hands of the virus and their neighbors. The previous version of the story Lander had expressed to me long ago was heavily watered down compared to this truth he'd finally spoken. I never could've imagined how much he'd faced at such a young age. Despite this new and deep sorrow, I still nursed a significant amount of anger for their dishonesty.

"I'm sorry," I murmured, wrapping my arms around my abdomen. "Truly, I am. For everything you've been through."

"Me too," he said.

"Doesn't mean I'm not still angry," I added quietly.

He drummed his fingers on the tabletop as we all sat mute, his lips pursed. Mrs. Robyn dried her tears and stared blankly down at her lap.

Lander said, "Now you want to hear about Cyntha, I suppose?"

"Please."

"You already know most of what happened. The night Cyntha was captured, I was running late because it's damn exhausting to have to carry around excessive weight every second of your life." Lander smacked his jacket with a hard thud of annoyance. "I could see Thamus storming down the pathway ahead of me, much too fast for me to ever escape. So, I whipped this out."

Lander reached into one of the inner pockets and pulled out a thick, coiled rope.

"I tied it onto a nearby limb and ditched my jacket, floating up above the tree, out of sight."

I was mildly impressed at his quick thinking, but refused to acknowledge it, lest he think I was no longer upset.

"Cyntha saw the jacket, too, of course, and she feared for both of our lives. For hers, that she might become sick, and for mine, that I would be killed by the city. That's when she lied about the boy who went missing. Cyntha didn't return to me that night, terrified. We had a small spat over it the next day, after I struggled for hours to climb down that tree and get my coat. Almost ended up another star that night." Lander rubbed the back of his neck. "Thank goodness Thamus was too much of a chicken and dropped it right next to the tree after figuring out what it was. I explained to Cyntha that she would be fine as long as we didn't touch."

He glanced sadly at his mother, with whom he'd lived so close to for all this time, and yet so far away. Taking a shaky breath, he continued,

"We solved our minor disagreement and continued as usual, except for the guilt that was eating her alive regarding our classmate. As I've already explained to you, three times now, Cyntha chose to kiss me before going to speak with Thamus. I tried to stop her, to tell her it was a terrible idea, but she gave me three good reasons. The first was not wanting to die without experiencing her first kiss. The second was the need for ammunition, something she could use to prompt the city to kill her after admitting she'd lied about the boy's identity. She was hoping he was still alive, that telling the truth would get him out of there. Her plan was, once he was freed, to tell them she was either exposed or already sick; that way, they could never torture my identity out of her. You know Ancthia. They wouldn't stop until they got it. Not unless they had no other choice. Cyntha swore she'd never sell me out, accepting death over it."

Cyntha's bravery struck a chord in my heart, one of pride and shame. Pride in how true to herself she was, willing to follow her plan through all the way to death to protect my best friend. Shame for the terror that I was currently paralyzed by, standing in her shoes.

Lander continued on, interrupting my moment of self-pity. "Cyntha's third reason was how much she liked me. Everyone knew that. It wasn't exactly a secret. I have to admit, she flattered me an awful lot, but I didn't feel the same." He scratched the back of his head nervously, and I figured if his face wasn't bruised and bloodied, he'd be turning red by now. "That's why Thamus heard us talking about you, Sadie. She . . . um, knew I had my eye on someone else."

Even though he didn't exactly admit it outright, his roundabout confession left the room horrifically awkward. Mrs. Robyn became suddenly interested in a piece of nonexistent lint on her dress, and Lander and I turned our gaze from each other, focusing on how fancy the wooden walls were today. I wasn't sure if I'd ever blushed that hard in my life. The room might've been silent, but my mind was screaming at my rebelling heart for fluttering warmly despite what I was facing. Lander had *lied* to me about who he was since the day I met him. How could I like someone I never even knew in the first place? And yet, I hated that I couldn't shake the thought that I truly did know the real Lander behind the lies.

He finally cleared his throat and continued on, pulling me out of my frustrating thoughts.

"I still don't think it was the fever that killed her."

I stared at him, incredulous at his continued denial. "You saw her collapse, Lander. You heard what Thamus said. Mrs. Fenter is dead, too. There was no mistaking her touch: She kissed you."

"Yes, but the kiss was way past the amount of time it takes for infection," he explained. "We never made skin contact again after that, just in case. And you forget, I was right next to Mrs. Fenter checking her when she collapsed. There was no fever. I know it when I see it."

I mulled over these two small details, trying to make sense of the possibility.

"You saw how quick Thamus was to try killing us today! He was also keeping an eye on Cyntha, waiting for her to drop. What if he realized she wasn't going to and decided to take matters into his own hands?"

"Yes, but what about Mrs. Fenter?"

"He'd have to make it believable, wouldn't you agree?" Lander tilted his head.

"I suppose it's possible," I reluctantly agreed, grasping on to this shred of hope he'd offered. "If Cyntha didn't catch it, there's a chance I won't?"

"There's a chance," Lander said slowly. "A small one. I'm not sure exactly how it works, other than you need to make physical contact. All the rumors that are floating around—that you can't even talk to someone who's been infected without being at risk—are obviously bogus. You and Mom are testament to that." He motioned toward me and Mrs. Robyn. "I don't know if blood is different than skin. Though I've always assumed it was the same. We're about to find out, though, I suppose."

"I suppose we will. And, should we find out that it is not as effective, then you won't be hearing from me, ever again, Lander Holland," I announced, scooting the chair back with an angry jerk. I stood, staring him down as coldly as I could despite the horrible soreness his story had inflicted upon my heart. "That is a promise." I turned on my heel, heading to the bathroom to wash off the blood and the despair that had settled into my skin.

"Wait!" Lander called out.

I paused. But I didn't turn around.

"Sadie. I'm really sorry, okay? I'm sorry this happened, and about Thamus and your mom. I was only afraid of losing you, of seeing him hurt you the same way he did Cyntha. Most of all, I'm sorry I never gave you a choice. You don't have to forgive me now, or ever. I need you to know that I do regret it. Deeply."

The sincerity of his apology tore me to pieces. I yearned to accept it, to move on, to pretend nothing had happened, but the heaviness of what I'd learned today—of what I may face—outweighed everything else. I couldn't find it in myself to reply. After all, what did it matter? Should I avoid the virus, I wouldn't be allowed near him, ever again.

12

I wasn't sure exactly what Mrs. Robyn told our teacher, but she managed to snag all the classwork we needed for the next month. I refused to speak to Lander unless there was no other choice. Mrs. Robyn and I were on decent terms, but there was palpable tension between us, since she'd taken part in plenty of the deception.

I understood why they didn't tell me. I understood the lack of trust and the trials they went through. I agonized over everything for endless, silent hours, trying to find it within myself to let it go, but I couldn't. Not after what happened with Mama, with the looming possibility I may never see her again, our argument still unresolved. I worried about her and the baby, hoping the stress hadn't caused any problems.

Despite the tension between the three of us, Lander and Mrs. Robyn were clearly much more relaxed now that their secret was out. When I entered the kitchen the second morning, I screamed so loudly Mrs. Robyn jumped about three feet, her frying pan clattering to the floor. Lander was upside down, cross-legged on the ceiling, casually tearing into a piece of toast.

"Good morning, Sadie!" he chirped, speaking with his mouth full as usual.

I stared at him blankly, stunned to see another human *floating* on the ceiling, but also because I'd never seen Lander without his jacket before. He was wearing a fitted black linen tunic, tucked into his pants to keep it from turning inside-out. Without his typical bulky article of clothing, he appeared much smaller, though his arms and entire torso rippled with thick muscle from heaving around his weights. He was terribly pale from lack of sunlight, a stark contrast to his olive face, although his face wasn't sporting its typical skin tone. The heavy bruising had become significantly worse, darkening and spreading the way bruises tend to do before getting better. The deep, inch-long split running down the left side of the bridge of his nose had scabbed over. I could already tell it would leave a nasty scar, adding to the jarring sight of my upside-down friend. I raked my eyes over him, got my bearings, and said nothing, still angry. I gave him a huge berth of space, avoiding this inconvenient, inversely protruding obstacle on my way to the table, and silently accepted the food Mrs. Robyn had prepared.

"Still pissed, huh?" Lander commented with an exaggerated sigh. He changed his voice to a shrill, mocking tone, attempting to imitate my voice. "Yes, Lander, I'm so very angry! You're such a liar!"

I chomped down onto my lip, fuming as I listened to his ridiculous mocking. I wanted to hurl a horrendous insult, but didn't exactly want to get another lecture from his mom on using terrible language. Instead, I hurled a fork at him. He dodged it expertly, knowing me enough to sense it coming, and continued eating as if nothing had happened. I was infuriated, but chose not to interact further, stabbing my breakfast as hard as I could in defiance.

"Lander! If you don't stop tormenting this poor girl any more than you already have, I swear!" Mrs. Robyn lectured her son, waving a large wooden spoon in his direction.

He recoiled, he and the spoon clearly having an unpleasant history, and shoved the last bit of food into his mouth. I watched, in both amusement and disbelief as Lander made his escape, crawling across the ceiling and into his room, shutting the door from the top.

"That insolent boy," his mom muttered, shaking her head.

Although he did wear his jacket on and off throughout the day, I came to discover that Lander spent a large amount of time on the ceiling, whether it be reading for school, snacking, or even taking a nap. It was frankly startling, a novel behavior from my point of view, and I found myself staring often. I wanted badly to ask him about it, but stuck faithfully to my vow of silence, working hard to both ignore him and not gape at this strange activity. He was amused by my struggle to keep the questions at bay—that much was obvious—and he followed me around like an irritating mosquito, trying to elicit some sort of reaction.

Mrs. Robyn kept us insanely busy with schoolwork, because we were both nearly three weeks behind and needed some sort of distraction. Lander had mentioned, in one of the rare moments he could manage to be serious, that he and his sisters had all fallen sick within four days of exposure. We all held out hope that if I made it through the fourth day, I might be out of the woods. The pair almost never left me alone, and I could tell by their constant scrutinizing, they were monitoring me for symptoms.

By the end of the third day, I had trouble focusing on the schoolwork. I sat at the table, repeatedly reading the same sentence, Lander upside down above me. Despite reading it for roughly ten minutes straight, it was as if I'd never read it at all, and I threw my book to the floor in frustration. When Mrs. Robyn and Lander peered over to see what the fuss was about, I stormed out into the garden, wanting to be alone for once.

They honored my silent request, and I stayed there, curled up on the bench until long after nightfall. Eventually, Mrs. Robyn came out to check on me.

"Sadie?" she called, "You better come in before you catch cold!"

"That's the last thing I'm worried about," I grumped, rolling my eyes.

She approached me quietly, wringing her hands together anxiously.

"Tomorrow's day four," I said flatly.

She nodded firmly. "Yes. Which means if you can make it past then, the chances that you've dodged a bullet are much greater."

"We can only hope."

"What comes before us is uncertain, but I can tell you one thing with certainty: staying out here in the chilly damp air doesn't help your chances of staying well one bit." She reached out instinctively to help me up and then hesitated, remembering I couldn't be touched. She slowly withdrew her hand, waving me forward to the door instead. "Come inside now, dear, and get something to eat."

I obediently followed, managing to get at least something down.

That night I laid on the floor of her bedroom, struggling to keep my eyes shut, as I feared the uncertainty of the next morning. I tossed and turned, tangling myself in the sheets and quilts, fending off short-lived nightmares during the infrequent moments I managed to sleep. After a terrible, fragmented night, to my complete and utter joy, I woke up, well. The small shred of hope that I'd been clinging to grew, and for the first time since finding out the truth, I believed that maybe, just maybe, I might make it out of here, unscathed. I was so glad to have made it to the fourth day, I even managed to say a few words to Lander, the question as to why he chose to hang out on the ceiling finally unleashed.

"As I'm sure you can imagine, it's pretty exhausting wearing that much weight all the time," he'd replied. "I have to flip around often so I don't get dizzy, but it's much less confining."

My curiosity finally satisfied, I exchanged a few curt sentences with him throughout the day, more than aware that if I was going to survive this, I'd never speak with him again. I was frustrated that I was even remotely blue about this thought after everything he'd done. I tried burying it under the burning bitterness, but it kept rearing its ugly head, a cool, numbing sensation among the fiery anger.

I managed to pull out my violin that evening, playing a handful of songs alone in the garden. The intensity of my internal thoughts were difficult to weave into the music, their complexities a unique commotion; something I had never experienced. I shoveled them out of my body through song, desperately seeking the relief of their absence. When I finally removed as much uproar as I could manage, I retired early to bed, crying exhaustion from the sleepless night prior. Mrs. Robyn and Lander exchanged worried glances at this behavior, wondering if it could be a sign of oncoming sickness. In reality, I was at peace, not only from having survived the fourth day, but from releasing my unbridled tension thorough song.

I awakened well again and again, hope growing with each new dawn. Lander's face was healing as decent as one could expect, with the bruising and swelling receding. The scab on his cut had peeled away to reveal a thick, pink, raised scar. As his face healed, I healed, the hope that I'd be reunited with my mama within reach. I was still short with Lander and kept telling myself it was anger. In reality, I'd realized I was nursing heavy sadness at our increasingly likely impending separation. Lander had been there almost as long as Mama. Despite everything, and despite how deeply betrayed I was, I couldn't deny the thought that one piece of my heart was being replaced at the expense of another.

I was stuck in limbo. Mama or Lander. Sick or well. Normal life or desperately hiding. The anticipation and uncertainty grew, piling higher and higher. I knew it was only a matter of time before everything would topple, crumbling downward.

Or in this case, up.

***

On the sixth night, I woke up with a start in the early hours of the morning.

My throat was dry and parched, demanding water, and I stood, trudging through the dark to the kitchen sink. I shakily filled a cup, desperately downing it in a matter of seconds, but it didn't do much to quell the hot and dizzying thirst. I squinted out the window while I filled the cup again, and the bright crescent moon hovering low above the peaks caught my gaze. A familiar sight. Though something was different.

I squeezed my eyes shut as I unsuccessfully tried to blink away the second moon that was oddly hovering beside it. The window was shut even though the house was unbearably stifling, and I wondered if maybe Mrs. Robyn had forgotten to open them tonight. Perhaps some cool night air would normalize my vision and relieve some of the thirst I'd developed from the heat.

I reached up to unlatch the window, momentarily forgetting about the cup I'd refilled. My elbow bumped into it, and it clattered to the floor with a spray of water, soaking my feet and the fringe of my nightgown. I bent down reflexively, trying to catch it before it hit the ground, but a sudden wave of dizziness struck, interrupting the attempt at a save. I braced against the sink, trying to steady myself, but the room continued to spin, and I was helpless to stop it.

As the world finally ceased its movement, I heard a groggy voice say my name from behind.

"Sadie? What are you doing?" Lander plodded closer, yawning deeply as he approached. "It's like, two in the morning, and you're already breaking stuff."

I clung to the sink, should the world decide to twirl once more. His feet splashed in the puddle I'd spilled, and I heard his footsteps stutter in surprise. After a brief pause, Lander popped into my field of vision from the side, water ignored.

"Hey, there. Spill your cup?"

"Kind of," I replied, hoarse, as I swallowed dryly. "Your mom left the windows shut."

He stared at me strangely, eyebrow raised, as his eyes flickered to the window and back to me.

"She did," he said slowly, frowning. "It's chilly tonight."

I shook my head. "No. It's hot. I need it open."

I reached out to try to unlatch it again, but Lander beat me to it, flipping up the hook and sliding the window up in one smooth motion, unable to take his eyes off me. Brisk air brushed past my face, and I closed my eyes in relief, though it took away only a fraction of the heat inside the room. Lander gathered up my long hair at the nape, draping it over my left shoulder in an attempt to help cool me off. A chilled hand pressed gently against the back of my exposed neck, the sudden icy touch sending a shudder through me.

"Any better?" he inquired softly, his tone having taken on a controlled hint of panic.

I shrugged, the audible fear in his words setting off alarm bells in my head. "What's wrong?"

He smiled, the expression not quite reaching his eyes and took my shoulders, steering me away from the sink. "Why don't you take my bed for the night? I'll open the window so you can sleep next to some cool air. It can't be comfortable lying on Mom's dingy old floor every night."

I was all too aware that he had dodged my question. That wasn't uncharacteristic in any way for Lander, but something wasn't right. I wasn't right, and we both knew it. As he guided me into his room, my legs grew suddenly weak and shaky. There was a small candle lit on his nightstand, the flame flickering along with the disturbance our movement made in the air. Simply seeing it made me feel even hotter, as if the fire was inside of me instead. My knees buckled as we reached the bed, and Lander scooped me up before I could hit the floor, swinging my legs onto the straw mattress.

"There you go, I got you," he murmured, resting my head into his soft pillow. He covered me with a light sheet and reached over the bed to the window.

"I'm sick, aren't I?" I asked tearfully as Lander struggled to open it, the wood having a bad habit of sticking.

He grunted with the effort, finally yanking it loose, the glass rattling as it slammed to the top of the track.

"You're going to be fine. I won't let anything bad happen to you," he assured me, still avoiding a direct answer.

"You said that last time too," I whispered, tears pooling in my eyes.

"I did, and I fully own up to my failure. But I meant it then, and I mean it now," he vowed.

I sniffled, the fever making my emotions rather haywire. "I'm still mad," I blubbered, lower lip trembling. "I don't know if I can ever forgive you for this."

He peered down at me sadly, eyebrows knitted tightly together, and he wiped away my tears with his forefinger. I noticed for the first time that night he wasn't wearing gloves, the skin on his fingers incredibly soft from their eternal confinement. "It's okay if you don't," he assured me, with a sullen, brittle whisper. I closed my eyes, trying to free them from the watery buildup and turned away, facing the cool night air from the window.

He stood beside the bed for a few moments before I heard him plodding off toward his mom's room. He rapped sharply on the door, raising Mrs. Robyn from her slumber. The latch clicked as she turned the knob, the hinges creaking eerily open.

"Lander? What's wrong?" she asked, worry breaking through the sleepiness in her voice.

Lander cleared his throat, inhaling sharply to keep his voice from trembling before he spoke.

"Sadie's got the fever, Mom. And she's got it bad."

13

The flame that had sparked inside of me raged, no end in sight. It engulfed every piece of my body—a dry, aching heat that refused to be controlled as it ripped through me. Lander didn't go far from my side, changing the damp washcloth he'd placed on my forehead as soon as it became hot. He pushed me to drink broth, water, and tea often, sweetened with honey to get whatever calories possible into my stomach. I was so weak I was unable to sit up without assistance, the haze of the fever weighing me down as heavily as Lander's jacket.

Distressing fever dreams plagued me nearly every time I dozed off, many of them an exaggerated, frightening replay of my last fight with Mama. There were a few consisting of Thamus punching Lander to a bloodied pulp, brandishing the silver knife as Cyntha's body materialized, lifeless on the floor in front of us while he bragged about poisoning her. The worst one was the repetitive scenario of floating off as I desperately grabbed for something, anything, to keep me grounded.

I often woke up screaming and thrashing, fighting Lander as he tried to calm me down. He held me tight until the terrors passed, screams dissolving in my chest while he mumbled soothing assurances into my ear. I begged him to bring me my mom, lashing out in delirious anger when he couldn't honor my requests, violently blaming him for everything. In my brief moments of lucidity, I apologized profusely after remembering how I'd talked to him. I knew why she'd never come, but I needed her badly right now. Needed her cool, healing touch amid the heat.

The second night, the fever intensified, weakening my body badly enough it failed to even conjure up nightmares. I was vaguely aware of Lander and Mrs. Robyn's terrified whispers at my increasing stillness, focusing in and out of their conversations. He'd changed the washcloth on my forehead again, wiping the beads of sweat from my flushed cheeks when he realized the fever was worsening.

Mrs. Robyn told him to soak me in a chilled bath straight away. Lander helped me out of my nightgown to my slip, and carried me to the bathroom, placing my limp body into a pool of cold water. Keeping my head above the surface proved to be a challenge, and after a solid ten minutes of struggling, Lander hopped in with me, fully clothed, propping me up against his sturdy chest. He splashed the water over my neck and shoulders, trying his best to keep me cool as I burned. And burned.

"Come on, Sadie. You can do this," he whispered into my ear, again and again. "You can do this."

I was barely able to make my lips work. "I don't know if I can," I whispered back.

"You can. And you will. I promised you, remember?" he said firmly.

How could I forget? He'd always promised that he'd keep me safe. And yet, here I was, in the jaws of the monster that threatened our entire world all because of him.

I was too weak to reply.

He dutifully kept at it, bathing every inch of my fiery skin in frigid water. But his efforts were fruitless. Because after over an hour of soaking, the bath hadn't made even a dent in my fever, prompting a surge of tearful panic in him.

"Mom!" Lander cried, "Mom!"

She raced into the bathroom, letting out a sigh of relief when she saw the rise and fall of my chest. I wanted to reassure her—to let her know I was okay. But even if I could, it would've been a lie. My body wasn't mine anymore. It had become a blazing fire, boiling itself from the inside out, refusing to be tamed by Lander's futile efforts. I only wished that death by the fever meant my lifeless body would float away—that he and Mrs. Robyn would be spared the agonizing task of burying me when this was all over with.

"What is it, son?"

"It's not working! Do we have enough money for ice? She's burning as bad as Lovena," he quavered. Thick drops of water fell on the top of my hair—down my face. At first, I thought he was splashing me again. But these drops weren't cold.

"We have enough money for anything she needs," she assured him. "Put her back to bed. I'll get ready to go to market."

Weighed down even further by a sodden jacket, Lander had great difficulty getting me dry and comfortable back in bed. Somehow we managed.

Mrs. Robyn stopped him before she headed out. "Should I try to find some fever reducing herbs?"

"They won't have any effect," said Lander. "Believe me. I know."

"And the honey? Do we still have enough?"

"Plenty. She can't get much down since she can't stay conscious longer than a few minutes. I-I've never seen her this sick before," Lander fretted.

"Neither have I," said Mrs. Robyn. "But you're doing a great job. I have faith she's going to be all right. I only wish there was more I could do to help. You're beyond exhausted."

"We can't take the risk. If you touch her, I'll have both of you to take care of. Not to mention, the unfortunate lifelong side effect," he said.

Mrs. Robyn sighed. "I know." Her keys jangled as she hesitated by the door. "I worry what this is going to do to her. Her family—"

"We'll deal with that when the time comes. First, we have to get her through this fever," interrupted Lander.

"Right. I'll be back shortly."

The door opened and shut. Mrs. Robyn's footsteps faded down the front steps as she rushed to the market. There was luckily a steady supply of ice in Ancthia year-round, due to the snow that settled upon the tallest peaks. Now, the price was nearly as steep as the mountains, since the rugged terrain made harvesting and travel difficult and hazardous. I worried that they wouldn't have enough money left for food, particularly since Mrs. Robyn was apparently skipping work to stay with us. Despite everything they'd done to me, I didn't wish them to starve.

I made a mental note to do an extra performance to pay them back when a sudden, terrible thought pierced me to my core.

How would I ever play music again while confined to a cage of weights?

***

It was an effective method, the ice, but it proved to be more miserable than the fever. Despite the relief of having something other than heat, my body fought hard to hold on to its fire, sending me into fits of violent shivering. I begged Lander to make it stop, to let me burn to death even though I knew he wouldn't. He paced the room, in his own sort of agony as he listened to my pathetic pleas.

I had no clue how many hours or days it took, Lander dutifully changing the ice as soon as it melted, but finally, the fever dropped, extinguishing its burn to a warm smolder. I woke up one morning, the haziness mostly gone, birds singing cheerfully out the open window. Frigid ice packs were still tucked all around me, an annoyance now instead of a misery. I was no longer shivering nor sweating, my internal furnace having mostly balanced out.

I noticed something warm and heavy atop my left arm, a stark contrast from the rest of my body. Curious, I turned my aching head to find Lander. He sat in a chair against the bed, folded over with his head resting on my arm, fast asleep.

"Lander?" I croaked, trying to pull myself free. His jacket hood was up over his head, the weight causing my arm to fall asleep about as deeply as he was. "Lander!" I tried again, louder when he didn't budge.

His head shot up, hair askew, including his eyebrows. His face had healed significantly, leading me to wonder how long I'd been out. The bruising had faded into dull shadows and the swelling had disappeared, leaving behind the pink scar from where the impact split his skin.

"Stop drooling on me." I complained with a groan, "It's gross."

Lander grinned brightly, seeing I was finally alert, and touched my forehead.

"It's almost gone! Sadie, you did it! You're going to be okay!" he shouted, choked up, his eyes shimmering in the morning light.

I managed a small, brief smile. I was more than relieved to have made it through the fever, as it was by far the worst one I'd ever experienced.

"Thank you," I whispered.

Sleepless, worry-filled nights were written all over his disheveled face. He'd made good on his vow to pull me through, and though I still harbored resentment, I was deeply touched by how much he'd cared. He took my hand and squeezed it tightly, our fingers interlaced without a barrier of thick leather.

The relief was short-lived, as the darkness of the next hurdle loomed over me. His celebratory mood quickly dampened when I asked him.

"When will it start?"

His face fell as he chewed on his bottom lip, giving my hand one last squeeze.

"It won't be long," was his solemn answer.

He was right. It didn't take long.

Later in the day, Lander sat in a chair in the corner, dryly reading out loud from a schoolbook on Mrs. Robyn's orders. She was horrendously worried about our educations and insisted that even mostly asleep, I could maybe pick up something. He droned on, making stupid jabs at the creative writing section.

"None of this author's ideas make any sense. Why in the world would Melvin go back to his hometown, knowing they were going to kill him?" Lander slammed the book shut, shaking his head. "It's supposed to be reading comprehension, but I can't comprehend any of these decisions!"

I was lying under a weighted blanket, one that he'd placed on me as soon as he removed the ice packs, weakly scowling at him.

"I honestly can't comprehend some of the decisions you make, either," I shot.

He rolled his eyes. "Even being on your deathbed won't keep you from being spicy."

I'd only said one sentence, but it was enough to make me incredibly thirsty. I slid an arm out from under the blanket to grab the cup off the nightstand when something strange happened. No matter how hard I tried, my arm would not obey. I struggled to force it down, to pick up the cup, only managing to knock it over. I wiggled under the blanket in a panic, trying to push myself upward into a sitting position. The blanket slid down from my shoulders to an alarmed Lander.

"Sadie, don't!" he warned, rushing to my side to yank the blanket back over me. We locked eyes, wide and fearful. "You'll hit the ceiling."

Even though it was expected, the reality of the experience shook me to my core. I couldn't control my own body anymore. I'd never live a normal life, doomed to spend my days crushed by a heaviness I could never be free from.

"I don't want it! Make it stop! Please, make it stop!"

Lander helplessly watched, distressed as I was. "I can't, Sadie. There's nothing I can do," he said, trying to keep his voice calm.

"You could have! Before any of this even happened!" I yelled, hot tears rolling down my face. "Get off me!"

He quickly obliged, stumbling backward as if I'd slapped him across his broken nose. I yanked the weighted blanket over my head, hiding everything but my mouth for air as I gave in to my sobs.

"Call out for me if you need anything," he muttered quietly, sensing I needed time alone. "I won't be far."

I cried until my minor headache turned into a pounding throb, huddled underneath the blanket where I was safe. When the tears stopped flowing, I laid still and quiet, watching a massive, electrically charged storm blow in. It hadn't rained in quite a long time, and for it to happen now was fitting. The rain poured against the roof, escaping through the open window to splatter on my face. I was about to reach out to pull it shut when I stopped in sudden fear. What if while reaching for the window, I somehow lost hold of the blanket? I'd go flying out and up into the thunderstorm, never to be seen again. My imagination ran wild at each scenario, as I laid face-to-face with the rumbling gale, the eye of the storm staring me down as it tore at the sky, the sky I might soon be pulled into . . .

The window suddenly slammed shut, shaking me out of my paralysis.

"Geez, Sadie, were you trying to let the whole house flood?" Lander chuckled, the thunder roaring overhead.

"Yes. I was," I muttered.

"Hm. In that case, sorry for ruining your plans here."

"Common problem for you," I retorted, muffled as I hid my face into the bedclothes.

Lander blew out a puff of air. "You don't have to keep reminding me, you know, it's kind of mean."

"That's why I said it," I grouched.

"All right now, wounded animal, you must be feeling much better judging by your terrible bite," Lander said, completely unbothered by my attitude as usual.

The bed dipped as he sat down next to me, and I shrugged weakly under the safety of the blanket. I was a lot better, despite the gaping hole in my chest left from such a terrifying change.

"Do you think you could join us for dinner?" he asked, peeling the blanket from atop my face to touch my cheek. "No more fever."

"It's been gone since this morning," I reminded him.

He paused before reluctantly pulling away. "I know. It's just . . . it's been such a long time since . . . I've missed this."

I grabbed his retreating hand at this heart-wrenching confession, giving it a tight squeeze as our palms melted together, skin against skin. The only touch I would ever have for the rest of my life. As devastating as that knowledge was, and as much as I wanted to deny it, the thought had my heart stirring in a strange and comforting manner. At least that touch was Lander. Even if I was pissed at him. We stayed that way for a few minutes until I unraveled our fingers, sliding my hand back under the blanket.

I resigned myself to my fate. "How do I do it?" I asked, unsure of how to even escape the bed.

"While you were out, Mom made you a jacket. It can be tricky to put on, but once you get the hang of it, it'll be a breeze."

I didn't want it to be a breeze. I didn't want any part of it, but I knew I couldn't stay here forever, within the safety of Lander's bed. He left the room momentarily, bringing back a heavy canvas jacket similar to his, albeit quite smaller.

"You'll have to slide it up under the blanket to put it on. If your core is held down, you'll be able to control your feet pretty easily, but wearing ankle weights or shoes is more than helpful," he explained. "I have both, if you prefer."

He shimmied the jacket under the blanket, and I slid it under my shoulders, pulling each arm into the thick sleeves. The combined weight of both objects made it a tad hard to breathe, so once the zipper was secured, I threw it off. I fought to keep my feet in control sans blanket, and after a few minutes of struggling, Lander took it upon himself to assist with the ankle weights. They were immensely helpful, as I was now able to swing them out of the bed.

I was still incredibly weak from being sick, and adding pounds of bulk to my shoulders proved to be in no way helpful. The instant I went to stand, I crumpled to the floor. Lander apparently expected this, as he caught me under the arms before I could make impact, carefully placing me back on the side of the bed.

"Things will be pretty wobbly for a while until you get your strength back," he told me. "Getting some actual food into you will be the biggest help."

The mention of food brought my attention to the gnawing pit of hunger growing loud and ravenous as the minutes went on.

"I think I can do that," I agreed, needing to satisfy the beast awakening within me. I didn't even know when the last time I'd eaten real food was, and the thought of a warm meal was more than tempting. Lander threaded an arm under mine, helping me to my feet. I had to lean on him the entire way to the kitchen table, the jacket incredibly heavy, but we managed, Mrs. Robyn delighted to have me upright.

"You're nothing but skin and bones, child! Here, eat up!"

She placed a bowl of chicken soup in front of me, the rich, savory scent tickling my nose. The worry of how much she'd spent to get the chicken was quickly overshadowed by the beckoning of a real meal, with actual meat, and I inhaled every last drop. It wasn't easy to manipulate the spoon while fighting the weight on my arms, but the intense hunger propelled me onwards. I was almost out of breath from the effort by the time I finished.

"It's great to have you with us, Sadie," Mrs. Robyn said, leaning in to kiss me on the cheek. She stopped herself before Lander could remind her, straightening her back uncomfortably as she cleared her throat. "Do you want some more?" she offered, indicating to the steaming pot still on the stove.

I shook my head, more than satisfied after having no solid food for almost a week.

"Thank you, Mrs. Robyn," I said quietly.

A strange sadness formed in my stomach as I came to terms with the fact that we'd never have the same physical closeness as before. I could read it in her face; the same starvation for meaningful, loving touch that mirrored her son's, living a life separated by a wall.

Lander was already on his third bowl of soup, observing the interaction closely. The way he was eating, I worried he might choke.

"Do you even chew?" I asked as he shoveled another spoonful into his gaping mouth.

He shook his head. "Faster if I don't."

"That's a teenage boy for you," Mrs. Robyn remarked, shaking her head. "Eats more than his sisters did, combined. And if you don't finish your damn schoolwork, you won't be able to get a good enough job to pay me back for eating me out of house and home!"

She rapped him lightly on the noggin with a wooden spoon. Lander completely ignored her.

After a fourth bowl Mrs. Robyn cut him off, stating that other people needed to have something to eat. He helped me back to bed, and I returned to the confines of the blanket, sleep threatening to take me nearly the instant I'd laid down. Suddenly remembering where I was, my eyes shot back open as Lander folded the jacket up on his nightstand.

"Where have you been sleeping?" I questioned, having all but taken over his bed. He dropped the jacket onto the wooden stand, creating a loud thump as the weight hit its surface.

"The chair, the ceiling, or the floor. Do you want me to stay in Mom's room tonight since you're feeling better?"

I was guilty about leaving him with such uncomfortable sleeping quarters. On one hand, I wanted to be alone to process the new changes occurring, but on another I realized how afraid I was. I had lost complete control over not only my body, but my life. One wrong move and I would end up gone, stuck in an endless, dark void up above the entire world never to return. How did he do it? How could he go along with each day so effortlessly, so calmly? Even though he was as weightless as I was now, it was as if he were a tree, rooted deep enough into the ground that even the virus couldn't yank him out. Lander was always there, steady and constant, holding it all together as everything fell apart around him. He'd held me down along with him, since my arrival in Ancthia, and through this entire mess. I was about to ask him to stay, when the nagging, repetitive whisper I couldn't quite shake washed through me like a cold breeze.

He did this to you, trapped you here for selfish reasons.

I tried to argue with myself, to be logical while staring into the face of who was supposed to be my best friend.

He didn't mean it. He was trying to protect me; to protect us both from being killed by the city.

The creeping thoughts poured in, bouncing around the walls of my mind.

If you had known, you wouldn't be going through this right now. You'd be at home, safe with your mom. Your life is gone. You won't even get to meet your new sibling. If Lander had never shown you the truth, you could've lived your entire life, oblivious to Thamus's job, the things he did to his family. Ignorance is bliss isn't it? But didn't you want the truth? That's what you begged Lander to tell you. That's what you sought when you told Mama about Thamus. You thought the truth would protect her, the same way Lander thought his lies would protect you. Which life would've been better? The truth you're in now, or the lie you'd been living? The lie where you were constantly at risk of danger, albeit unknowingly?

The conflicting words shouted louder and louder and I squeezed my eyes shut, begging them to stop when Lander ruffled my hair gently. He pulled me out of my head, almost dizzyingly so, and gave me a sad smile.

"I know it's a lot to process. I'll be right next door if you need anything."

Shoulders drooped, he turned to leave the room. Each step that took him further away tore at my heart, widening the pit of loneliness that had settled within it.

Before I could think, I yelled out, "Wait!"

Lander stopped and peered over his shoulder from the corner of his eye. His chin was tilted in that adorable way of his, the fresh scar visible on the side of his nose.

"Stay. One more night. Then you can have your room back," I begged. "I-I need you."

I hugged myself tight under the blanket, heart pounding as he silently tried to read me. He twisted around.

"I'll be right here, Sadie," he promised, and returned to the chair in the corner of the room, curling his knees up to his chest. He leaned his head back, peering over at me through heavy-lidded eyes. The panic that had gripped me at the thought of him leaving melted away. Lies or not, I knew I'd be safe as long as he was here. That was one truth I could always be sure of.

Rain pattered against the roof, a gentle rhythm of a soothing song. I briefly thought that a melody might spark from this noise, but it slipped away faster than I could process it, as did my consciousness. As I fell into a warm, deep slumber, I almost thought I heard Lander whisper back.

"I need you too."

14

Walking around carrying the weight of an entire other human on your back was challenging enough. As was having to fight your feet and arms in an endless dance for control, as they tried to race toward the sky faster than I could stop them. But perhaps the most difficult part of dealing with the effects of this virus was taking a shower.

"Okay, remember what we discussed," Lander shouted through the bathroom door, trying to coach me through it. "Tuck your feet up under the cabinets before taking anything off. That'll keep you from flying upward. When you remove the weight, reach for the handle outside the shower door. You'll have to yank yourself over with it. Slide inside the door and use the handles. It gets slippery, so be careful! If all else fails, the ceiling is your best friend, only gotta be careful getting there!"

"All right! I'll give it a try!" I said, nervous to remove the weights.

This would be the first time I was completely without them. It was also the moment I figured out the actual reason why Lander's bathroom was fitted with a conglomeration of random handles. I was under the assumption the house was previously owned by an elderly person; the fixtures there to help them in and out of the bath. Now, I'd learned the true reason, the handles and I staring each other down as I prepared myself for this challenge.

I did as Lander instructed and tucked my feet up under the bathroom cabinet, the ledge smooth and worn from years of my friend doing the same. I took the ankle weights off first, since the next part was rather intimidating; I didn't quite know what to expect, having yet to experience the full effect of weightlessness. Slowly pulling down the zipper, I readied myself, shimmying my feet into a snugger position. My jacket slipped off my shoulders almost instantly, a loud thud rattling the mirror as it hit the floor. I had been prepared to become a feather as the weightlessness took over, my body fluttering around on a gentle breeze.

It was nothing like that.

The only way to describe it would be as if gravity completely switched directions. I wasn't weightless or floaty; everything was as heavy as it had been before. No, it was like being pulled upward with an incredible force, almost as if I was falling backward. The shock of the unexpected sensation startled me, and I panicked, my feet slipping out from under the cabinet. I managed to grab the sink in time to shove my feet back to safety, holding onto the wooden frame for dear life.

"What is this?" I shrieked, afraid to let go.

"How are you doing?" Lander asked. "Did you make it to the shower?"

"No! Why does it feel like this? I'm still heavy, but in the wrong way!"

"Yeah, so, it kind of looks a lot different than it feels," Lander said, his explanation coming way too late.

"And you didn't think to mention this before?" I hollered, knuckles turning white from holding on. The tops of my feet burned from the wood pressing hard into them. I was going to have to move, and soon.

"I'm so used to it at this point I forgot how most people view it! Sorry! You need to hurry and grab the first handle or your feet are going to be hurting all week!"

"I know!" I huffed, trying to figure this out.

My dress was still on, and I worried it would be impossible to get off while holding onto the handle. I sucked on my teeth, bracing my feet tighter and let go of the wood, using my hands to quickly release my dress and undergarments. As soon as they hit the ground, I grabbed on for safety again, catching a glimpse of my pale and angular face in the mirror. I still looked pretty rough from the fever and hoped that a few weeks of good food and proper sleep might make me appear more like myself.

I cried out as I reached for the handle, gripping it tightly with one hand. Once secure, I yanked my other hand over, stretching halfway across the bathroom.

"Did you get it?" he asked again from the bedroom.

"Halfway," I grunted, and slowly pulled my feet free. They shot to the ceiling at an alarming rate, heels slamming hard into the wood as they made impact. "Ouch!"

Everything was so different, so backward, my entire body now horrifically out of control.

"I know that hurt," Lander commented, sucking on his teeth. "I've broken a few toes doing that."

"Not helpful!"

"Sorry."

Now that my feet were on the ceiling, I had more control over which direction my body was going since that's where they were begging to be. I could understand now how Lander sat upside down with such ease; walking on the ceiling was similar to walking on the floor. The most difficult part was getting up there without "falling."

I managed to climb into the shower, holding onto the handles. The only issue was I was now completely upside down. I stared down the spigot, trying to figure out what to do next. I couldn't shower this way, lest I wanted to inhale water the entire time. After a few moments of thought, I finally decided on a strategy and placed my feet flat to the ceiling as if trying to walk along it. I knew I'd have to let go of the handle for this to work, and counted to ten, finally brave enough to peel my fingers off the sturdy wood.

Squatting onto the ceiling, I swapped places with my feet and my hands, performing what one could call an upside-down handstand. Pushing my legs down further, I hooked my foot into a handle and bent down to grab it. I had to count to ten again for my nerves but managed to let go and take the handle on the opposite side of the shower. I stood upright in a forced manner, a gymnast holding herself on a set of bars. I had done it; I was right side up and ready for a shower at last!

There was only one small problem. I'd forgotten to turn the water on.

I cursed loudly.

"Sorry, I forgot to tell you to turn the water on first," Lander's voice floated in sheepishly.

"I'm glad you're not going into teaching because you're not doing a good job of it!" I declared. He stifled a laugh. "It's not funny!"

I glanced behind me at the faucet and then to my hands, locked onto the handles. I'd have to turn around somehow. This was impossible! After a few failed attempts to spin toward the faucet, I ended up turning the lever with my toes, sending a spray of frigid water right into me. I cried out at the sudden cold, shivering until the water warmed up.

Now came the next problem: soap. There was no way I could do this while gripping both handles. As Lander had explained, I may have to go either upside down or hook my feet under the grips as I did at the cabinet. I was reluctant, the tops of my feet still aching from their previous encounter, but there wasn't any other option. Lander had said the last time he tried tying his feet to the bars, he'd dislocated an ankle. A type of injury we couldn't risk seeking help for as a survived. I got my feet up under the handles nice and secure, and went about my shower, the warm water a relief from the week of suffering I'd endured. For the first time in a while, I was finally invigorated and calm.

Nearly finished, preparing myself to get out, I dropped the bar of soap. Acting on instinct, I bent down to get it, the slickness of the soap and water causing my feet to slip off the bar they were hooked under. I fell upward, and hard, almost knocking the breath out of me.

"Sadie! You good?" Lander shouted.

Water dripped down my face and hair into the shower below as I lay, splayed out atop the ceiling as if I'd fallen flat on the floor. I saw stars, the impact jarring my head spectacularly, and I blinked them away as I tried to figure out what to do next.

"I'm fine!" I replied, even though I was not, in fact, fine.

"Do you need help? I mean, I've been helping you in the bathroom all week so it's not like—"

"Shut up!" I screamed, face turning scarlet at the memories I'd love to erase completely from existence, not just from my head but from the entire universe. "If you *ever* mention that again for as long as you live, Lander Holland, I will strangle you to death personally with my own two bare hands!"

He paused thoughtfully before giving me the most irritating reply: "I forget you can do that now."

"Ugh!" I yelled back in frustration.

It took an immense amount of effort, maneuvering, and strategic placement of each limb, but I ended up getting off the ceiling, finishing the shower, and getting dressed. I stomped out of the bathroom and past Lander—the stomping part not entirely intentional due to the weights—glad to finally be done with that mess. For now. I didn't know how I was going to do this for the rest of my life. I wished I had Mama to guide me. She always knew exactly the right thing to say to get me through the hardest moments. I missed her terribly, the hole in my chest growing larger with each passing day. I wondered how the baby was doing, how she was doing, if she missed me the same.

I sat in solitude in the large windowsill of one of the kitchen windows, leaning my head against the glass. The clouds strolled casually by, blissfully unaware of the mayhem and despair below them. I envied them, in a way. To be free of all the chaos on the ground, of a terrible fever that had destroyed life as humanity knew it. I'd spent all my life running from it, and for what? I'd been caught. My family was torn into shreds, my entire life turning on its head. My father was lost to it, and now I was lost to it. Or was I? I was still here. Contagious for the remainder of my life, but here, nonetheless. Mrs. Robyn had lived all these years with Lander and managed to avoid any and all touch. Could I maybe do the same with Mama? Spend the rest of my life in her company, and yet so utterly far away?

I sighed, allowing my sorrows and fears to go haywire when I noticed someone familiar walking down the street. My heart stuttered as I recognized who exactly it was, and I immediately shouted for Lander and Mrs. Robyn.

"Lander! Mrs. Robyn! It's Thamus!" I turned to hop out of the windowsill but ended up falling hard onto the floor, the awkward weight of the jacket throwing off my balance. I was starting to understand why Lander had always been clumsy and slow. Dressed this way, it was impossible to do anything gracefully.

The pair raced to the window, watching as the man turned into the small pathway of the house.

"Mom, do you have it?" Lander asked, the seriousness in his tone agitating the butterflies in my stomach.

His mom nodded, tightening the grip she had on her pocket. I realized she likely hid a knife there, in the event Thamus tried to pull a fast one again as he did in Mama's house.

"I'll talk to him," she said firmly.

Thamus had attempted to kill her son, breaking his nose and scarring his face in the process. Mrs. Robyn was a force to be reckoned with, and when it came to her last surviving child, she would stop at nothing to protect him.

"No. We go together," Lander told her, placing a gloved hand on her arm for reassurance. "We're a team, after all."

They smiled at one another and reached the door right when a few quick raps sounded from the wood. The instant the lock *clicked*, I heard Thamus step backward down the short stairs, an attempt to avoid getting close to such contamination as us. Warm light flooded across Lander and Mrs. Robyn's figures as they stood in the doorway, staring out toward Thamus with a challenge on their faces. I could see the resemblance between mother and son in the way that they stood, the angles of their cheeks and jaw, both held taut in contempt for the man before them.

"Good morning," Thamus called out, keeping his distance from the door.

"What do you want?" Mrs. Robyn shouted back to him.

"Oh, I was only swinging by to check on how things were going. Your face has healed up decently, Holland," he said casually, in a grating sort of way. This was no casual visit.

I heard Lander whisper to Mrs. Robyn, asking if he was allowed to curse at Thamus. She whacked him in the head with her identically gloved hand, answer a clear *No*. I knew she'd donned the gloves in case the situation put her at risk of touching her son.

"It's none of your business," Mrs. Robyn said to Thamus. "Now get off my property. We're not welcome on yours, you're not welcome on ours." She grabbed the door handle, ready to slam it in his face.

"It is entirely my business, and Sadie's. Surely, you'd want her mother to know what became of her daughter?"

They both glanced over to where I stood, completely helpless in the face of this situation. I knew despair was written all over my face. Hearing him mention my mother tore at my heart.

"What do you want us to tell him, Sadie?" Lander asked gently.

I opened my mouth to speak, but the words dissolved faster than I'd hit the ceiling earlier. Instead, I moved my feet forward, fighting both the weights and my own hesitation to stand tall, face-to-face with the man that started it all. His mouth twitched up into a gleeful grin as he took in my sallow face and weighted jacket, placed snugly over my skirts. As pleased as he appeared, I wondered if this had been the plan all along. He lifted his bearded chin.

"That's all I needed to know," Thamus simply said. He turned, waving us off as he trudged back down the path.

"Wait!" I screamed, hot with anger. "That's it? That's all you have to say? Mama didn't send you with a message?"

Thamus stopped, turning back around, the smug sneer still plastered on his face. "Nope. That's all she wanted to know. If you'd be returning or not."

I didn't believe him, especially with his secretive violent history, and I crossed my arms, shaking my head. "I don't think you're telling the truth."

Thamus chuckled. "Things are not always as they seem, as you have become acutely aware." He gestured toward Lander, whose jaw tightened up at this accusation. "She had nothing else to say to you."

I bit back the tears prickling at my eyes, trying to keep control over myself, something I was sorely lacking as of late. "I have a message for her if you please."

"And what would that be?" said Thamus with a raised eyebrow.

"Tell her I miss her. That I love her. And I'm sorry."

Thamus stroked his beard. I hoped he was committing my words to memory, to deliver the words I'd spoken, but I wasn't relying on it in any means.

"Very well. But I wouldn't expect a reply. After all, there's risk of transmission based on verbal communication, is there not?" Thamus knew how untrue that theory was. Yet I also knew he'd stoked that fear in my mother. "She has a new baby to think about; a new life at risk. I have no doubts she will go to whatever measure possible to do right this time, since she couldn't protect her last child."

My heart sank all the way to my feet. To her, I was no more. Nothing different from an aimless cloud passing by. Sure, I was standing right here, alive and well. But at the same time, I wasn't. I'd changed to the point my own mother didn't want me—had already replaced me, even. I didn't die, to be tossed into an early grave—didn't float off into the sky. And yet, I had somehow been lost to the fever.

"Go to hell," Mrs. Robyn spat from over my shoulder. "And unless you have a message from her mom, you'd best not show your face around here again." She patted her pocket menacingly, in full mama bear mode, as Thamus chuckled, shaking his head at her threat.

He twisted around, conversation over, and headed down the street, disappearing around a distant corner.

The instant he was out of sight, my focus shifted from an outside enemy to an internal one as I stood facing the world for the first time. The void above me. A massive, empty sky, a gaping mouth, ready to swallow me whole should I lose the weight holding me down. I panicked, stumbling backward from its reach, the soft breeze I'd once cherished now grabbing me—the claws of a monster. I fell to the floor, unbalanced, much to Mrs. Robyn and Lander's surprise, and rapidly scrambled back to my feet. I made a mad dash toward the bathroom, the only room in the house lacking a window; the only room that was truly safe.

"Sadie, wait!" Lander called out. Mrs. Robyn stopped him as I slammed the door closed.

I leaned against it, panting to the point I feared I might faint.

"Give her some time, son. She needs it," she said.

15

I spent the next few days moping and avoiding windows. The weather had become a lot warmer, and Mrs. Robyn had kept them open, allowing the air to circulate through her stuffy home. I'd shed at least one of my skirts to compensate for the added warmth of the jacket, wondering how I'd ever survive a hot summer this way. I worried I might have to spend the entire season stuck on the bathroom ceiling, my new favorite room of the house, should the heat become too stifling. I spent hours in there when everything became too much, fending off a nosy Lander and concerned Mrs. Robyn. She was worried I might be having stomach troubles, offering various home remedies of which I vehemently refused, assuring her that was not the case.

Lander hadn't yet brought it up, but he watched me curiously as I skittered past each window, fascinated by this new behavior. I ignored his piercing gaze from the rafters, trying to focus on my schoolwork while sitting at the end of the table farthest from the window. Mrs. Robyn assigned us a certain number of hours of schoolwork daily, bringing our completed assignments to Miss Poe once a week. I'm not sure what she told our young and nervous teacher, but whatever it was, we had been approved to complete our work from home, on the condition it was in a timely manner.

Despite the choice to work upside down, Lander's handwriting was exquisite, which irritated the living daylights out of me. I sat in my spot, squinting at the paper, struggling to move my hand smoothly in the presence of heavy arms and lack of light. Each messy stroke had me muttering curses to myself.

"You know, it might be easier if you scoot over toward the window," Lander said casually, having finally decided to acknowledge his observations. "You'd at least be able to see."

"I can see fine right where I am," I asserted, continuing my work, trying to ignore him and focus. The absence of his scribbling pencil alerted me to the fact that he was watching, making it even more difficult to continue. My mistakes increased, and I finally got sick of his silent observation. Slamming my pencil down on the table, I lifted my eyes upward, glaring at him.

"Why are you staring at me?" I demanded.

"Because you're acting weird," was his reply. He narrowed his eyes, reading me as clearly as he always did. "You're scared of the windows."

I averted my gaze back to my paper, making a feeble attempt to finish my work. "Am not."

"Are too. You haven't stepped out into the garden since you've gotten better."

"Have you ever thought that maybe I haven't wanted to?" I argued, trying to keep my tone even and controlled as the thought of stepping into the garden made me lose all sense of control.

"I have. And I've thought that maybe the weather wasn't the best. But it's been great outside. Mom has asked you to join her out there multiple times. You've been hiding out in the bathroom, the only room that doesn't have a window, all the while creeping around each open window as if it were a ticking time bomb. You're frightened of it. The outside."

Spot on, as always. There wasn't even a point in denying it.

"So, what if I am?" I retorted, spitting venom to mask the shame.

"We're going to have to fix that."

I jerked my head back up at him with a feral bolt of fear. "No! Absolutely not! I won't be going out there now, not ever! Heights terrify me, you already know that, and to . . . to be permanently threatened with flying off at any moment? You can't make me!"

"You can't stay locked up in a dark hole forever, Sadie. That's not living."

"I don't care! I'm not living, anyway! I'm cut off from my family, can't take a normal shower, and have to worry about the freaking sky of all things!" I threw my arms into the air in exasperation, and they fell back down almost immediately, as heavy as they were.

Lander sighed, chewing on the inside of his cheek. "I haven't had a pretzel since I've been stuck up in here with you. I think it's time you treat me to one."

"My coins are in your closet. Have at it." I waved him away, scribbling carefully on the paper set before me.

Lander crossed his arms. "You're going, too. It's not up for discussion."

"Nope. I'll be right here when you get back," I sang, focusing with such intensity on my schoolwork I couldn't even process what I was supposed to write.

Lander tossed his clipboard and pen over his head, the paper fluttering as the clipboard clattered to the table. He crawled across the ceiling into his room and jumped expertly toward the floor, grabbing onto the frame of his bed. I found his weightless dance fascinating, watching carefully from the side of my eye as he worked, movements smooth and rehearsed and effortless. Despite how heavy it felt—being yanked upward—he was the embodiment of why they called it weightless.

Lander finally hit the floor when he secured the jacket over his shoulders, and hopped up, grabbing a handful of coins from his closet. They weren't mine, though.

"Let's go, Sadie."

I shook my head and gripped the table hard. "I said no," I warned him, peering around him in the direction of the bathroom, wondering if I could run fast enough to hide and lock the door.

"And I don't care. You're coming with me."

"You can't make me!" I screeched. "Good luck carrying the table down the street, because I'm not letting go!"

"Look, I know it's scary. I was afraid the first time I left the house too. But as long as you pay attention and keep your zipper to your chin, you're not going anywhere. Promise." He dug around in one of his pockets, pulling out a handful of his hidden rope. "Here. Take this. If you're ever afraid, tie yourself down. Having something to hold on to helps a lot."

I hesitated, my brow furrowing as I debated whether to accept. Lander promised. He said I'd be okay. But the lies. He'd told me so many lies. How could I be sure this wasn't yet another?

"I have more. Take it," Lander insisted, pushing the rope into my palm. I rubbed my fingers over the heavy cording, the rough texture scraping gently against my skin. "You're not alone, Sadie. I'll be there."

I'll be there. Our eyes met. Beyond the lies, the secrets, the deception, that's how it had always been. Me and Lander, against the world. And through all of this, the changes and loss, his unwavering presence was the only thing that had stayed constant. The one truth that had always been. In that moment, I chose to hold on to it, as tightly as I held onto the rope he'd given me.

"No more secrets, Lander," I said quietly. He tilted his head quizzically, indicating for me to explain further. "You betrayed me by lying since the moment we met. Promise me there's nothing else? That you'll never do it again?"

He stared at me with conviction, his eyelashes fluttering as he took my hand, crossing his pinky with mine. "Pinky promise. If I ever betray you again, I'll pay you back with my life." He was so serious, so genuine, I believed him fully, and finally let a small portion of the hole in my heart to close up. I was still empty, still in pain, and likely never would be completely healed. But this was a start.

"I'll go with you."

***

I did go with him, but it wasn't without a fight. He had to drag me out kicking and screaming, the two of us hurling insults and profanities that made me glad Mrs. Robyn was away at work. I'd had more than enough of her wooden spoon, which she skillfully wielded the instant either one of us stepped out of line. I hyperventilated as he dragged me down the street, frantically checking the sky every few moments to make sure it wasn't sucking me in.

"Quit acting ridiculous! You're already outside, and you haven't gone anywhere, obviously! You owe me this much, for everything I've done for you in the last two weeks!"

"I don't owe you anything!" I argued, tripping as he sped down the street, faster than me for once.

"Yes, you do! I took care of you while you were burning with fever, throwing my own sleep and hunger to the wayside and for what? To be denied even a pretzel for my efforts?"

"You can have a damned pretzel whenever you want! I told you where my money was!"

"It's not the same, Sadie! What if I gave you money for a specific birthday gift instead of buying it for you? It doesn't have the same meaning!"

"I can't stand you sometimes, Lander Holland!" I said bitterly, tripping again. "If you're going to be dragging me around like this, can't you at least slow down?"

Lander laughed but obliged, slowing his pace to a crawl as I gripped his arm to the point I wondered if his hand was going numb. It certainly appeared rather purple, peeping out from the sleeve of his jacket.

"Isn't this entertaining. Now I'm the fast one," Lander teased. I wanted to hit him so badly, but the fear of letting go trumped any desire for violence.

We finally made it to the market, purchasing a set of pretzels from Lander's favorite stand, and we sat in our usual spot in front of the fountain. The cool mist from the water was more than welcome as hot and sweaty as this jacket made me. We sat in silence for some time, gnawing our delicious snacks as I grew calmer being away from the house. I kept my eyes trained to the ground, as seeing the sky made me feel rather faint, and I didn't dare let go of Lander's arm, holding on to it for dear life.

Holding on to Lander as if he were a part of me was how Inala found us.

My heart skipped an incredible number of beats as I noticed her long black braid among the sparse crowd, with a terrible frown of spitting hatred directed at us. Lander noticed her right as I did, and Inala tore through the crowd, pushing bystanders out of her way as she locked in.

"I knew it!" she yelled. "You're both cheating liars!"

I almost laughed. She had the lying part down.

"Inala, calm down, as we said before, it's not like that," Lander insisted, holding his hands out in front of him as if he were under arrest.

"How can you say that when she's sitting right up against you, *wearing one of your jackets?*" Inala indicated to my confining outfit, the only thing holding me to the fountain right now.

"Stop, Inala! It's not—" I said, but Lander interrupted me.

"There's a lot you don't know about me and Cyntha," he explained calmly to the girl in front of him, the veins in her pale neck standing up in rage. "We were never together."

"That's the most ridiculous thing I've ever heard! You know how much she liked you, and then there's all the time you two spent together. You were her first kiss!" Inala argued, growing more hysterical by the minute.

"We did kiss, but, as I said, it wasn't like that. And neither is this."

"Then why don't you explain," Inala declared, crossing her arms and tapping her right foot on the street below us.

Lander worked his jaw as he decided how to approach this. I was starting to realize why he became stuck in such a web of lies. This wasn't exactly something with a simple explanation. To understand it fully, he'd have to reveal what he was, what we were—a truth that could kill us and Inala.

Instead of forcing him to speak up, to spin a story to keep the peace and our secret, I took over. Lander had been through enough at this point. And Inala's constant insistence that we were doing something wrong had me at my breaking point. The frustration and pain that I'd been through over the past few weeks won over, landing its mark on Inala, who was honestly innocent in all of this.

"It's none of your business anymore, Inala. Cyntha's gone. It doesn't even matter," I snapped coldly, the words painful to say to my once great friend. They left my tongue as prickly needles, leaving me numb and throbbing as if poisoned. "Leave us alone."

Inala appeared as if she'd been stabbed, and in that instant, I knew for a fact there was no friendship left to mend. It was over. Time wouldn't heal these wounds as I'd previously thought; neither would an apology. As Inala stared at me, as shocked and broken as I was on the inside, I immediately wanted to take it all back, to apologize. I wanted to tell her the truth, even though it was impossible. Inala was only trying to protect her friend, even in death. And I'd all but punched her. Her crossed arms unraveled at her sides, and she squeezed her hands into tight fists.

"If that's how you want it," she quavered. She spun around and ran off, wiping away tears as she went.

"Thanks for the save, Sadie, but that was kind of a crappy thing to say," Lander admitted from the corner of his mouth, tearing back into his pretzel.

"What else could I have done? I didn't want to lie to her, but I couldn't tell her the truth, either," I said, swallowing back the lump in my throat. "It's not safe for either of us."

Lander squinted, staring thoughtfully off into the crowd. "That's how I felt before," he stated, taking another bite of his pretzel. "Every time I was with you."

We didn't speak the entire walk home as my mind shifted perspectives, and I couldn't help comparing it to the shift I'd experienced with gravity.

Everything had gone upside down.

***

I had trouble keeping my spirits up as I dutifully worked on boring schoolwork, chores, and once daily walks around the city with Lander. I'd become gradually used to leaving the house, repeated exposure greatly reducing the fear of flying off. Windows were no longer a source of terror, and I laid out in the garden on occasion to watch the wind rustle the plants. Despite having overcome it for the most part, I still couldn't stare down the sky without experiencing some semblance of faintness. Lander had to shove my head between my knees on more than one occasion when I let my anxiety get the better of me.

Mama dominated my thoughts the more time went on. Where was she? How was she doing? Did she miss me the same? Many days I struggled getting up in the mornings, the weight of grief heavier than any jacket Mrs. Robyn could've ever crafted for me. My own sadness was swallowing me up as intensely as I worried the sky would, until I could stand it no longer. I was trying to write a four-page essay, my handwriting still lacking any improvement when I shoved the tip of my pencil into the paper, shattering it. Lander glanced down at me from his perch on the ceiling, pleasantly amused as he waited for me to do something else unexpected.

"Lander—I have to see her," I urged, the desperation finally reaching its peak. He thoughtfully twirled his pencil in his fingers, understanding immediately what I meant.

"When do you want to go?" was his reply, primed and ready for some sort of break in the monotony of our recent everyday lives.

"Now," I said.

He didn't even hesitate. Lander immediately got himself together to leave the house. I didn't fail to notice the knife he'd hidden in his jacket's inner pocket, knowing exactly what it was for should we come across such obstacles.

Despite the familiarity of my surroundings, the journey back to my old home was surreal and unsettling, as though I were walking through a dream. Something was different, but I couldn't quite place it. I fruitlessly searched to discern what was wrong. The stones, the gardens, and even the rats were exactly as I had recalled. But the longer my gaze lingered, the world passing by as if nothing was amiss, the more the truth became glaringly obvious. My surroundings hadn't changed. I had. I was a stranger in my home, one that belonged anywhere but here. I wondered if it was real, or if Thamus's words had simply gotten to me.

Approaching the house, now the home of a stranger, the memory of our last adventure came crashing back. This was where I'd been exposed, where I learned the truth about Lander, Cyntha, and Thamus. It was the last place Mama and I spoke, in heated anger and a fit of fury. I was no longer safe standing at the foot of the stairs. The old door loomed above me, mirroring the peaks of the mountains that loomed over the city. My legs were frozen to the spot, and I shivered, chilled to the bone despite the heavy warmth of my jacket.

"Do you think she's home?" asked Lander, trying to pull me out of the dangerous depths that was my mind. I shrugged, unsure of the answer.

"The last time we talked, she said she lost her job. She was doing odd jobs around the city, but Thamus was providing most of the support. Now that she's pregnant, I'm sure she can't do much of anything."

My throat was dry, and no matter how many times I swallowed, I couldn't make the cottony sensation go away. We lingered at the bottom of the steps as I worked up the nerve to do something, anything. I'd been determined earlier to see her, to beg for forgiveness, but now, standing face-to-face with the situation, I was crippled with fear. Fear that Thamus was right, that she hadn't anything to say to me. I was afraid to face the reality of my life and the promise I'd made to Thamus. Would he come after us for not upholding our end of the deal? Surely, Mama wouldn't put us in harm's way. She was my mom. My everything. She loved me, and I loved her.

Reassuring myself with the knowledge of her love, I powered myself up the stairs, loudly knocking on the door. Seconds ticked by, dragging along into minutes. My anticipation nearly reached its peak. What would happen if she opened the door? I imagined Mama reaching for a hug, of me having to push her away. I'd promised Thamus I wouldn't tell her what he did, so I hadn't a clue what to tell her about my new . . . condition. Panic gripped me. I hadn't thought this through. How could I approach this without ruining everything? What if Thamus was the one who opened the door?

I stumbled back, nearly falling down the stairs at the sudden thought of Thamus. But nothing happened. No one was home. The door didn't open, and not even an inkling of footsteps sounded from inside. I was relieved and disappointed—more so relieved that I wouldn't have to come up with something on the spot. The decision to come here without a plan was quite rash, to be honest. I turned around, taking the steps heavily one by one back to where Lander waited. As soon as I reached the road, a gasp caught my attention, pulling my gaze from the street to the person ahead of us.

Mama stood, seconds after having come from around a corner, the basket of groceries she'd been holding now scattered on the street. She had one hand over her mouth, the other protectively on her protruding belly, staring wide-eyed in horrified shock. An apple went rolling in my direction, bumping along the ground in an almost gleeful manner before it slammed against an askew stone, coming to an abrupt stop.

"Mama," I called out, voice trembling. "It's me. Sadie."

She didn't move, face growing pale as the rolling clouds above us. Tears welled in the corners of her eyes, her shoulders heaving slightly as she kept herself as silent as possible. She shook her head, taking a step back. Mama gripped her belly tighter, as if protecting her baby from me. From her other baby.

"Mama. It's okay! Unless you touch me, you won't get it. I promise! Talk to me! Please, talk to me!" I begged, my voice becoming shrill as I came to the realization that she wouldn't. She'd never talk to me again. An uncontrolled sob ripped through my throat as the finality of it all crashed down onto me with the weight of a thousand suns. "Please. I love you, Mama. I'm sorry. I messed up. I wish I could go back and change it all, I wish we could be one big happy family. I want to meet my new sibling! I want to live my life with you, with us, the way it used to be! Please, Mama. I can't hurt you, not unless you touch my skin! I'm still your daughter. I'm still Sadie."

Mama stepped away again, now refusing to even look at me. She stared at the ground as tears fell heavily into the stones, leaving dark splotches where they dispersed. I screamed at her to say something, anything. I pleaded for her to yell at me for being stupid, for not listening to her, for ruining everything. I needed her to acknowledge me, even if it was only in anger, so that I knew she still cared.

She remained frozen to her spot, unable to run or move, to even make a sound while she cried for fear that a response would infect her. I watched, devastated, my chest ripping apart as I witnessed my own mother deny me. And for what? For being weightless?

"I'm still Sadie," I said one more time, my voice trailing off as I concluded that this was pointless. Thamus was right. She didn't have a message for me. The fear of what I'd become was greater than her love for me. I should've known when she never came knocking while I was deathly sick. I should've known when she didn't search for me after our fight. I should've known when I confronted her with that conch shell. She hadn't been afraid of what could happen to me. She only feared what could happen to her and Thamus.

It was as if I'd become a ghost. As if I had died long ago and she moved on, my sudden appearance dredging up a life she'd longed to forget. Maybe that was what I'd become. I was as good as dead to her, after all.

Lander took my hand, breaking his silence seeing that Mama wasn't going to break hers.

"My mom loved me more than she could ever fear some stupid sickness. I'm ashamed of you, Mrs. Cleamont."

He gently led me around her trembling figure. As soon as we were behind her, she bolted to the house, slamming the door. The groceries were as forgotten as I was, a bruise already forming on the discarded apple. The moment the door latched shut, I broke down completely into racking, guttural sobs as the sting of her rejection tore me apart. Lander somehow managed to carry me home as I cried, the combined weight of rejection and my jacket too much for my legs to bear.

When we arrived at his house, or at this point, our house, he gently laid me down in his bed.

"Is there anything you need?" he asked quietly, knowing full well there was nothing he could do. I shook my head.

"I need to be alone," I choked out through gasping hiccups.

"I'm sorry, Sadie. I truly am," Lander said helplessly.

I was unable to muster an answer in my current state, so he let me be, patting my shoulder once before shutting the door. That's where I stayed for the rest of the day, the tears dampening his pillow to the point I feared it would need to be wrung out. Eventually, they stopped flowing, from either how swollen my eyes had become or straight up dehydration, I wasn't sure.

At some point, long after the sunlight faded from the windows, Mrs. Robyn came to check on me. I couldn't bring myself to move or acknowledge her. She must've figured I was asleep, covering my curled-up form with a quilt. I thought she was about to leave the room when she surprised me, sitting down on the edge of the bed. She rested her hand on my shoulder through the fabric.

"I'm sorry for everything, dear. As a mom myself, I find it difficult to understand. I won't lie and say I wasn't terribly afraid when Lander found me on the way home all those years ago. But I was willing to risk living the same life he does so we could stay together. He's my son, my baby, my everything. My heart breaks for you, Sadie, especially since you're caught in this mess because of us." She pulled her hand away with a sigh. "If you ever need a mom, I'll be there for you. Even if it means risking it all."

I was wrong thinking I couldn't produce any more tears as her heartfelt words brought up an entirely new flood of emotion. She patted me, as I cried for the thousandth time that day, staying until I finally gave in to the welcoming darkness of sleep. I didn't know what time it was when I awoke, but she was gone, the spot in the bed where she'd been sitting still rumpled. As I turned over in the bed, jacket holding me down in place of Lander's weighted blanket, I found she had left me something in her absence. I reached over, picking it up to see what exactly it was, finding a thoughtful, laborious gift:

A pair of handmade leather gloves, just my size.

16

Lander tried nonstop in the coming days to pull me out of my misery all to no avail. I was stuck inside the darkness to the point I could barely even get out of bed, having to be dragged out into the kitchen for each meal. Mrs. Robyn mandated that I join her in the garden every evening, offering me tea, books she'd borrowed from some of her wealthier friends, anything to get me to interact. Lander still forced me to walk around the city, hoping that the change in scenery would help lift me up as it had previously. These walks were slow and painful, as watching people go about their everyday lives happy and joyful made my depression even more noticeable. After a few unsuccessful trips, Lander changed our route to include the outskirts of the city, where people were sparse, hoping that nature would have a greater soothing effect.

I appreciated their efforts but preferred to stay alone, letting the world go by while I stayed still as if frozen in time. After days of no improvement, Lander finally got fed up and stormed into his bedroom. I figured he was coming in there to launch another lecture on how I needed to get up and walk, but today, he had come up with something completely different. Something that finally made me turn my head and perk up.

"Sadie isn't Sadie without music," he said, picking up on the small flicker of life in my eyes as he held up the violin case. "Today, we're going to figure this out."

I hadn't even thought about my instrument since everything happened. Seeing this part of my life, the most familiar and comforting piece gave me hope that I'd long since abandoned. Music had pulled me through the darkest days of our coming to Ancthia. It helped me deal with the loss of my father, giving life to the instrument he'd made me. Music cleared my head and organized my thoughts, allowing me to say everything I wanted to without ever having to open my mouth. It gave structure and balance to my world, one that had turned completely over. Maybe this would be the thing I needed, to return to who I was, buried deep inside under the heavy weight. After all, Lander was right. I wasn't me without music.

He sat the case on the end of his bed, and I scooted over to it, the metal latches cool and familiar underneath my fingertips as I flipped them open. The scent of the finished wood—of my father—tickled my nose, warm and comforting as I brushed the dust off the violin's body. With the edge of my thumb, I plucked each string one by one, the notes having gone sour from sitting still for so long.

"It's out of tune," I whispered, excited by the soft reverberation of the strings within the wood.

"I can't even tell, I swear I'm tone deaf," Lander said, eliciting the first smile I'd created in days.

I tightened the strings accordingly, until each note was satisfactorily within range, the shiny strings quivering with the same excitement I was brimming with. This instrument was my heart, the thing that kept me pumping, and I held it in my hands, the smooth wood as light and airy as I once thought weightlessness might feel. But we quickly found there was a minor problem. Or, rather, a major one. My arms were heavy to the point I couldn't hold it up for longer than a few seconds, my bow arm in particular. I sawed at the strings, off balance and squeaky, as I fought the jacket that held me down. The terrible noise had me cringing, and I repeatedly tried to make the sounds work with me to no avail. Raw panic gripped my chest. Seeing this fear, that I was unable to play even one normal note, Lander proposed a different idea.

"What if we try strapping you down to the bed? That way your arms will be free from the weight," he suggested, pulling out another hidden stash of rope from his nightstand.

"It's a good idea in theory, but then I'll be fighting my arms in the opposite direction," I wailed, truly terrified that nothing was going to work. I'd finally found a sliver of normalcy to this strange and unfamiliar life, and I was already facing the dreadful possibility of another loss.

"Don't worry! We will come up with something!" He thought for a minute, eyes darting between me, the violin, and the ceiling as he cooked up another strategy. "I always find it much easier to perform finer skills such as writing while upside down since everything pulls me down like it's supposed to. It might be tricky to get the hang of, but it's worth a try."

I considered this, recalling the few times I'd been stuck on the ceiling. Remaining upright was typically more comfortable for my head. But if I was going to make this work, I'd have to try something different, or else lose the last piece I had of myself.

With some help, I managed to get onto the ceiling and sit upside down without incident, cross-legged as Lander tended to prefer.

"All right, are you comfortable?" he asked, peering up at me, our heads almost touching.

Surprisingly, I was. Other than the slight disorientation from seeing the entire world upside down, it was the most normal I'd felt since being sick. I eagerly reached for the violin that Lander carefully held.

"Yes! I'm ready to try it!" I said. He grinned up at me, gingerly handing over my father's work of art. This way was easier than wearing the weights, but it still proved to be an incredible challenge. My violin constantly attempted to fall down (or up, in this case) meaning instead of fighting my arms, I fought the instrument. I squeezed it under my chin, trying to keep it steady as I worked the bow into the strings. The sounds I created weren't as scratchy or coarse as before and a fountain of hope bubbled up in my heart. I might be able to do this, with practice.

I danced the bow across the strings, a melody unfolding under my fingers. My heart sang as the music danced out of me, breathing life into my soul as the largest piece of who I was fell back into place piece by piece, covering the void gaping heavily open. For a few moments, I was Sadie again. Even weightless, I was the hopeful, curious best friend of Lander, ready to take on the world together. I wasn't troubled or in pain anymore. Only one thing mattered: the melody inside as it erupted forth, exploding out of the dam it had been held behind for so long. This was the best moment of my life thus far, reuniting with the one thing that made me, me after such a long separation.

Until it wasn't.

I took one of the notes slightly too hard. I'd forgotten for only a moment where I was and what was happening, the music consuming my awareness. But this slight misstep was all it took, my violin dislodging from my chin. To my absolute and utter horror, I completely lost my grip, sending the instrument clattering upward onto the floor. Lander tried to catch it but failed, and I watched, helpless as my entire life shattered into a hundred splinters.

I stared in shock, bow still in hand, unable to process what I had witnessed.

"Sadie, I—"

"Pull me down!" I screamed, flailing desperately for the ground. "Pull me down now!"

Lander grabbed me by the shoulders and twisted me upright with a grunt of effort, helping me slide the jacket on as fast as physically possible. The instant I could walk, I fell to my knees in front of the broken violin, my broken life. I shakily sifted through the scattered pieces, searching for the inscription my father had left me on the inside. It had always been visible if I peeked through the holes in the front, a small, hand-carved note that I'd never touched until today.

To my dearest daughter, Sadie.

Sharp and jagged was the wood, but I didn't care. I gripped the inscription so tight my hand bled, the splinters tearing into my skin.

"Sadie, I'm sorry, I—"

"Get out!" I screamed. "You've ruined everything! Everything! I hate you, Lander Holland! I hate you! I hate you!" I yelled it repeatedly as Lander backed out of the room, tears in his own eyes, but I couldn't bring myself to care. I was ruined to the point I couldn't feel anything anymore. It was all too much. My life, my family, and now, my music had shattered before my eyes.

And so had I.

***

Lander stopped trying after that.

We both went through the motions of each day without laughing or joking, Mrs. Robyn unable to get any sort of reaction out of us. She even brought home pretzels one day, hoping it would finally evoke a grin from her son, but he wouldn't even look at them. Neither would I. I was so empty I barely even noticed how Lander didn't hang out on the ceiling anymore. He kept his jacket on, staying low to the ground, face hollow and lifeless. I was sure it matched mine, judging by the way Mrs. Robyn watched us both with intense worry.

"You two need to get outside," she'd tell us, knowing it was doing no good. She tried forcing us, threatening punishments or grounding, but how could you ground someone who never left the house?

One particularly bad night, we sat quietly around the table, the only sound the wind howling through the windows. I stared at my plate of food, glancing up once to see Lander doing the same. There was nothing behind his sunken eyes, no glimmer of sarcasm, stupid jokes or lively antics. I remember thinking that if I could feel something, anything, it would probably be sadness. It was my fault, after all, since the moment I shattered, Lander shattered. Typical Lander. He'd follow me anywhere, even if it was toward his own destruction. That thought brought up a strange, horrible stirring inside of me that I hadn't experienced in weeks, as if some semblance of despair for my sullen friend was trying to come up. As quickly as it came, it sunk back down, far into the void of emptiness.

"Can at least one of you speak?" Mrs. Robyn pleaded, slamming her fork down on the table. "It's been a month! We can get you another violin, Sadie. I know it was your father's, and I know how difficult it is for you to play in this state, but I've been working extra to afford you one. You'll play music again. We'll make it work and you two can go back to normal."

Lander didn't budge, continuing to stare lifelessly, his once voracious appetite absent. I slowly lifted my eyes to his mom, to the lines of worry deeply engraved in her forehead.

"Thank you. But I don't want it," I said flatly, unable to muster even a hint of emotion into my voice.

"You can't go on this way forever," Mrs. Robyn said, eyeing us as we sat, devoid of anything resembling life. Whether she was trying to convince us or herself, I didn't know.

Seeing that she was finished with her food, I took my full plate over to the sink and retreated to her bedroom floor, the place where I spent nearly all of my time these days. Lander followed suit, softly shutting the door to his room. I heard Mrs. Robyn's defeated sigh. She was as close to giving up as we were, having run out of ideas at this point.

I slept deeply and quietly, my mind as silent in my sleep as it was in the day. I no longer dreamed. There wasn't enough light or color within me to muster them, even subconsciously. Every night was as dark as my life had become, and I welcomed the veil of numbness that sleep provided with open arms.

Except for this night in particular.

I didn't know if it was Mrs. Robyn's comment that had finally triggered it, or if it had been simply on the way since my complete and utter breakdown. At some point during the night I heard a vague rustling noise, as if someone was walking around. I didn't care in any way what it was at first, as caring was another emotion that I didn't have the capacity for. It didn't last long, so I drifted back off to sleep, figuring it was either a mouse or Lander, using the bathroom during the night. Despite initially being unbothered, it wasn't much later that I woke up from the relief of unconsciousness from a strange sensation bubbling up in my gut. It was hard to recognize at first, since it had been so long since I felt anything, but when I figured it out I sat up, startled. I almost lost my grip on the weighted blanket and hit the ceiling.

Something was wrong. Very wrong.

I pulled on my jacket and released myself from the confines of the blanket, stumbling out of Mrs. Robyn's room and toward Lander's. His door was open. He never left the door open. Lighting a candle as quickly as I could, I searched the small room for my friend, expecting to see his dark head of hair snoring gently upon his pillow. There was nothing. The bed was empty. So was the closet, and under the bed. The bathroom. The kitchen. I searched in a frenzy, Mrs. Robyn somehow remaining asleep through it all. I finally stopped my search when I came across a small piece of paper, folded up neatly underneath his unlit candlestick. I almost couldn't read it, hard as my hands were shaking, the sweat on my fingers wrinkling the paper as I unfolded it.

If you seek to find me, count the stars. I'm sorry. For everything.

"No," I quavered, knowing exactly what it meant.

As I raced down the street, running until my lungs burned and my legs roared at me to stop, our trip to the ocean replayed through my mind over and over again.

I like to think they don't suffocate. That once they pass the clouds, they become another star.

My feet thundered against the dirt pathway, as loud as my pulse in my ears. I didn't care if the gate guards found me. I didn't care about anything. Except right now, I did. I cared that Lander thought his life was over since mine was ruined. I cared that he might float off into the sky out of reach. I feared the threat of loneliness that he'd warded off since I came to Ancthia. It was all too much. I should've known. Lander was never quiet or solemn, he was my outgoing, goofy, smiley friend. He didn't let anything get him down. Did he truly believe me when I said I hated him? I could never hate him, for as long as I lived. Was I nothing more than an empty shell of who I used to be? Yes, but I was still somewhere in there, and I needed him. *I needed him.*

I was stopped in my tracks as I slammed into a new wire fence that blocked the small footpath Lander and I had once taken up the side of the mountain. I violently shook the chain links, needing them to move out of the way. When they didn't budge, I frantically raced down the line of fencing, screaming his name, my voice raking against my throat like the serrated end of a knife.

I searched for a shadow in the dark, for any sign that he was still here on this side of the fence to no avail. The boulders played tricks on my eyes in the lack of light, and I raced up to one after another hoping they were Lander. I was moments away from attempting to scale the fence when I tripped over a soft pile on the ground, not far from where the field met the structure. I landed flat on my face, dirt flying up my nose and in my mouth. Sneezing and spitting, I whirled around, clumsily patting around for what I'd tripped over. Dread sunk into my chest as I searched, for deep in my heart I knew exactly what it was. And that knowledge terrified me. I couldn't breathe, couldn't think. The faster I worked, the slower time moved. I feared I'd never find it; hoped I wouldn't because I wanted to be wrong—to be stuck in the middle of some crazy dream my messed-up brain had conjured. Maybe the semblance of emotion I'd experienced earlier meant things were waking up, and I'd soon emerge from this living nightmare. I couldn't see in the dim moonlight, so it took me much longer than it should've to search the ground, but eventually I was successful. And when my hand finally made contact with the object of which I sought, I wished I had never found it.

It was Lander's jacket.

17

"Oh! Sadie, you scared me! I didn't know you were still here," Jena said, hand to her chest in surprise.

I wiped my hands on my apron, flour dust going everywhere as I gave Jena an apologetic grin.

"Sorry, I was trying to finish up tomorrow's batch," I sheepishly replied, placing the fresh bowl of dough onto the rack to rise.

"Don't sweat it, I'm glad to have someone here as dedicated as you!" she beamed with pride, her bright red hair peeking out in all directions from under her kerchief. "I almost forgot, we had a few extras today; do you want to bring them home to your mom?" she swirled around, grabbing the small basket of extra pretzels off the sales rack, going to hand them over. I wasn't wearing my gloves, having finished rolling out the dough only moments before, so I tilted my head toward the counter, indicating that she should place them there. It was too risky; if our fingers accidentally touched, it was all over.

"Thank you. I'll grab them in a moment, my hands are filthy!" I held up my flour-dusted fingers, wiggling them to demonstrate. She laughed, her green eyes crinkling up as she did.

"Always a mess! That's the sign of excellent work. You've been here almost four years now, correct?"

I nodded, wiping up the countertop with a damp washcloth, sweeping the excess flour into my palm to discard. "It'll be four years next week."

"We'll have a special sale for you, then. Starting Monday! The four-year anniversary of the best baker around."

I grinned, embarrassed about such a fuss, but glad to be valued. "Thank you. I appreciate it."

"Anytime. I've got to head out now. See you in the morning?"

"See you in the morning."

She slid out the back door, shutting it gently as I finished up my kitchen duties. It seemed longer than four years; I was hired here when I turned fourteen, the earliest one could work in Ancthia. I'd refused to attend school on account of both my unfortunate condition, and the inability to bear seeing Lander's desk empty. Or worse, filled by someone else.

After two years at the house, Mrs. Robyn told me I could only continue schooling at home if I found something to do in my spare time instead of moping around. We sealed the deal, and I applied at one of Lander's favorite pretzel stands. It was almost therapeutic, being able to create the one thing Lander loved the most other than me. I'd failed miserably at giving him what he needed most—myself—in my broken state, the pieces much too far gone to put back together. But making his favorite snack allowed me to give him something back after taking away his entire life. Crafting a tribute to his short, hell-like existence here in the city. The scent of the baking bread brought him back to me in whispers, and I often pretended he was still there, waiting eagerly for the next batch to get the best pick.

The grief never left me, although some days were better than others. For the most part, I was only going through the motions, smiling when expected to, answering with the appropriate emotions to display a point without being robotic. Mrs. Robyn could see right through it, but never mentioned it, her own eyes displaying a constant, lonely emptiness. She did a much better job at hiding it, from either years of practice or a drive to live on and honor her destroyed family, I wasn't sure.

I locked up the bakery, as the sun was hanging low over the peaks. We closed early on Fridays, since Jena wanted to get home to her family on her favorite day of the week. I hated it. I'd rather stay here late into the evening, baking batch after batch, handing them out to the delighted children that waited and watched from the window. It reminded me of when I stood on the other side, waiting as eagerly as them, excited to see Lander's face light up brighter than the stars above as I handed him his gift.

Watching the stars was one of my favorite pastimes now, and every night I attempted to count them, despite knowing it was completely impossible. I hoped that by counting each one, I might get lucky enough to come across

Lander's. I wanted him to know he was found among the masses, that he still mattered to me.

My other favorite pastime was the one I was heading to, my daily ritual that allowed me a small bit of peace throughout my never-ending internal chaos. On nights I stayed late at the bakery, I took my lunch break at exactly this time, refusing to miss even one day. As I trudged through the streets, the weights on my shoulders slowed me down as usual, and I wondered if I'd arrive before them.

The park was situated near the center of the city, up against Ancthia's large lake. The area was small and sparsely wooded, a few hundred yards across, with a modest playground. It had swings and monkey bars, playhouses and pretend markets. Lander and I visited here when we were younger, spending hours running around through the different structures. There was one slide in the entire park, the metal a rarity in Ancthia, and children often fought over it. But not my brother.

He was a mirror image of Mama and me, something I was grateful for as I didn't want to see any part of Thamus in him. I would've loved him anyway, of course, but it was less painful this way. He'd entered littles that year, having finally come of age, and was a strong, proud little boy. I didn't know his name, the distance between us always being too great to catch Mama's voice calling him over. I took my spot on the small hill above the park, climbing up high into the tallest oak. It wasn't the easiest climb with the weights, but I wasn't as brave as Lander had been that night with Cyntha, when he had nothing to hold on to but a rope. Nestled into the top of the tree, I leaned against the abrasive bark. In this spot, I had a clear view of Mama and my brother's favorite evening spot.

I'd arrived earlier than usual, since the bakery had closed, but I didn't mind waiting. It was peaceful here, among the branches, the arms stretching toward the heavens where Lander was. I felt closer to him here. Searching for his closeness in everything I did was something that happened subconsciously anymore, it was all I desired, at any moment of the day. I wanted him back so badly the numbness I typically held was overshadowed by the sharp need for his touch.

Today, as I rested in my spot, I nursed the pain as I noticed Mama and my brother approaching, his small figure bouncing up and down as they arrived.

He let go of Mama's hand, racing off to the swing set, checking often to make sure she was still watching. His golden-brown hair, identical to mine, brushed across his ears as he hopped into the swing, taking off back and forth from the sky to the ground. He was lively and youthful, as I had once been, the world at his feet. I watched as he climbed as high as possible among the structures, fearless and untamed. He never missed a beat, graceful and coordinated while he conquered each challenge. I was incredibly proud of this little boy I had never met. Watching him play, living a life unconfined, brought forth a small smile to my lips. Mama may have forgotten me after all these years, but a piece of me lived in this boy, whether she knew it or not. I only hoped he never had to experience the same hurt I had at her hands, and got to live the life I was supposed to, fearlessly.

After nearly an hour of play, the pair retreated, my brother still bounding with energy as they disappeared down the street. The air had taken on a chill as I jumped out of the tree, crashing to the ground as I usually did. It took about a half hour to walk home, my feet slower than usual as I carried something different inside of me I couldn't quite place; something reminding me of finality.

Mrs. Robyn was home, the windows glowing with gentle candlelight, as I saw her shadows bustling about the kitchen. I gripped the basket of leftover pretzels tight as I entered, wishing I'd find Lander on the ceiling, his once favorite haunt, begging me to hand him the biggest one. He wasn't—no surprise there—and I sat the basket on the table in silence as Mrs. Robyn warmly greeted me.

"Welcome home," she said, hesitating to give me a hug due to both of our naked hands. "I've got dinner on; it should be ready shortly. I see you have an extra treat for us tonight." She eyed the pretzels, eyebrows knitting tightly together at the reminder of her son.

"Yeah, I made too many," I said flatly.

"You've been doing that a lot lately. Are sales down?" she asked, rhythmically stirring the pot on the stove. She took the wooden spoon out, the once rounded edge now flat from many years of use, and placed it on the stovetop.

"No," was all I said. I found it hard to keep any kind of conversation going, even with Mrs. Robyn. There wasn't enough left inside of me to keep creating meaningless words. We typically sat in silence, although some nights she poked and prodded as if I were a pile of burned-out coals, hoping one day to find a spark hidden beneath the ashes. Tonight was one of those nights, and she huffed in frustration, turning toward my slumped figure at the table with crossed arms.

"Sadie," she said. I already knew I was in for another lecture. "I can't watch you continue doing this to yourself. When are you going to stop playing the victim and start your life? It's been six years!"

I stared blankly at the basket of pretzels, any sort of answer lost on my tongue. I wanted to say never, but mustering the energy to even try was too much.

"What you're doing is not living. I understand what happened to you was terrible, and you've lost a lot. I've lost, too, Sadie! I've lost everything! But I keep going for them. Lander always made it work."

"Until he didn't," was my only reply, and the instant the words left my throat I wanted to take them back. "I'm sorry. That was rude," I immediately mumbled an apology, not wanting to cause any further pain for the woman I now called Mom.

"You have to stop," she calmly demanded.

"I can't," I spat, exhausted of having these discussions.

"You won't!"

"How many times do I have to tell you? I refuse to stop because if I let go, then I have nothing left! I want to feel the pain, I want to miss him terribly, I want to hate my life because feeling anything, *anything* is better than nothing! At least when it hurts so bad I can't even breathe, it means he was here, and he was *real*."

My words rang out in the kitchen, echoing against the cozy wooden walls. The candles flickered as if unsure which direction they should run. Mrs. Robyn's face didn't change, fully expecting this response.

"All I'm trying to say is, at some point, you have to move on. That's all."

She turned around, picking her spoon back up to stir the pot. She was right. I'd been feeling it a lot lately, the fatigue of fighting both endless despair and weightlessness. I was tired; so very tired. I was ready for something different.

"Mrs. Robyn?" I whispered. I wasn't even sure she'd hear me, I'd said it so quietly. The woman was as sharp as a tack, though, and peered over her shoulder in surprise.

"What is it, dear?" she replied, turning back to face me.

"Thank you. I am grateful for you. Always will be."

She smiled sadly, eyes teary as the words I spoke were the most genuine I'd shared since Lander left.

"You're always welcome."

The rest of the meal was hushed as usual, and Mrs. Robyn headed off to bed. I took a quick shower, washing the flour out of my hair, staring at myself in the mirror as I untangled the long, damp locks. The process of removing my weights never got easier, the tops of my feet having an almost permanent ache from holding myself under the cabinet. As I stared, I eyed a small scar piercing the corner of my left eyebrow, a reminder of the day after Lander left. A group of children had seen fit to throw rocks at me in the street as I lay in an alley covered in dirt. I had collapsed there on the way home, clinging to the jacket in shock. The children approached me, laughing and jeering, as I fought them off, begging them not to touch my skin as they tried ripping the jacket away. They'd labeled me as deranged, which was honestly quite fitting, and threw handful after handful of heavy stones. Only one hit my face, doing the most damage, the rest bruising up my back through my heavy, weighted jacket. Honestly, I didn't care when it happened, and I didn't care now, the scar as much a reminder as the pain was that he was once here.

I went outside to lay in the garden, counting the stars the same way I did every night. They glittered above me, as I had seen the moonlight do once above ocean waves. The conch shell I'd found that night stayed in Lander's nightstand. It hadn't been touched in years, covered in a layer of dust at this point, as the breath of the ocean lay in wait, deep within its depths. I counted and counted, losing my place a handful of times when clouds passed over where I watched, temporarily darkening the lights. At some point, I finished, my mind at peace for the first time in ages as I came to terms with my decision. The decision to move on.

"You want me so bad, you can have me," I whispered to the sky, as if its millions of tiny eyes were watching with anticipation. With one swift movement, I yanked down the zipper of the worn, faded jacket Mrs. Robyn carefully crafted long ago. The instant the ends slumped to the side, the force of the sky grabbed me harder than it ever had before, my arms effortlessly slipping out of the sleeves. I almost panicked, wanting to roll around and grab at something, anything, but knew it would be fruitless. Instead, I lay there on my back, face up to the sky as I had done every night since Lander left me, and counted the stars again, wondering which ones I'd end up next to.

***

It was peaceful, floating into the sky.

I'd fallen asleep right before dawn, as the stars faded into the background, the dark void becoming lighter and lighter as the sun replaced the moon. The wind rocked me back and forth, as a mom did to her newborn baby, the movement soothing and familiar. As I swayed in the warm sunlight, coming in and out of awareness, I noticed I had reached the line of clouds. They were bright and soft, a golden yellow hue along each curve of its ever-moving structure. They never stayed still, ever changing and shifting into various sizes and shapes. Every once in a while, one would engulf me in its journey, the world going white and quiet until it decided to spit me back out.

I wondered if Lander's journey had been this peaceful, when he slipped out during the night. Had we touched the same clouds; traveled the same parts of the sky? Did he ever look back down to see the ocean one more time? How far had he gone, in the last six years, and would I ever catch up to him on this endless journey up to the stars? Mrs. Robyn surely realized I was gone by now, the thought tugging fiercely at my heart. She never left me, no matter how bitter I'd become. Some days I wondered if she did it out of obligation or out of the goodness of her heart. Or maybe it was because I served as a reminder of her son, being the last thing she had left of him. After all, he'd made me what I was. Even if it was all an accident.

I floated along aimlessly, becoming thirsty and hot as the intensity of the sun pierced my skin. My arms hadn't seen sunlight in many years, meaning their discomfort was much greater than that of my face. The relief of the clouds was beyond welcoming, as the thick vapor kept me shielded, at least temporarily. I completely lost track of time, dozing off or falling unconscious at various, unscheduled moments. There was daylight, and there was night, and then I was thrust back into another, searing day. Eventually, the dehydration hazed over my mind, my lips cracked and bleeding. And right when I was about to succumb to sleep once again, I was sure the shouting I heard from to my right was a hallucination. I thought about turning my head to see and ultimately decided against it, the movement not worth the effort. Instead, I let the soft breeze pull me under once again, briefly wondering if it would be the last time I closed my eyes.

***

The amount of noise had grown ridiculously irritating.

There were voices and beeps, clattering and clicking. It sounded as though an entire crowd of people were frantically putting together a massive, never-ending project. Every time I had finally gotten comfortable upon the cloud of which I lay, something cold and annoying would jostle me, disturbing the deep rest I was trying to continue. I wondered if I might be in a storm, but the lack of dampness and rain made me think otherwise. I tried to make sense of what I was hearing underneath the heavy blanket smothering my mind, but nothing was working. The more it went on, the greater I fought against the thickness, trying to find some logic in it. I was no longer thirsty or hungry, which was strange, and the burning of the sun had been absent for what appeared to be quite some time. Although time had been long forgotten the instant I was pulled into the sky.

My awareness awakened along with my eyes as I struggled to open them. After the latest loud noise startled me enough to lift the fog lingering in my head, I desperately needed to see what kind of strange cloud I was stuck in. I groaned with the effort, eyelids heavier than any jacket had ever been, and a burst of unnaturally white light blasted me in the face. The sudden brightness prompted me to fling an arm up over my head, blocking the piercing assault, and I blinked in both surprise and wonder at what I saw.

I was in a room, starched and white, with lights scattered along the ceiling. It wasn't a cloud that I was sitting on, no, it was a long white bed, the sheet that lay over my legs unwrinkled and as bleached as the walls. To my right was a thick, large window, with a scene I could barely comprehend, and I left my curiosity regarding that for later, when I could figure out exactly where I was. There was a young woman at the foot of my bed, staring at me in surprise as she bent down to pick up the clipboard she had dropped. Her hair was blonde and long, pulled into a ponytail down her back. She wore clothing matching the white theme of the room, and there was something odd about her that took me a moment to place it.

She wore pants instead of skirts.

Startled, I almost sat straight up but stopped myself on account of not having my jacket. I'd made the mistake of hitting the ceiling before, and sometimes my neck still ached from that unfortunate encounter.

"Oh! You're awake!" her high-pitched voice rang out as she took in my shocked face. "How are you feeling?"

My throat was dry as I went to answer, the sound nothing more than a croak. "Where am I?"

The woman raised her eyebrows at my confusion, as if she wasn't expecting to answer such a question. "You're in the hospital on Isle Sordenya, within the capital city."

"Isle what?" I echoed, wondering if this was some sort of insane dehydration-induced dream.

"Sordenya." She glanced down at her clipboard, taken aback at what she'd found. "Oh. I'm sorry, I didn't realize which room I was in. This isn't my end of the hall. I only heard your pump beeping, and I came to silence it for your nurse."

"Didn't realize what?" I demanded, needing some sort of explanation. "My what is beeping?" To my side was some sort of strange contraption with flashing lights, a bag of what appeared to be water trailing down to one of my arms. The thought of something digging into my skin was more than unnerving. I went to rip it out, too creeped out by the invasive device, but the woman stopped me by placing a hand on my arm.

"Don't do that, you'll hurt yourself! Stay still, please, I'll go grab your nurse."

I yanked my arm away out of reflex, conditioned from many years of avoiding any and all types of intimacy on account of my contagion. "You can't touch me!"

"It's okay!" she tried to explain, backing out of the room, making sure not to take her eyes off my unruly self. "Mendy! The new arrival is awake!"

I wiggled my body underneath the blanket, trying to see down the hallway at what was happening when I noticed something else entirely strange. I had nothing but a light sheet over me. The blanket wasn't weighted, and when my arms were uncovered, they were completely within my control. Waiting for whoever Mendy was already taking much too long. I decided to risk hitting the ceiling to see if I was correct. Surely, my neck could take at least one more impact.

"Mendy!"

The strangest thing happened, and something sang within my heart that had long been forgotten, a note of joy and hope and living a normal life. For the first time in six years, I threw back the blanket and stayed. I didn't hit the ceiling. My legs didn't float off. Neither did my arms. I was sitting in the bed in a skimpy white gown, completely and utterly free.

"What in the hell . . . ?" I gasped, for a moment wondering if I'd done it, if I'd let go of my weights and floated off. Or if I'd awoken in the past, the last six years only some sort of strange fever dream. There was absolutely no way. I'd had the fever; I'd become weightless. There was no cure, reversal, or any sort of treatment known in the entire world. It simply wasn't possible. This couldn't be real. But when I saw the bubbly red sunburn dotting my arms, I knew it had to be; that everything truly happened. There was no other explanation. I had left my jacket behind that night in the garden while Mrs. Robyn was asleep in her bed. I was among the clouds for days, watching the sun rise and set while rocking along the wind as I floated upward. The shouting I'd heard in the clouds wasn't a hallucination. Someone had rescued me from the sky.

I sat straight up, in the process of getting out of the bed when a middle-aged woman with dark curly hair and matching, smooth dark skin came barging into the room.

"Sit your bottom back down this instant before you cause a whole lot of paperwork for me!" she ordered, pointing at the bed I was trying to escape. I obeyed immediately, the air of authority coming from this woman equal to that of Mrs. Robyn's, a brief flash of a wooden spoon in the back of my memory.

"Please, tell me what's going on!" I begged her.

She grabbed the askew sheet and held it up, a silent order that I was to lay back down, or else. I did, the sheet fluttering down in one sweep to cover my bare legs, not a corner out of place. How she did that in one move was a mystery to me. The woman touched my arm gently. This time I didn't flinch away, her confidence more than enough to keep me still. She smiled broadly, excited to share her next words:

"I'm not allowed to tell you much. Someone will be here shortly to discuss everything. But what I can say, is welcome to Sordenya, capital of the floating islands."

I stared at her, dumbfounded.

"The-the floating *what*?" I stammered, unsure if I'd heard correctly.

"The floating islands. See for yourself," she motioned toward the windows, wanting me to look, to understand, to see.

And for the first time in my entire life, I did.

I saw everything.